GRADING SCALE

A Novel

John C Morgan

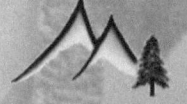

Selkirk Publishing LLC
Coeur d' Alene, Idaho

For my family
Kim, Tim and Kyle
And
for all the dreamers
of this world.

CLAIRE

Claire sighed deeply, wondering if she'd ever be able to return to her home with the Human Race. She longed to touch the face of life again, to feel its warmth and fervent desire for self-expression. She enfolded herself within her sinuous white feathered wings, wings she'd not used for eons, become like the fallowed winter fields on the world she longed to walk again.

Expelled from the legions of her peers at an early age, Claire had banished herself to a secluded corner in the Angelic Universe, afraid to face her peers. Shame drove her away and shame kept her crippled, leaving her to exist in utter desolation. She'd sat with a heavy heart for an eternity, with only fleeting thoughts of her former life. Even though she'd been relegated to the most menial of tasks among humans, and unable to enter into their daily affairs, they now brought her solace in this forsaken place she'd fled. Her memories were her only connection to any semblance of her purpose as an Angel, the only hope she had left within herself, now all but a distant flicker of light. Her heart ached for the chance to get her hands dirty in the emergence of life on Earth – the Humankind.

The Ranks of Angels had swelled with the assent of modern Man, as their mental prowess expanded and searched for meaning in life. Angels were charged with helping the Human Race discover creation and their place within it, guiding them along their myriad of diverse cultural paths. Claire longed to be part of the foothold on this young planet, but she was new to the Angelic Realm and had to wait her turn. At least that was the acceptable way for her to act; the way Angels were supposed to act.

She'd gone too far and broken her solemn oath to not interfere and had saved a young girl from certain death in a swift-moving river in the south of France, in AD 214. And for that, she was chastised and expelled from her apprenticeship on Earth. Angry and saddened, she'd run away, too ashamed of herself to accept their help. "They'd never find her," she had vowed.

Claire had locked herself away in self-punishment and hid from those sent to find her. And, even though she'd been expelled from the Ranks, it was always meant to be a temporary condition, a time away to reflect; but she'd disappeared long before, never hearing the full explanation of her discipline, and terms for her absolution. She'd fled hastily in her guilt and never looked back, feeling spurned and unable to look upon their Angelic faces for one more moment. Many helpers were sent to find her and return her to the fold, some coming so close she was forced to flee into the innermost bowels of creation, scattering herself to the winds of light and formless substance. She'd ventured so deep into unfamiliar territory, she feared she'd never be able to find her way home. Claire fell into a dispiriting chasm within herself, alone, and with only her shame as a companion.

With boundless eternity stretching out around her, it was here, in the wilderness of her thoughts she remained, waiting and hoping to find herself, consumed by this place without time or feeling. It became her life, for how long, she could only guess. Seclusion became her friend, her ally, as she fashioned her home in the wilderness, one with snowcapped mountains and rushing creeks, and her primitive domed dwelling of woven branches. It reminded her of her life in France, where she'd saved the young girl, and forever changed both of their lives. Claire always hoped the girl would be beautiful and marry a loving and kind man. She dreamed of them often, and took long walks in the mountains of her world, always walking towards the next rise, the next bend in the path, so wanting to see her dreams revealed; the couple's castle by a pristine azure lake, with their children playing on its shores. Claire's heart swelled with pride whenever she thought of them and the possibilities in life for the young girl; a life she'd saved from certain death.

Claire sighed deeply once again, lost in time and place, and longing for a life back in her home among humans.

ARTHUR

Arthur Organ's Web Design class was a place of laughter and even a prank or two, often employed by him as a way over the parapets, which teens used as defenses against adults. He often joked it was trench warfare when it came time to confront the charged issues of teens, making him laugh at his illusion of authority so casually brushed aside, swept away, and trodden under foot. Two students, in particular, were adept at the time-honored cause of rebellion: Frank, lordly ruler of misery to all who would defy him, and Linda, whose icy blue stare could slice and dice one in a heartbeat. Seeing them in action made even him cringe, as they so adeptly went about their task of unraveling another student's psyche. They were unstoppable when united in cause.

Today was such a day. His explanation of the midterm assignment due in five days drew groans and cries from many of his students, but not Frank and Linda. They'd joined forces, whispering across the aisle, plotting their nefarious deed together in plain sight of their teacher. Arthur chuckled to himself, wondering what it would be this time.

"Frank. Linda. Did you have something to share with the class?" Arthur asked pleasantly enough, hoping to catch them midway in their scheme. They both eyed him with a wary, contemptuous sideways glance. Yes, he'd tripped them up alright.

"Please, do share, won't you." Linda folded her arms tightly while Frank seemed pleased, a wry smile beginning to form. He cleared his throat with an attention-getting guttural growl. The class seemed to sense a showdown in progress, turning all their attention to their two peers, completely ignoring their teacher's mere existence as a figurehead planted in the front of the room – just someone who took up space in the room.

"Yes, Mr. Organ," he snickered at the sound of the name, as did the class. "I do have something to say about the assignment. You're asking us to spend hours in research on the Internet in order to compose our Web pages. We have other classes you know." Frank said with a punctuated sneer.

He's pleased with himself, Arthur smiled at the two of them. "Why, yes you do have other classes Frank, and I hope the other midterms are as much fun as this one. If you will remember, we've already done what you're referring to, the 'hours of research', in the many assignments leading up to the midterm. I'm quite sure because you've already expressed your displeasure in class on numerous occasions during the past five weeks. Linda will get you up to speed since she did all the work for you anyway." Arthur cocked his head ever so slightly as he fixed his gaze on Linda, who was now glaring at him. "Gotcha," he whispered under his breath.

The period bell rang just as Linda's pursed lips were poised to spit some venom his way. It was lunchtime, so he had some alone time to contemplate the possible outcomes, which were brewing in this opening round of conflict. No one lingered in the classroom to discuss the assignment, not wanting to endure the wrath of a scorned Frank and Linda, who posted themselves just outside the door, waiting to assault anyone who dared to suck-up to the teacher. Frank's sardonic smile filled the window beside the door as it closed behind the last student to leave. Arthur gave him a little waggle of his fingers and a pleasant adult smile, meaning – nice try.

"Enough," he mumbled, reminding himself to relax. He pulled out his brown paper lunch sack from the bottom desk drawer, releasing the aroma of a well-deserved lunch, and instantly producing a soft sigh of relief. What was it today? His mouth watered in anticipation of a leftover slice of meatloaf between two thick, hand sliced pieces of his favorite bakery pumpernickel, with lettuce, tomato, dill pickles, a dash of ketchup laced with horseradish, and a generous grind of black pepper. Arthur was a man who easily pleased both himself and others, with his pleasant yet stout physique, bushy brown hair, soft brown eyes, and the warmest of smiles, which spoke of his kindness. He was comfortable inside his own skin, except on rare occasions with people like Frank and Linda. For some reason unknown even to him, they could disrupt his normally tranquil composure, and thrust him into a befuddled state; but only on rare occasions though. Today was not one of them. He opened the sandwich's plastic bag and took a big bite, savoring the chilled texture, smells and salty taste, and the bite of coarse ground pepper in his mouth. He forgot all about Frank and Linda, being pleasantly lost in his lunch, and the thought of a weekend getaway just two days from now.

"Arthur," the distant, yet familiar voice, sounded faintly inside his head. "Arthur, I need to speak with you."

A piece of sandwich flew across his desk when he greeted his friend. "Hi, Sandy." His words muffled by a full mouth. "How are you?" He knew this high-ranking Angel from the many missions they'd shared together. He liked her both as a partner and as a close friend, having learned a great deal from her through the centuries. "Yes Sandy," he said, the words again muffled by another bite of his sandwich. "What do we have to talk about?" He swallowed the wad in his cheeks, as she began to appear by his side. Sandy had on well-worn designer jeans, a tank top with a rhinestone rainbow, pearly clouds, and a contemporary angelic presence with the caption: "Angels do it on the fly."

"Nice touch," Arthur grinned, looking up at her radiant angelic face and flowing red hair.

"It's for you, Arthur, because you're such a great partner. You have an addition to your current assignment. You're to find Claire and bring her here."

The words fell on him like bricks, each one finding its mark, and bruising an old wound he carried within him. "How? No one has ever found her. She doesn't want to be found. So why do you think I can?" Suddenly he felt weak in the knees, and he was sitting down.

"The Higher Ups wouldn't have asked if they thought you couldn't find her. You were there that day in southern France. You watched it all happen and knew that nothing could stop Claire. She was your charge and you paid dearly for her actions. I watched you suffer the loss of her for the longest time, never wanting to take on assignments again, and never wanting to venture out of your protective shell. I remember Arthur and so do you. That's why you're being asked to find her. She's been hiding way too long and you're to find her this weekend."

Sandy's aura was bright and distinct now, encompassing him, and radiating through her semi-transparent wings folded around him. The Higher Ups were delivering a message through Sandy because he'd believe it all the more coming from his old friend. Claire's innocent actions had stunned him those eighteen hundred years ago. She'd only done what she thought was the right thing to do, the loving thing to do. She'd jumped into the swift, turbid spring runoff to save a life, in order to give life back to the young girl. He'd done nothing, as if frozen in time, while he watched her pour out her heart, risking her own new and fragile life. His heart had swelled with pride and it was the moment he knew how completely he loved this young Angel. He stood now, just as he had then, his heart racing, his head swimming with feelings for her, knowing he loved her still.

"I know Arthur. I love her too. That's why it has to be you. This is her chance, my old friend. It's an important assignment and will test the both of you. Arthur, it's Claire's ticket to redeem her life, the one she was meant to live. Are you listening to me?"

Sandy's wing thumped him on top of his head, getting his attention. "Yes Sandy, I hear you. How could I not hear you? You're drilling the words right through me with that aura of yours. This weekend? Do I get any clues? Special talents? It's kind of a big place out there – the Universe of the Angelic Realm. Two days to find someone who's been in hiding since AD 214? It's a tall order, but I'll give it my best shot." Every hair on Arthur's physical body was standing at attention, his skin bristling with electricity, the room blurred and he was somewhere else. Sandy was showing him the way, a starting point at which to dive into the Realm. "Okay. I'm in," he said, his mind filled with thoughts of Claire's self-inflicted exile.

"Good," Sandy punctuated with a wing to his head again. "Sorry to fly away so soon. I have things to get ready for you two. Until we meet again, you take care, Arthur." Sandy's voice once again sounding distant.

Arthur was still holding his sandwich in his left hand, which was poised somewhere between the desktop and his mouth. He looked at it oddly, his mind still ajar. It somehow appeared out of place with what just happened, but these sorts of things happen when on assignment in a physical body among the human population. The moment passed quickly as his stomach growled for another bite, which he obliged by shoveling the rest of the sandwich into his mouth. He closed the paper bag and returned it to the drawer. Claire was on his mind for the first time in a very long time. He choked on the last remnant of the sandwich, sending little bits of it flying. Sometimes he forgot what he was doing, not remembering he was wearing a physical body. He wiped up the tidbits from the desktop with a napkin, thinking of his young student of long ago.

"Claire, Claire, Claire," he mouthed quietly. The vision of Claire leaping into the river, eighteen hundred years ago filled his mind. He smiled at the outright audacity of her actions, and of her first real assignment among humans in a physical body. "Where are you, Claire?"

CLAIRE'S WORLD

Arthur spent the next two days in a daze, wondering how in the Angelic Universe, he'd ever be able to find Claire. No one else had. Even Sandy had not spoken to him about Claire through the centuries, during which he'd held his concerns for her close to his heart, and never spoke her name to anyone.

Frank and Linda were mostly quiet those two days, which he was grateful for, and didn't bother to ask them how they were doing on the midterm assignment. Besides, who was he to question their place in life – to each their own – something he'd learned through the years of walking among human beings.

When the final bell rang on Friday at 3:30 p.m., he hurried out of the building to his well-used late model Chevy sedan he'd inherited. It had more miles than the manufacturer ever thought possible, and more dings than he could count. Not his first choice, but he had to take whatever he was supplied, with no questions asked. He'd replaced Cindy a little more than a month ago, for reasons unknown to him. He often wondered how well she'd dealt with the Frank and Linda duo – they were the assignment after all. Born into well-to-do yet troubled middle-class families, both Frank and Linda had inherited more than their fair share of emotional baggage. Cindy's, and now his job, was to study and learn about them, helping where they could, but mostly staying out of their way, allowing them the right to orchestrate their lives.

What he'd learned throughout his many assignments, was everyone lived a life filled with mysteries, awe, and for some, more suffering than seemed fair; but for each life, there was an overriding purpose being fulfilled, and its unfoldment wasn't complete until the final breath. Arthur had seen many a life turn for the better in the brief, but final moments before their death. He let out a long sigh, clearing his mind of the many images of past assignments, and buckled his seatbelt. "Better focus," he mumbled.

He started the engine and got in line to exit the school grounds. Now here was an experience every Angel should be required to endure – his opinion. It's amazing that anyone ever got out of the parking lot alive: what with cell phones glued to ears, foot to the floor on the gas pedal or brakes locked up, heads turned anywhere except out the front, and hormones gushing out of every pore. He chuckled at the exaggeration. He got his turn in record time this day because two girls were busy talking on their cell phones, allowing him to slip into their place in line.

Sandy told him she'd meet him when he got home, and true to form, she promptly scooped him up as soon as he'd parked – no fanfare, just gone – poof. His heart raced in anticipation of the adventure that lay ahead. Claire was to be found; his charge from eighteen hundred years ago.

The ignition key was still dangling from his fingers when he departed, and in an instant he was hovering somewhere in the Angelic Realms with Sandy by his side, overlooking a deep canyon with a rushing turquoise river at its base. He wondered who lived in this beautiful little corner of the Realm. Every Angel had their own private retreat while on assignment, giving them a place to think and recharge away from their assignment.

"Arthur, pay attention. I'm going to stuff your mind with possibilities and likely-hoods, for where I and others, think Claire may be hiding."

As Sandy spoke the last word, he reeled with the onslaught of all kinds of stuff. Some of it even brought up memories from his and Claire's past. He didn't question, just swallowed, reminding him of his training in Angelic Boot camp. When Sandy was done, shortly after she'd begun, she was aglow in golden light. "Must have been a lot of stuff from the Higher-Ups," he mused quietly to himself.

"Yes," Sandy said. "From the Higher-Ups. Now go find your good friend Claire and bring her right back here. I'll be awaiting your return. And yes, this is my retreat home from time-to-time."

Sandy smacked him in the behind with a wing to send him on his way. He sailed over the canyon, sweeping past her to say thank you and goodbye. Sandy's stuff took over as he turned away from her and headed for the rim of the two-mile deep canyon. There was a quiet popping sound as he left her little corner of the Realm and picked up speed on a predetermined path, compliments of Sandy and Company. He didn't have the slightest idea where he was headed, and that was okay with him, not really knowing where to find Claire anyway. He settled in for the ride, thinking of his young, vivacious student, Claire, who was stunning to see in action. The old memories were just as new and clear as the day they happened, causing his heart to race, even in this body. He veered sharply away from the route he was on, feeling an old memory coming from afar. Something was drawing him off Sandy's path, something familiar. A world lay below him, or at least part of a world – he couldn't see it all through the star rookery in front of him.

He banked steeply, dodging in and out of the newborn stars, sweeping down into the beautiful world below. He stepped into Claire's world atop a mountain deep with snow, the wind swirling the powdery flakes in little eddies in between boulders. The sun was shining in a rich blue sky, and stars curiously dotted the horizon above the coming blackness of night, the star rookery among them, creating an impressionistic scene of nightfall rising on the horizon – opposite of nature.

"Claire," he called out to the valley far below. If this were Earth, he'd be in the Himalayan Mountains, looking down tens of thousands of feet into the valley. "Claire," he threw his voice literally far into the distance, the echoes coming back in waves. He scanned the valley below for signs of life, anything that spoke to him about his young student. There in the distance, was a small round structure in a clearing on the valley floor. As he saw it, he started to move towards it, gliding down from the heights brushing the tops of the trees with his wings, twisting and turning with the landscape. He stopped just above the small dome-shaped hut on an outcropping of rock to look for her.

The dwelling was primitive, to say the least, but perfect for someone who'd exiled herself out of shame. She wasn't there, so he dropped silently down the slope, landing directly in front of the hut. It was twelve feet across, and a foot shorter than his seven-foot stature. Twigs woven expertly together laced cedar-like branches to shed water and insulate. He bent to smell their intoxicating aroma, nothing like cedar, but green and earthy with a hint of mustiness. He walked around it, seeing footprints all around her camp, and a parade of ones leading off on a narrow path into the woods. He squeezed through the tiny arched entrance, finding a bed of similar makings in one corner, with a small fire pit in the center of the hut. It was cold to the touch, so she must have been gone all day – however long that was.

He exited and followed the path through the woods, walking briskly ahead of the rising arc of nightfall. The path meandered from clearing to clearing, sometimes crossing a small babbling brook, before it began to climb, heading towards a cliff with a narrow ledge cut into it, wide enough for one person to pass. It wound along the cliff face at a steep incline, before opening to a long grassy ridge, and climbed towards the base of the sheer face of the mountain where he'd landed – the highest peak in the range.

It was there he found her, picking flowers and berries, which she placed in a small basket that hung on her arm. The moment he saw her, she reeled around to face him with surprise on her face. Their eyes met and he flushed so hard the color reached his wings and tinted their feathers with a pink glow. With the look of surprise on her face still there, he bridged the distance between them; stopping so close her warm breath caressed his face.

"Claire," he said in a hushed voice. "It's Arthur. Do you remember me?" The heat in his face was growing, embarrassing him to the point of distraction. In the quarter second that had passed, a long time by Angelic standards, she remained in the same pose, the same expression of surprise, her lips never moving to form a greeting, her blue eyes locked on his. He tried to calm himself and lose the flushed state, but when Claire spoke his name, the words rushing through him, deepening his color.

"Arthur?" She whispered into the silence of her world.

Her eyes delved deep into him, searching for the memory of his name. She took a step back, looking exposed and fearful. "Yes, your teacher from long ago." He said as softly as possible. "I was there. Remember? You saved the young girl from the river in the south of France and then you fled, never to be seen again, until now. Claire, that was eighteen hundred years ago. Have you been here the whole time?" He winced at asking too much of her all at once. "Sorry," fell from his lips as she retreated and collapsed into the tall grass and flowers by the narrow path up the ridge.

He knelt beside her, stroking her face, completely taken aback. Angels don't faint. "Claire. I'm sorry if I frightened you. I know you've been alone for so long. Please don't be afraid of me." He brushed her auburn hair aside and kissed her on the forehead. He listened intently, trying to hear her thoughts, but she was nowhere to be found. After a time, he decided to carry her back to the

18

shelter where she'd been living. He scooped her into his arms and carried her down the winding path as darkness set in, emerging from the blackness of the forest by her shelter. He laid her on her bed and started a fire for warmth and comfort. He sat on the other side of the hut and waited for her to wake.

There in the flickering firelight, he thought of her those many years ago, and of how proud she'd made him feel. Such a daring Angelic Soul, placing a human life above her own on her very first assignment, and sacrificing everything of herself for the child. She was just as beautiful now as then, perhaps having made peace with herself, and her decision to live alone in a world of her making – still in the Angelic Realm though. He wondered what she'd thought about through all those years, being so completely alone in her thoughts and in her little world, and he questioned why he'd not seen any animals in her quiet corner of life. Did she really want to be left alone? Was it wrong of Sandy and the Higher Ups to interfere in her life by sending him?

"Sandy," he spoke softly. "Is this wrong of us to do?" He waited for a long time for her to answer, thinking she'd not wanted to answer his call. But she did, telling him in the gentlest voice he'd ever heard from her, to be patient with her, this was the right thing to do. He nodded to himself, deferring to Sandy's wisdom, and sitting quietly by the fire, he waited for Claire to wake.

Morning came late to the valley, the sunlight blocked by the mountains and then filtered through the tall trees. He hadn't moved all night. The last flicker of fire had passed hours ago, leaving him in darkness for most of the night, till midmorning. The faint light which came through the narrow archway threw only the dimmest of shadows against the walls. It dawned on him that his aura was not lighting the hut at all. Even in the darkness of the forest, he'd projected no light whatsoever, carrying Claire down from the ridge last night – very strange for an Angel's aura not to light the way. Claire was still not awake, her body wrapped in her wings just as he'd laid her hours ago. Sandy had not told him anything about what to do for this situation, except to be patient. He didn't understand why he couldn't hear her thoughts – he could always hear his students' thoughts when needed. It was a part of his job and often proved helpful to his students. He moved to her side feeling a need to be close and listened intently, finding only an empty feeling inside himself, a hollow that needed filling.

"Sandy," he murmured. "What's wrong here? I don't understand the silence coming from Claire." Her answer didn't come until the sun was overhead and the inside of the hut was bright enough to see its woven branches and the placid expression on Claire's face.

"Arthur, you haven't been able to hear Claire, because when she fainted, I took her Soul with me to see the Higher-Ups. They wanted to understand why she'd chosen to remain alone for so long and to help her understand that she was still a member of the Angelic Fold. I'm sorry to have left you in the dark all night, but I didn't have the opportunity to explain before I took her. Forgive me, old friend."

"Yes, of course, you're forgiven. When will she wake up?" Arthur stood hunched over inside the hut and stretched his wing, touching the sidewalls he beat them forcefully, stirring Claire's garment and some of the dried cedar leaves on the dirt floor. "Give her back to me, Sandy. The Higher-Ups don't know how hard it is for young students – they've forgotten." Arthur folded his wings and knelt again.

"Don't start Arthur. I will not go there with you. She'll wake soon enough. But if you must, try calling her name, she knows your voice."

Arthur bent close to Claire, breathing in the earthy fragrance of her hair. "Claire, come back from your slumber. It's a new day and the sun is up high in the sky. We could go for a walk and pick some flowers like you were doing when I came. It's Arthur, your old teacher. Wake up Claire." He rocked back on his heels and stirred the air with his wings, in hopes of disturbing her slumber. "Claire," he called out loudly, sending a chill down his back. He was getting frustrated, not something that happened often at all – maybe twice in his life. The first was when she disappeared and he felt responsible.

"Mmm," she murmured softly.

"Claire," he whispered in her ear. "It's Arthur, you old teacher. Wake up, Claire." Her eyelids fluttered, lifting ever so slightly. She murmured something he didn't catch. "Hey, sleepyhead, nap time's over." He smiled, happy to see her waking. Her eyes opened all the way and she looked up at him with curious, sleepy eyes.

"Arthur? What are you doing here?"

He laughed aloud. "Well, that's a long story. Interested?" She stretched a little, unfolding her wings from their tight embrace, and rubbed her eyes and face. Her intense gaze found him and pierced his heart.

"You scared me. How did you find me? And what are you doing here?" She asked again.

"Can you sit up?" His feelings boiled to the surface, making him blush. Gathering his composure, he helped her up and then stood to give her some space to think and get her bearings. "It's been a long time." He watched the recognition grow on her face, remembering the centuries of self-reflection she'd endured – all of her own free will. She rubbed her eyes again, nodding.

"Help me up Arthur. I want to go outside in the sunshine. It smells like smoke in here. Did you make a fire?"

He offered his hand to pull her to her feet, and then ducked out through the doorway, taking several steps away from the hut. The sun was directly overhead, warm, and inviting. He felt better now that she was awake, but had many questions. They would have to wait though, at least until she was more aware of being in a familiar place. She stepped through the doorway, having only to bend slightly and spread her wings in the sunlight, turning and arching skyward. She stretched her hands toward the sky and flapped her wings, lifting off the ground a few feet, and then settled back down.

"Arthur. How did you find me? Did you have help from, you know, the others?"

"Sandy helped me. She brought me close to your world, but I think it was your need to be found, which guided me to the mountaintop." He pointed towards the tallest peak.

"I forget . . . Is she your teacher?" Claire wiped a tear that had appeared just as she mentioned the word teacher.

"And yours too. Remember?" He could see she did because it brought the tear to her eye. She remembered something of the incident long ago. "I was there with you. I was your teacher, and Sandy mine." Claire's legs slowly folded under her, collapsing her to a seated position. Her face showed the same fearful look as when they'd met on the path.

"Help me to remember, Arthur." Claire's eyes pleaded.

"Let's go for a walk, shall we." He said, extending his hand to her. "I like the ridge where we met yesterday. Could we go there?" She nodded, taking his hand and pulled herself up. Her hand was trembling slightly as they walked into the woods on the well-worn path she established through the many years in exile. He was happy to be with her again, reminiscent of days past, but all new to him again. He wrapped a wing around her, drawing her close, doing what little he could to comfort her, his student of long ago. His heart raced forward down the path in anticipation of what lay ahead, hopeful for his charge, that she might recover her will to live a meaningful life.

Claire stopped trembling halfway to the cliffs, breathing a deep sigh of relief when she saw them. Clearly, she was at home again, and ready to talk about deeper issues than what they'd covered on the path through the woods. He let her lead on the narrow winding ledge carved into the cliff face. The home she'd made for herself impressed him with its grandeur and imaginative landscapes, truly a beautiful world, all except for her hut, which was austere and wanting, but perhaps fitting for her frame of mind.

He stepped up beside her when they'd exited the ledge, taking her hand again and swinging it gently as they walked up the ridge. Claire stopped where she'd dropped her basket full of flowers, picking the basket up and examining its contents, removing the wilted ones.

"For you Arthur," she held a small bunch of tiny white flowers out to him. "I'm sorry I was so afraid. Thank you for coming to help me."

Again, a tear appeared in her eye as she thanked him, the basket shaking in her hand. Claire nestled into his arms and wrapped her wings around him. He was melting inside, his Soul stirred by the power this youngster held over him. "I missed you," he whispered, his face buried in her hair. Her eyes gazed up into his, filled with liquid love.

"I missed you too, Arthur."

They sat in the tall grasses and flowers and spoke of many things. He tried his best to answer her questions, as she did for him. It was the best day he'd had in a thousand years. "No, eighteen hundred years," he corrected himself.

THE ASSIGNMENT

It was dusk as they descended from the ridge and returned to Claire's hut for the night. He built a fire, while she gathered a few plants in the fading light, from the meadow and forest for a vegetable soup, a habit she'd opted to keep from her days in the south of France – Angels don't eat. He'd not noticed a small cooking pot in the hut until she took it to the brook to fill. There was a lot he'd not seen of her world and wished they could stay here for awhile, but it was not to be. After finishing the pot of soup, which he thought was quite good, he could hear Sandy calling to them for their return. While they sat by the fire, Sandy took them from Claire's home of eighteen hundred years to her place in the Angelic Realm, perched on the edge of the vast canyon where he'd left on his journey. It was too soon, but then he didn't really have a choice in the matter.

"Welcome, Claire. I'm Sandy, and I am so very glad to see you once again."

Sandy didn't wait for her to acknowledge, she took Claire by the hand and led the way down into the canyon, and river below. As they approached, a dwelling by the river came into view, something he'd missed on his first visit to Sandy's retreat. It was a modern, glass and fieldstone marvel of design, molded into its natural desert setting, with the turquoise waters of the river flowing a short distance away. They landed on a flagstone path, which led from the house to the river, surrounded by a desert in bloom. Sandy had quite the getaway.

"Home sweet home," she said, folding her wings. "Let's go sit by the river for a while, and talk of your assignment."

Again, she didn't wait for an answer, taking off down the path with Claire in tow. He fell in behind them listening to the rushing river up ahead. Sandy led them to two ornately carved wood benches facing each other by the river, surrounded by small cactus in bloom. He had to hand it to her; his getaway wasn't nearly as dramatic as this, or as beautiful. He had a log cabin in the mountains, period. Sandy sat down and patted the place next to her, motioning to Claire. She dutifully sat next to her, across from the one she wanted to be next to, making a face at him. He smiled at her, projecting what his heartfelt. Sandy eyed him like she used to when he was her student centuries ago.

"I'll get right to the point of this gathering. Again Claire, welcome home. Arthur, your assignment will take you and Claire back to your home on Earth, where you will continue with your current assignment. Claire will live with you, assuming the body of your sixteen-year-old niece, daughter of your deceased sister Josselyn, who died in a car accident with her cousin, Beth. Claire, these are not real people, to answer the question you're about to ask. Arthur, you will also have Beth's daughter living with you, who is also sixteen years old. You may remember Rachel, who you both knew from the south of France. Claire and Rachel are cousins and will both attend the school where you teach and are a part of your assignment. Rachel is no longer among us, as she Fell from Grace some sixteen hundred years ago. You and Claire will retrieve her from her prison in the Depths of Darkness to which she has descended, for a second chance at her life in the Angelic Ranks."

"Hmm, second chances. That's unusual." Arthur made himself pause to think of what not to say. "How can I possibly accomplish my assignment with two inexperienced Angels, much less with one who has Fallen?" He bit his lip to keep from saying what he really wanted to say about the knuckleheads in charge.

"Knuckleheads? Really Arthur." She laughed.

"Sorry. No offense implied." He lowered his head.

"Well, those knuckleheads want to give Rachel a second chance, because she witnessed what Claire did, and they think that she was unfairly influenced by the incident. She was also on her first assignment at the time.

"What did she do?" Claire asked.

"Rachel killed a man to stop him from raping a woman on the streets of Paris, AD 414. She lost complete control of herself in a rage, which speaks of a deep-seated anger she'd acquired while living in the physical realm. The man was her assignment, as strange as it may sound. Anyway, the Higher Ups think she deserves to be tested. That's part of your assignment, Arthur. You're the Assessor, and the grading scale will be tough on her this time. Claire will be graded by you as well, only on a different scale of course."

Claire groaned audibly, her head turning as far away from Sandy as it would let her. Arthur had never seen such a cold shoulder given to another in their ranks. "Tough assignment Sandy. Am I on trial here too?"

"Don't start Arthur. I warned you before about that, and yes, it is a tough assignment. We reassigned Cindy because we didn't think she could handle it as well as you. You were chosen specifically for this one, because of your experience, and because you were Claire's teacher. Rachel was added only recently. I have faith in you Arthur. You won't be alone on this one; I'll be available if you need me. If either of you has questions; now would be the right time to ask them. You'll be leaving in a little while."

"And if I fail," Claire asked. "Then what? Will I join the ranks of the Fallen?"

Sandy shifted her position on the bench to face Claire. Arthur had seen this look before, and it was usually accompanied by a tongue-lashing; not a pretty sight to behold. Sandy took it all in stride though, softening her voice and posture.

"Claire. Arthur will afford you every leniency, as you made but a small mistake on your first assignment. That and you've punished yourself for way too long; but it was your choice, for which we did not want to interfere. If you'll but remember your birthright of free-will, then I know you'll do well."

Arthur interrupted Sandy, standing and walking away towards the river, weaving in and out of the yellow and red blooming cactus. He'd heard enough to know he was about to react and say something he would most assuredly regret. He could hear Sandy's, 'Tsk Tsk', in his head. He ignored her rebuke and continued to the river's edge, looking straight up at the edge of the two-mile-high canyon wall. It was magnificent, he had to give her credit. He returned to the bench and sat down, seeing that Claire was still upset.

"I'll be leaving now. You may use the house until it's time to go. Talk to Claire about the assignment, Arthur. It's an important assignment." Sandy said, fading from view.

He breathed a sigh of relief at her exit, why, he didn't know. He walked Claire back up the path to the house, wanting to hear more about her extended absence from the Ranks, something unique among Angels, especially one so young. He also wanted to discuss their assignment, which he had to admit was quite unique – no, more like unheard of; but he did feel honored to be a part of it and relished in the Higher Ups' trust in him, which didn't come easily in the Ranks of Angels. He opened the glass door for her, stepping into a large room with a high flat-beamed ceiling of spruce. They sat by the open fire pit in the center of the room on a southwestern styled sofa, which faced the river.

"Where should I begin, Claire?" He mumbled, stretching out on the sofa. "That didn't come out quite right," he said to himself. "Claire, tell me how you feel about our assignment." He looked her straight in the eye, listening intently, and still unable to hear her thoughts. "It's okay to be nervous around me. You've been alone for so long. I would imagine this is a very difficult situation for you, one without your consent I might add. But, it's the way things are done in our Ranks – orders given, orders carried out. Sandy can be abrupt at times, but she is always fair, and always looks out for us. Tell me what you're feeling right now. You know I care about you." Her eyes, awash in tears, shot up to meet his. She leaned into him, laying her head on his chest, her eyelids slicing through a tear, sending it cascading down her cheek and into his lap.

"Just hold me, Arthur. That's all I want for now."

He extended his wings around them, enveloping them both in a cloistered peace. In the quietude, he whispered to her about his life as a teacher, and about how much fun it was to have a physical body to inhabit. It hungered, and thirsted for life, clinging to the mind that made choices, and then hung on for dear life through every experience: happy, sad, angry, proud, all the wildness of life contained in physical form. He told her she would love it so much when it came time to leave, there would be incredible sadness it was done, and time to move on to a new life; but there would be much ecstasy in a life well lived.

When Sandy came for them, they had not moved, and together, had fallen into a dream-like state, where they could rest, free of what lay before them.

DEPTHS OF DARKNESS

Sandy took them gently, in their entwined dreamlike state, stopping some moments later, high above a busy Angelic World, where all below paused to look up at the three of them, their eyes bidding them farewell, with wishes for courage and faith in their mission ahead. Arthur was overwhelmed with their love, never having received anything remotely close to their send off. Claire gazed intently on Sandy's gold tipped wings shimmering in the sunlight, extending beyond those of Arthur, sensing for the first time how special she was in the Angelic Ranks – leader of many, servant of all. Arthur took her hand and together with Sandy's, raised them in salute to those below, thanking them for wishing them well on their mission. His wingtips were flashing a golden hue as well. She didn't think to look at hers.

"See Claire, you are welcome here, and held in high esteem. Hold this moment in your thoughts always, fall back on it if needed, because it is a place to find and center yourself if ever you should need it. Emblazon their faith in your mind that you might never be lost again." Claire was shining like he remembered her. She was ready.

Sandy led them from the tranquil place in what seemed to him as no particular direction, but it was evident they were moving away from the Angelic Realm, and into a place even he had never been. Darkness slowly enveloped them, pulling them down with increasing intensity, deeper into the unknown. Sandy stopped their descent just short of the roiling, absolute blackness ahead.

"I'll be leaving you now, but will be with you when you call me. Remember your birthrights, for in the depths of darkness you will feel alone and lost. If your light should go out, do not be concerned with what cannot bring harm to you. You are an Angel, Claire, and the darkness has no power over you. Arthur, I have given you the path to follow to Rachel. Do not stray from it. You will find Rachel in a despondent state, but deep down in her there lies a memory of where she came from. Call it from her, lead her to it, and you will succeed. Go in grace that you may come back to us."

Sandy enveloped them in a brilliance, which threw back the darkness, and then she was gone. He stood with Claire at the entrance to darkness, a little unsure of himself, but ready to follow orders and plunge into the unknown. "Well," he said quietly. "Here we go," taking the first step.

"Arthur," Claire's voice wavered. "Don't let go of my hand."

Together they took the first and only step into the dark abyss, and there was no going back from it, as it swept them down, dragging them into a place, he'd never been. He gripped her hand tightly with both of his, not knowing what to expect, as they could not see the way ahead. Claire gasped and held him close when hands extended from the darkness all around them and tried to latch onto them as they descended. Desperate decaying hands raked over their bodies, unable to grasp them, but trying in desperation to escape their entombment in the darkness. "Claire, don't be afraid. Remember what Sandy told us: 'darkness has no power over you.' "We'll be fine." He felt his strength sucked from him, his faith clawed at by the desperate beings they passed, but he held fast to his faith, knowing this would pass.

"I have faith in you Arthur," Claire whispered in his thoughts.

"Thank you, Claire. I've not heard your voice in my thoughts for a very long time. It is a comfort to me." Arthur felt better now than he had in ages, even with their encasement in darkness. They were together again.

The hands left them and they slowed, as the faint outline of a cavern appeared ahead, the first thing they'd seen since departing. A large silhouette became visible as they approached. They were walking on their own now, taking hesitant steps on the uneven rocky floor of the cavern. Claire sucked in her breath and stopped when they both saw how small Rachel was next to this mountain of midnight blue, a beastly looking thing, which had its clawed foot firmly wrapped around Rachel. She was turning the same color as him, with all but a tinge of dirty white at her wing tips. It was sucking the life out of her, that much was apparent. The beast paid them no mind until he called out to Rachel, wanting her to know she was not alone.

"Rachel," his voice swallowed by the darkness. There was no echo like in a cavern on Earth. "Rachel, you're not alone."

The beast clutched her even closer to it, staring down at them with black eyes and an ugliness oozing from it like a festering wound. Rachel had not looked up, perhaps lost in despair, and unable to hear them. He turned to Claire. "She's one of us. She'll hear us both if we concentrate on who she is – an Angel. They stepped to within inches of the beast's foot, where Rachel lay encased in its claws. She nearly disappeared in the size of it, clutched as if she were a prized possession.

"Rachel," they said in their thoughts. "Awake, Rachel, we have come to take you home. Arthur reached out and laid a hand on her wing, which was protruding from between the three-fingered claws of the beast's paw. Arthur focused his thoughts like Sandy had told him to do, creating a link with Rachel to her past and the world where she belonged. Rachel's head rose from the beast's foot, opening her bloodshot eyes to see who was speaking to her.

The despair in her eyes wasn't easy to look at, hauntingly empty and pleading their last look of any hope for life.

"Rachel, try to remember who you are," he said aloud. This caused the beast to stir, growling its displeasure, and drawing Rachel up into its massive arms. As she disappeared into it enormous limbs, the beast snarled at them, barring yellowed teeth and a decaying breath of death. He stepped back with Claire to reassess the situation. Sandy had told him it might not be as easy as just showing up and saving the day, and she was right.

"What do you think we should do, Claire? That didn't seem to do the trick."

"You saw her eyes, Arthur. She wants to be helped but is completely unable to stop the beast from emptying her of life. Sandy told us our light would leave us, but it didn't mean we'd be helpless."

"She said to keep the faith and it would cut through the darkness. Maybe we should address the beast. It used to be something or someone else before it came here, so maybe it could remember a little of its real self, enough that it might want to release Rachel out of regrets." Claire said.

Arthur raised an eyebrow, looking at the thing towering over them, a little bit intimidated. "Let's talk to it like we would a person." Claire nodded with hopeful eyes rising to his. "But what to say," he mumbled, as Claire's voice rose above his.

"We're sorry you're in pain. We know you probably didn't mean to hurt yourself or others. You're more than this. You're a person who once loved, who cared for others and had people caring for you." Claire spoke softly and firmly, each word crisp and lean.

Arthur nodded for her to continue, as she was having an effect on the beast. It was looking at them, not snarling or growling, but looking with wide sad eyes. Rachel's head appeared from the beast's arms, as it seemed to relax its grip.

"We want to help you remember who you were before you were here. Nothing can take that away from you. Try to remember who you were, what your life was before. Know that you're forgiven for whatever you did. Touch my hand and try to remember."

Arthur watched as Claire stepped towards the beast and reached up with her hand. He tried to not be afraid, summoning from deep within himself all of his strength, all of his faith and understanding, and reached out to Claire, sending it all, and his love for her. She was as fearless now as that day in France.

"Touch my hand. Let us help you be free of this place."

The beast groaned loudly, its free paw snatching Claire from the cavern floor, and raising her up, groaning all the while, like it was in pain. Arthur swallowed his doubts and called out to the thing. "We can help you if you let us. We care about you and want to help." His words returned in a faint echo from a distant wall. The beast's head snapped towards the direction of the echo, perhaps never having heard one before. A deep wailing groan echoed through the cavern, rebounding off the walls, a deafening sound building upon itself. The beast moaned in pain, agony filling its ugly face, and lowered its arms, gradually releasing Claire and then Rachel, leaving them laying on the cavern floor. The beast went silent, with only its breathing audible, in shallow halting breaths. Arthur quickly gathered Rachel in his arms from the cavern floor, Claire helping him with her wings, which were dangling and catching on the jagged boulders strewn about on the cavern floor. Together they retreated, stepping back a ways before turning to hurry away. The beast did nothing to stop them as they retreated to the entrance of the cavern.

"Sandy, we could really use your help now to find our way home. Can you do that now please?" Arthur said in earnest. As promised, Sandy reached out to them and guided them back the way they'd come, only this time, there were no hands clutching at them, and the way was lit by their aura, albeit a bit dim by Angelic standards. When they left the place of darkness, there was a quiet sucking sound as the opening closed behind them, leaving him to wonder about the gravity of their situation, if they too had accidentally fallen by the wayside and been sucked down into everlasting darkness. He shivered at the thought, glad to be done with the task.

AWAKENING

Arthur shook off the chill as they entered Sandy's retreat home, and as much as he hated to admit it, that black hole in the universe had changed him – shaking him to his very core. Admitting to himself he was afraid and had doubted his powers while in the dark place troubled him, but Rachel was free now, and that's what mattered. He laid her on the sofa in the living room and started a fire in the sunken pit because Rachel was deathly cold when he'd picked her up in the cavern. She was dark blue and cold, with the same fringe of dirty white on the tips of her wings not having changed much except their dark blue tint had lightened in places. Rachel's Fall from Grace had drained the life out of her and was replaced by what she thought her punishment should be, evidenced by the dark place she'd taken herself. If they'd stayed longer or had strayed from Sandy's path, they probably would have begun to look like Rachel. Sandy appeared next to Rachel on the sofa, looking down at her, with wings stretched wide.

"It was difficult, I'm sure, but you succeeded just as I knew you would. Poor thing," Sandy said, gently stroking Rachel's head. "She must have suffered greatly."

"Did you see where she was in that dark place?" Arthur glanced at her sideways, wondering if Sandy really understood what had happened to Rachel. Sandy's brow furrowed when their eyes met.

"Of course I saw. I observed through the two of you." Sandy said quietly.

"You were there? You saw and heard everything? Arthur bowed his head, sorry he'd questioned her.

"Yes, Arthur. I know it was difficult for you both. The depth of Rachel's despair was a challenge for me as well. The death of an Angel is not a pretty sight, as you both now know. But Rachel will recover thanks to you and will begin her life again."

Sandy vanished as quickly as she'd appeared. "Why does she do that?" He gazed down at his new charge laying half dead on the sofa.

"Perhaps because she is busy," Claire said. "What are we to do now? I don't think I can help you with Rachel."

Claire took a step back from Rachel, looking scared of what could have happened to her. "Actually Claire, you're the perfect one to help Rachel. You understand a little of what she went through, because of your self-imposed banishment from the Angelic Ranks. Why don't you sit with her awhile, touch her, and get to know her in this state? So when she is well, you will have an appreciation for everything she went through. You saw the utter despair in her eyes in the cavern. You heard the mournful cries of the beast when it knew where it was and why."

"I don't ever want to hear that sound again," Claire said despondently. "It would be a horrible place to die."

Arthur took Claire's hand and sat with her on the sofa next to Rachel, in hopes she would talk to her. Sandy really hadn't given him any instructions on how to help Rachel, and he had no experience in these sorts of matters. It was all new to him, but Sandy was confident that he and Claire would figure it out. Claire moved a little closer to Rachel's head and laid a hand on her cheek, stroking it and humming to herself. Arthur closed his eyes to listen, carried away by the feeling Claire was emitting with her voice. After a bit, she began to sing quietly, swaying with each stroke of Rachel's cheek and hair.

"If these words would find an ear and then
to lay upon your heart. I rejoice in knowing
all is not lost, for I have found a new friend
and hope to know you well. So lay in quietude
with new found peace, that we may walk again,
together as one under starry night skies.
Emblazon my heart and let your words fall
well upon my ear. To see you rise to greet
new life that all may be well within your heart.
Rise Rachel to meet the day. Lo I await your
eye's new gaze, which so warmly falls upon my face.
Our love is not lost but only awaits, the longing
to feel its gentle bright touch. Walk with me on your
new path in sun's bright glow. Rise, Rachel, to
greet your new day."

Arthur was taken far away by Claire's song, to a place he'd not been much, except in times of trouble; a place where hope could lay hold of him and lift him up. When he opened his eyes, Claire was glowing brightly and Rachel's eyes were fluttering and her dark blue color gradually fading to a powdery blue. Rachel's eyes opened as Claire stroked her wings, wiping away the darkness and terror of the cavern. Tears rolled down Claire's face, dropping into Rachel's hair, brightening it to a clear glossy black from the dull midnight blue. Rachel looked up at Claire, her eyes welling up with tears, awake for the first time in centuries. The suffering was gone from them, their clear light brown color alive with new life. Rachel slumbered, no more in despair; awake now with her Claire, a newfound friend. The faintest of smiles laid hold of her face, as she reached up to touch Claire's cheek, her lips murmuring a thank you, as the room filled with light from Sandy's return with five other Angels. They surrounded the three of them on the sofa, singing softly of their friend's return. Arthur had no words to describe what he felt for his Claire, his student of long ago.

"And so your journey begins. Your paths are woven together for the three of you. Thank you for the light you bring to life; Arthur, Claire, and Rachel." Sandy whispered to each.

The others left them at song's end, leaving a warm glow in the room, and in their hearts. Arthur was still a little dazed from Claire's depth of clarity and understanding, which she had displayed. For one so young, she had a deep wisdom and command of her words. Something must have happened during those eighteen hundred years alone, something he'd only seen after centuries of guidance by the Elder Angels. It made him wonder all the more about this mysterious rebel, who banished herself out of shame.

"So young yet so wise," Sandy answered in his questioning mind.

Sandy moved to stand in front of Rachel, who had since sat up, and unfurled her wings, encompassing the three of them on the sofa, beating them gently, stirring their feathers.

"You have come to this place from far below, where darkness is the way of life for all living things. Let its lingering memories draw you nearer your source of light and inspiration, that you may serve well the cause set before you. You have taken the first step on your path together; one of many yet to come, all of which will test you to the very limits of your resolve and strength. Remember this day, so you may draw upon each other's gifts, and stay the course of your challenges. You shall rest here for two more days so that Rachel will find her strength once again."

Sandy silently instructed him on the assignment and his role in helping these two wayward Angels to fully recover and grow to be teachers in their own right. They were a family now, both here and on their assignment together. Sandy gave him enough to get started, without saying what the outcomes might be. That was always up to the mentor and student to work out together.

"I must leave you now, and I won't be back. Arthur knows how to reach me. I will always be there to help whenever you need me. Until we meet again, I go with you in my heart."

Sandy's wings beat as she faded from the room, leaving behind three feathers from her wings. "It's kind of her trademark, to leave us a part of herself," Arthur said, holding the one, which had fallen into his lap. They always had a sparkle to them and this time was no exception. He tucked his into a niche in his wings, where many others lingered. Claire twirled hers in her fingers, making it sparkle even more; looking to Arthur for what would come next. She appeared anxious to get started on their assignment together, ready to leave behind the cavern of darkness and the memory of her own exile.

"Do you feel up for this Rachel?" Claire asked. "Are you ready to venture into the unknown world of teenagers?"

Rachel managed a weak smile, continuing to twirl her feather, appearing hypnotized by the sparkles it gave off. "Shall we get started?" He asked, shifting his position on the sofa. "Rachel is getting better, and you Claire, look impatient to begin. We have two days to sort through our assignment, while Rachel continues to improve, and hopefully, she'll recover by the time we leave this place. The next stop will be my home in Washington DC, with you two as orphaned cousins, both in sixteen-year-old female bodies and juniors in the high school where I teach. You won't assume the physical bodies until we arrive at my house. So let's get cracking."

Arthur spent the next two days instructing his charges in the ways of human teenagers. He explained that they would be subject to all the hormonal rushes and the like, which the human female body experiences. He stumbled while talking about sex to them, blushing like any father would, tripping over his feelings for Claire. He could almost see Sandy looking down at him, shaking her head at how easily he was influenced by his past, and admonishing him, 'to work it out'. He knew that he would, so for now, he let himself fall into his excitement to be with Claire again, the rest could wait until later.

HOME

Leaving Sandy's place in the canyon was the easy part, harder, was the abrupt arrival at his home with two recovering Angels thrust into the bodies of female teens. He was used to dealing with a physical body, having done it hundreds of times. Claire and Rachel were a different story. Not realizing that living in a physical body can seem an overwhelmingly claustrophobic experience, both Claire and Rachel were anything but calm, cool and collected for the better part of an hour. He busied himself with homework, which he'd left undone, knowing full well they would have to work it out for themselves. So, there they stayed, in his living room, him on the couch buried in homework on his laptop, and them, jumping from the couch to the hall mirror, alternately admiring their new bodies and bemoaning their plight. It was an amusing scene and it all passed fairly well, he thought. No one was bleeding, no torn clothing, no broken windows, and no Bosco the cat getting underfoot.

He waved at Bosco who was perched on the front windowsill peering in, his mouth opening and closing with incessant meowing. He retrieved the two laptops, which Sandy had provided. They contained their class schedule, what not to eat in the cafeteria, and a long detailed summary of teen lingo, so they could at least understand what others were talking about. He handed them the laptops on their way upstairs to bed, urging them to respect each other's privacy at home, and not leave the bathroom a complete mess in the morning. He would be sleeping on the futon in his study, giving them the upstairs to themselves, except they had to share his bathroom with them. After he let a very annoyed Bosco in, he followed them upstairs to get his pillow, the extra comforter off his bed, and his toothbrush. They were already in Claire's bedroom talking up a storm, comparing class schedules and the like. The thought of two teen girls in his home brought a smile to his face on the way back down the stairs with Bosco. This weekend had to have been an all-time record of some sort, for strange happenings and new beginnings. He and Bosco would have to do some serious adapting in the days to come.

Nodding off to sleep, the weekend's events were parading through his mind, and how neatly Sandy had altered time, by cramming what seemed like an eternity into his weekend. Angelic time was different from the way humans measured the stuff. The girls were giggling when he drifted into a deep sleep, but it was not the sound that woke him four hours later.

It was 3 a.m. when the blood-curdling scream hit him like a brick and snapped him into an adrenalin-induced wakefulness. He stumbled up the stairs and into Rachel's room, flicking on the ceiling light, and finding her curled into a tight ball under the covers. She was shaking uncontrollably and drenched in a cold sweat.

"Rachel," he squeezed her shoulders with both hands. "Wake up! It was only a dream, Rachel." She opened her eyes, the terror etched on them and her face.

"It was here," she sobbed. "The beast was here in my room."

She clutched at him, wrapping her arms around his waist. "It was a dream, that's all." He peeled her arms off him, helped her to sit up, and rubbed her back to help wake her from her first night terror. Claire stood beside them looking worried. He patted the bed and she sat down, laying her head on his shoulder, her hand reaching out behind him to stroke Rachel's head.

"I had the same dream. We were in the cavern and Rachel was screaming, held captive by the beast. But, I knew it was only a dream." Claire said.

"It was so real," Rachel sobbed. "It was sucking the life out of me all over again."

"Yes, but you're here now, in your bed with Claire and me. It was a dream. You're safe now and the beast can never hurt you again." Arthur rubbed her back vigorously. "Here," he said lifting her chin with his other hand. "Look at me. You're alright now." He stood up to let Claire take over. She could do a better job of helping her. "Oh, by the way, nice PJs." Sandy had left them matching pink ones with little angels fluttering everywhere among puffy clouds. Rachel looked down at the angels covering her and giggled with Claire.

"Good night." He kissed them both on top of the head. He wondered how long the memory of the blue beast and the darkness of the cavern would haunt Rachel. Sixteen hundred years she'd endured that place. He shivered at the thought, as he climbed back under the covers. He fell asleep having a one-way conversation with Sandy about how ill-prepared she'd left him to deal with Rachel and Claire, to say nothing of the fact she expected them to be able to dive into their assignments. He thought it a little unfair, even by Angelic Standards, to expect so much from the two young Angels. He'd have to take it up with Sandy in the days to come, broadcasting the thought loud and clear, knowing she'd hear him.

Bosco woke him at dawn, with his incessant gravelly meowing from his perch on the planter outside his window. He let him in, stopping to make coffee for himself and orange juice for the girls, all the while, Bosco following his every step and rubbing his leg. Bosco was a big tomcat and had tripped him many times getting underfoot when least expected.

"Hey, you girls awake up there?" He called up the stairwell. "You don't want to be late your first day of school." He heard the bathroom door close and the water running in the shower. He nodded, smiling, at how different it was to have company in his home – and two teenage girls at that. He stepped out onto the porch to retrieve the morning paper, taking a deep breath of the crisp fall air, a little ritual he'd come to enjoy before his morning coffee. The one thing he liked best about having a physical body was the taste of coffee in the morning, and then breakfast, and lunch, and dinner, and snacks. Food was definitely a motivator for him, kept him coming back all those years of assignments. He was most fond of his assignments in the Asian countries, because of their insanely spicy cuisine. After he'd made a batch of French toast and on his third cup of coffee, the girls sauntered into the kitchen with Bosco in tow, all looking a wee bit disheveled. "Morning. School starts in fifty minutes and it takes ten minutes to get there." A hint he hoped.

"Morning," Claire said, sitting down.

Rachel mumbled something he couldn't make out but took it as a good morning. "You'll get used to having a physical body in no time. Anyone hungry?" He poured them both a glass of juice and waited for their eyes to light up with the first sip – and he was right. "Good stuff, eh?"

"Awesome," their voices piled on top each other.

"Breakfast's on the stove," he pointed to the skillet keeping it warm. "I need to get ready while you're eating." He excused himself and went to shave in the powder room under the stairs. When he emerged, they were admiring themselves in the hall mirror. "You both look beautiful." He said cheerfully, to which they giggled. He handed them the jackets Sandy had left for them and held the door on their way out. They were actually a little early, which was always a good thing to be on the first day of school. It was a sunny November morning as the three of them chatted away on the six-block walk to Woodrow Wilson High School, where the two young Angels would get a second chance at life.

WOODROW WILSON HIGH SCHOOL

Claire sat down in the back of the classroom on a chair she removed from a stack along the back wall, for her first day at school, ever. She and Rachel had found their way to their respective classes using the map in their notebooks, which Sandy had provided. Her first class was English with Ms. Letrell on the third floor. It was 7:45 a.m., and so far, she'd not said hello to anyone, and no one had even noticed she was a new student. She shifted in her chair and fiddled with the zipper on her notebook, uncomfortable in her new body and surroundings. The trouble with this arrangement was, she still thought of herself as an Angel, not a teenage girl. Also fresh in her thoughts was the home she'd fashioned in the Angelic Realm and the solitude of the place. The boy at the desk in front of her turned around and smiled directly at her. She felt herself grow warm in the face and her thinking fogged. "Hormones," she mumbled.

After an awkward pause, she smiled back. "Hi, I'm Claire."

"Jeff."

Ms. Letrell entered, causing Jeff to turn back around, and several students to hide their cell phones in their backpacks. Ms. Letrell was looking directly at her, motioning for her to come up front. Claire dutifully walked to the front of the classroom, feeling warm again, knowing it showed on her face for all to see. "Hi, see the new girl, who's embarrassed and blushing," she thought.

"Class, this is Claire, who comes to us from California. Welcome Claire," Ms. Letrell patted her on the back.

She returned to her chair, as there were no desks available in the room of eighteen students. She liked that she was in the rear of the classroom because no one could look at her without turning around to do so. Ms. Letrell began class. They were reading Chaucer from the 14th century. Clair had no idea who that was but liked the discussion.

Claire waded through Western Civilization next, and then Algebra and a Human Development class before she met up with Rachel for lunch. The cafeteria opened out into a large atrium with tables and chairs, large planters, and lounge chairs grouped together. She found Rachel sitting by herself on the edge of a planter. She sat next to her, balancing her tray on her lap. Rachel was sullen and said little while they ate the chicken salad, breadsticks, and string cheese, washing it down with something called 1% milk. "Hey, if this stuffs only 1% milk, what's the other 99%?" She held up the container to Rachel. They laughed together, which was the first sign of life coming from her new sister – cousin actually. "Hard morning?"

"You have no idea," Rachel said. "My first class was American history, and this guy seated in front of me starts hitting on me."

"Don't let it get to you, Rachel. We'll get the hang of this place soon enough. Besides, you're a very pretty girl, much better looking than me." Claire said, trying to cheer her up. "You know what? I got embarrassed in the first two minutes of English. I blushed so hard I must have looked pink." They both giggled. "Hey, we have Theater together. That'll be fun." Rachel's now bright and cheerful face, made Claire feel better than she'd felt all day, except for maybe the French Toast, which Arthur made this morning. They left the atrium for their next classes a few minutes early, checking the map in their notebooks. Sandy had left them each a note and lunch money in a pocket in the notebook. The note read: "Put your best foot forward." It had confused both of them. Which one's the best? They'd have to ask Arthur when they got home.

Claire entered the Applied Science classroom and found an empty stool at the lab table by the windows. Their teacher, Mr. Boswell was late getting there, so she introduced herself to the girl next to her, saying she was new to the area. Lu was Oriental, pretty, and soft-spoken. Claire liked her immediately and was beginning to feel a little comfortable with school, certainly more so than in English class that morning. Mr. Boswell entered pushing a cart with some sort of machine on it, with a shiny metal dome attached to a two-foot column with a pedestal. He plugged the cord coming from it into the side of the lab table up front and flipped a switch, causing a humming sound to start.

"This is a Van de Graaff generator, named after the American Physicist. It generates an electrostatic charge, which can have interesting effects. Ms. Jackson, would you be so kind."

The petite girl with shoulder-length blond hair stepped to the front by Mr. Boswell and his machine. He had her step onto a black mat and put her hands on the metal dome, whereupon her hair stood straight out in a big frizzy ball after a few seconds. Claire didn't have a clue why that would happen.

"Who can tell me what is happening?" Mr. Boswell asked.

One of the guys up front gave an adequate explanation, which Claire didn't understand; something about an electrostatic charge covering the outside of the girl's body, driving her hairs apart from each other. Mr. Boswell pointed to her to come forward. Claire looked around and then back at him. "You mean me?" He nodded and motioned her to the front again, so she slid off her stool feeling embarrassed, again. She was sure she was blushing for all the class to see. Mr. Boswell patted her on the shoulder, trying to comfort her and introduced her to the class and handed her a frosted glass tube. She moved it closer to the metal dome and it flickered to life. She nearly dropped it she was so surprised, and it must have shown because the class snickered. "It felt funny," was her description. When she returned to her stool, her hand brushed against a girl's bare arm and a spark flew from her, shocking the girl. They both jumped a little out of surprise and a dash of pain. Mr. Boswell continued his explanation, and by the time class was over, she understood a little bit about static electricity. She walked part of the way to Theater class with Lu, who introduced Claire to all the latest tidbits of gossip going around, leaving her scratching her head as to what it all meant. Claire liked Lu a lot, glad that she'd made a friend, and was actually looking forward to school the following day. She entered the Theater classroom, intending to sit next to Rachel, but those seats were taken. She found an empty one in the front row and tried to make herself invisible. Mr. Clark, their teacher, came in with Ms. Newman, the production coordinator and head of the Music Department, which she learned when Mr. Clark introduced her. It seemed the two departments were hard at work on the Christmas musical. He asked his two new students to stand and introduce themselves, which she and Rachel did without embarrassing themselves.

Ms. Newman had both of them join her by the piano and asked Mr. Clark to take the rest of the class to the auditorium to begin rehearsal. They'd join them later. Ms. Newman warmed them up and Claire discovered she was definitely a soprano, while Rachel's husky voice was a strong Alto. Everything was going fine right up until it came time to sing a couple of bars of a song from the musical, that's when Claire froze up. Ms. Newman told her it was okay to be nervous and had her sit next to her on the bench. With a wave of heat rushing through her, Claire's hauntingly clear voice laid hold of the song and infused a rush of emotions into it. Claire giggled gleefully at the intensity of feelings coursing through her body and was very aware she had no control of what was happening to her. She was overheated and wavering on the bench so much that she grabbed it with both hands to keep from falling over backwards. Ms. Newman smiled and patted her on the knee.

"That was a good start, Claire Tate. Now let's give Rachel a turn."

Rachel surprised all three of them with the intensity of her gritty, yet wistful voice. Ms. Newman had her do a couple of exercises for her diaphragm, showing her how to breathe and draw the notes down deeper. Rachel's face lit up with what it did for her voice.

"This musical has several duets and I would like to hear you two sing together."

Claire got up and stood next to Rachel, almost giddy with anticipation. Ms. Newman pulled out a different sheet of music and played it halfway through for them, then asked them to hum the first six measures. Then she played their respective part separately, giving them each a chance to learn their part. When they sang together, Claire felt something energizing and inviting going on within her. On their third go-round, Ms. Newman signaled to the audio-video tech to record it, playing the piano much louder than before, making Claire and Rachel sing louder, just to hear themselves above it.

"Let's hear that please," she said to the young lad.

Stunned by what she heard, Claire could hardly believe it was them singing.

"With a lot of practice, you two will bring down the house with this song." Ms. Newman said. "We lost two members of the cast and I think you would be perfect for the parts. Is that something you'd like to do?"

Claire and Rachel's eyes locked in a gaze, which spoke of centuries of pain and sorrow, but that wasn't what they felt at this moment. Just behind the hidden sorrow, lay a pool of eternal love they had for each other. They had to sing together, there was no other answer.

"Yes, Ms. Newman. We'd love to." Claire responded for both of them.

Claire was walking on air as she left with her sister. She hadn't had this much fun ever. They talked nonstop on the way home and couldn't wait to tell Arthur or Bosco for that matter.

Arthur had left them a note saying he'd be a little late, having to catch-up on some work in the computer lab. It also said he was bringing home dinner, but if they needed a snack, there was leftover spaghetti in the fridge from last week. The note on the container said to microwave for two minutes.

"What did you think of your first day?" Claire asked.

"Besides lunch and singing with you, the rest was mostly passable, a little weird but in an okay way. This body will take a while to get used to, but I really liked how it sounded singing with you. Did you feel the same way when she played it back for us? I got shivers up and down my back."

"Yeah, me too." Rachel said, shooing Bosco off the countertop. "Guess he wants something to eat. I'll go look for his cat food."

Claire looked down at Bosco, who was rubbing her pant leg like there was no tomorrow. She reached down and picked him up, hearing and feeling his motor running. "You're a strange sorta guy," she said stroking his head, to which he turned up the volume. Rachel rattled the cat food bag and Bosco leaped out of Claire's arms, his hind claws digging into her belly. "Ouch!" Claire pulled her shirt up to find three tiny dots of blood. "This is weird," she murmured. "I've never bled before." Rachel came over to look.

"Sorry. I didn't mean for him to do that."

They both looked down at Bosco doing a face plant in his food bowl. They looked at each other and laughed. Rachel got her a paper towel off the roll to wipe up the blood. "This is weird," Claire said again. "What do think about this physical body thing?"

"Yeah, I'm not quite sure about anything yet. I'm still trying to get my head around being free of the beast. I was so scared last night that it was happening all over again. I was afraid you and Arthur were just a dream."

Claire hugged her, remembering how scared she was last night. "We're both a little broken, so it might take some time to fix ourselves. But singing together . . ." Claire gave her sister a kiss on the cheek right as Bosco flew between them and out of the kitchen,

"Hi, I'm home," Arthur called out from the front door. "Ow! Bosco that hurt."

Claire giggled with Rachel.

"We're in here," they said together, giggling again.

Arthur came into the kitchen with Bosco in his arm, setting him down to hug the two of them.

"Hey. How was your first day at school?"

Claire hid the bloody paper towel behind her back. "Guess what!" She said excitedly. "We're in the Christmas Musical. We get to sing together." Claire glanced over at Rachel, passing her the towel behind her back to throw in the trash can right behind her. She was embarrassed because some of her insides had leaked out.

"Bosco's handy work?" Arthur asked, eying the two of them.

"What?" Rachel said.

"This." He said pointing to Claire's sweatshirt.

Claire looked down at a small blood spot showing through. "Yeah, he got a little excited about us feeding him. I found out cats have sharp claws–good to know. "I'm hungry too. What's for dinner?"

"Chinese," he said handing her a sack with heavenly aromas. "Let's eat at the kitchen counter."

Claire placed the contents on the counter, including some sticks of some sort. She handed a set of them to Rachel with a curious look. Rachel shrugged her shoulders and got three bowls out and knives, forks and spoons. Claire got a jug of milk from the fridge and three glasses, smiling at Arthur, who was watching the two of them in his kitchen. "Not used to having company?" Claire asked. He shook his head and parked himself on a stool at the end of countertop, and opened all the containers.

"You'll want to try these," he said handing them each a set and broke his apart. "Down here, it's customary to say grace before a meal."

"Okay." Claire raised an eyebrow. Arthur said a short version of what was more of a thank you for this assignment, than a blessing for the food. It was all new to her anyway. She broke her sticks apart, eying them like something to throw on the fire.

"Here," he said. "Hold them like this and tap them together a few times. Then pick up the big pieces of chicken first."

Claire giggled when Rachel flipped her first bite onto the floor, bringing Bosco over from his food bowl. Both she and Rachel turned pink from laughing as Bosco purred loudly, absconding with his booty.

Claire tried the chopsticks but used two fingers to steady the bite across the dangerous open space between bowl and lips. When the first bite of Kung Pow Chicken hit her tongue, her mouth exploded with saliva, her nostrils drinking in the smells. "Oh Arthur, this is wonderful!" She exclaimed, latching onto another big piece of chicken.

"One of the perks of assignments is all the different foods," Arthur said with bulging cheeks.

Claire's head bobbed in approval, her smile reaching nearly to her ears – at least it felt that way in her new body. She stared at Rachel, who was stuffing her cheeks like she'd not eaten in years, which was true. She had suffered greatly in the cavern, so she deserved to relax and enjoy her freedom. Claire still had lingering thoughts about the place and the picture of her sister's lifeless form held captive by the beast. At least in her own self-imposed banishment, she had food to cook, and a warm hut to shelter her. She had her life.

"It will go away with time," Arthur said. "For both of you."

"What will?" Rachel mumbled.

"The cavern . . . you know . . ." Claire hesitated to mention it at all. "Sorry."

"Yeah, I know," she said scooping up a wad of noodles between the sticks and into her mouth, leaving several draping on her chin, before they disappeared between her lips. "Can we not talk about this right now please, or this yummy dinner will wind up tasting like the cavern smelled – old, musty, and filled with the stench of death."

"Sorry," Claire said again. "You're right as always. You should have heard us sing together, Arthur. It was so much fun and we sound really great together. Ms. Newman made a recording and played it back for us. Ask her to play it for you tomorrow." Claire got so excited she forgot all about dinner. This was something more important, more exciting than Kung Pow Chicken and all the other stuff. She could hardly wait until last period tomorrow. Bosco stretched his paw up onto her lap asking for more chicken, which she obliged with several smaller pieces. She was truly happy for the first time in a very long time and glad to feel alive again.

ROUTINES

The morning was crisp and clear, biting her cheeks and making her fingers tingly, reminding Claire of the cold sweat she'd awakened to last night. She'd dreamed she was in the beast's claws, having the life drained out of her, and unable to do anything to stop it from happening. She shuddered at the thought. "Rachel, did you have a nightmare last night?" She wished she hadn't asked, but she had to know if she was having the same nightmares her sister was having. Rachel stopped several steps ahead and turned to face her, with a hint of worry showing. A wave of loneliness swept over Claire, just like it had so often in her world, leaving her cold and afraid of what pain awaited her in her new life.

"Why do you ask?" Rachel finally responded. "Did you?"

"Yes. I woke up in a cold sweat. I was helpless and being held by the beast. I don't know how you managed to keep yourself alive all those years. I think I would have given up." Claire took her sister's hand in her and gazing into her brown eyes, she felt truly alive again, like she had in France so long ago.

"I'm sorry. It's a horrible place to die. I tried to cry out for help for years, but no words would come from my lips. It was the same last night . . . so real." Did you dream that too?"

She nodded. "I know it bothers you to talk about it, but I have to because it bothers me you're in pain about it still. Being there for me was the worst thing I've ever experienced. I can't imagine how bad it was for you."

"I'm sorry if I have hurt you. I don't want to do that, ever. What was your home like, the place you exiled yourself to? Was it nice?"

"I tucked myself away in an obscure corner of the Realm and created my home. I filled it with mountains and tall trees, and it had a path through the forest that I walked every day. My shelter was a hut made of cedar-like branches where I would build a fire most nights to cook with and keep me warm. It must have been a pleasant enough place, as I was there for eighteen hundred years. It didn't seem like a long time, but time in the Angelic Realms really doesn't exist like it does here. I'd have to say it was a paradise compared to where you were." A picture of the path through the forest and her picking wildflowers on the ridge flashed in her mind. "You changed the subject. Did your dream bother you a lot?" Claire winced at her stupid question. "I'm sorry."

"You have no idea what it's like to be completely powerless and have your life slowly sucked out of you. The waves of searing pain were unbearable, as I disappeared into a dark void with the beast grew stronger from my life's essence. I don't expect you or Arthur to ever completely understand because you weren't trapped there, you were only there long enough to rescue me."

The pain in Rachel's eyes grew wide and deep and drew them together into each other's arms. The centuries of anguish all came roaring to the surface in their young bodies, bringing forth an ocean of tears as they clung to each other on this second morning of school. Never had Claire thought she could love someone with such utter abandonment. "Sisters for life," she whispered into Rachel's thick black hair. She wanted this moment to live on forever.

"Hey, you two alright?" The deep male voice said.

Startled, they pulled apart, staring at the bespectacled boyish face atop a gangling body.

"Jake? Hi." Rachel said.

"I stopped because you looked like you were crying, Rachel. You okay?"

"Um. Sorry. Girl stuff – you know. Oh. This is my sister, Claire. Actually my cousin." Rachel said wiping the tears away on her sleeve.

"Hi, Claire. We better hurry, or we'll be late." Jake said and jogged away.

They ran across the school grounds following Jake's bouncing backpack and then split up to go to their respective first-period classes. She entered Ms. Letrell's English class, finding a desk in place of the chair she'd sat in yesterday. She hung her coat on the backrest and sat down for her second English lesson. She waggled her fingers at Jeff when he turned around to strike up a conversation. She looked past him at their teacher.

"Good morning everyone," Ms. Letrell said. "Claire, I have a textbook for you."

Claire went up and got her text, tripping on the way back on a boy's feet, which were now in the aisle. That's how she met Frank Richards, the same Frank that Arthur had in his Web Design Class. She knew that because . . . She couldn't think of how she knew. Murmurs filled the room as she collected her wits and the text from the floor and continued on to her seat, flushed with embarrassment.

"Not one more sound." Ms. Letrell commanded, holding up her hand. "Frank Richards, you owe Ms. Claire Tate an apology."

Frank, slow to show any emotion, turned to face the back of the room and made sure their eyes didn't meet.

"Sorry," his woeful voice trailed off.

He turned back around with a pint-sized grin on his face. "Pathetic," she whispered under her breath. Claire wanted to yell at him, but instead, she vowed Frank Richards would never catch her off guard again. At least she didn't have to see his rich-kid, arrogant, didn't give a damn about anyone face, until Theater class later in the day.

The rest of English class was uneventful, and for that matter, so was the rest of her day. With the exception of Theater class, there wasn't anything special going on for the rest of the day. She did get a note from Mr. Clark delivered to her in Science class though, reminding her about rehearsal at 3 p. m. in the Theater classroom, adjacent to the Theater. She'd have to race over to Arthur's classroom after class to tell him they'd be home later than usual.

Rachel was sitting in the back of the room when she returned and had saved her a seat next to hers. Claire sat down, read the single sheet of paper Rachel had handed her. It was about the Christmas Musical, Do It For Love: the rehearsal schedule, coordination of lighting, sound, sets, and any special effects like snow flying, and the like. She and Rachel would be doing catch up to the rest of the cast, who had been in place for over a month. The only reason she and Rachel got the parts was that the two sisters playing them had to be out of town the week of the performance, for family reasons. Ms. Newman wasn't very happy about that, not having found out until the week before she and Rachel had shown up. Claire didn't care how it had happened, all that mattered was they would be singing together.

Ms. Newman gave them the script with their speaking lines, blocking, costume attire, and the sheet music to three duets of their characters, telling them to see Mr. Clark in a piano rehearsal room next door. They spent the next hour learning the music and the way Ms. Newman wanted them to approach their parts. Mr. Clark was patient with them and worked with an intensity, which left them both exhausted. They walked home in the dark after rehearsal not saying a word, but they both liked how their bodies felt – tired yet deeply satisfied.

Arthur had dinner ready when they walked in, being the astute mentor he was – having listened and known they were tired after a long day. Mr. Bosco weaved between their feet, welcoming them to his home. Claire flopped down in her chair at the dining table and let out a long sigh. "Smells good. Thank you." Rachel sat beside her and promptly dug-in, as the last word spilled from her lips.

"Hungry are we?" Arthur chuckled.

Rachel nodded, only half looking up from her plate of roast chicken. "That's my sis," Claire said to herself and began eating. "Arthur, do you have a Frank Richards in your class?" Claire asked between bites.

"Yes, I do. Why?"

"Because he was rude to me in English class. He tripped me for no reason at all, and he was rude in his apology, which Ms. Letrell told him to say to me. Is he always like this?"

"Pretty much. He's got a chip on his shoulder, I think because his father is a Washington DC Council Member from our Ward, and rides him a lot. I don't know much. I took over from Cindy a month before I found you in your corner of the Realm, so I'm still getting up to speed with Frank Richards and Linda Connor, who are both in my class. They're a part of my assignment and yours. We're one big happy family, the Richards', the Connors', and us."

"Who are Frank and Linda?" Rachel asked.

"You'll see soon enough Rachel. You'll both need to remember that you're here because your mothers died together in an auto accident a month ago, and the court awarded custody to me, your uncle. They were both single parents, never having married their wayward boyfriends if anyone should ask."

"Arthur, did Sandy strip us of all our Angel privileges? You know, our powers." Claire whispered, almost afraid to ask. She'd run away after all and hid from her Angelic duties for such a long time.

"For the most part, Sandy left it up to me. You're both on probation, so-to-speak. For now, it's important for you both to acquaint yourselves with your new lives, and we'll see about those other things as we go along. You might remember that your voices are in my head when I remember to listen. I'm getting used to this arrangement too, you know."

"So you can hear us?" Rachel yelled in her thoughts.

"Yup. We're on a three party line." Arthur grinned. "But only if you direct your thoughts to one of us – mostly. I won't be listening unless you ask me to."

Both she and Rachel jumped at the sound of Arthur in their heads but giggled at the thought of such an outrageous thing. "How about Bosco," Claire said in her thoughts. Bosco came running at her call, jumping into her lap and nestling down, his motor running full throttle.

"And there you have it. The dishes need to be done if you would please. Oh, and Bosco made a little mess in the pantry. He knocked a glass jar off the shelf. Thanks."

"So, this is how it works in regular families," Claire said in her thoughts, as they cleared and loaded the dishwasher, with Bosco rubbing their legs the whole time. Rachel finally booted Mr. Bosco out the back door, since he was being such a pest.

SHOWDOWN

Claire lingered in bed the next morning, thinking about her assignment, Frank the jerk, and Linda, still an unknown. What exactly was expected of her and Rachel? What could these two wayward Angels do for these two screwed up teens? She wondered if all Angels on assignment were kept in the dark, on how to go about helping without breaking the rules. Or, was it just them, and their special needs: one in from the cold – as in a runaway; and one back from the brink of nonexistence for all eternity – one of the Fallen. Quite the pair. She curled herself up inside her fluffy comforter and spoke to Rachel in her thoughts about their day at school, and how cool it was to be able to talk like this.

"Sure beats the pants off of what the blue beast was filling my head with – major pain, anguish, and thoughts so dark I don't even remember them. Life's good now. See you downstairs for breakfast." Rachel's wispy voice ended with a giggle.

Claire rolled out of her sweet repose to attend to all her bodily needs and get ready for the day at school. A physical body was definitely more work than she thought it would be, but it was fun: to shower, then brush and blow dry her hair and highlight her facial features with the makeup kits, which Arthur had provided. She was enjoying living in a beautiful female human form, one that she had a lot to learn about, but the possibilities intrigued her. She'd already noticed a lot of boys watching her in the hallways between classes, making her nervous and self-conscious, but in a good way according to the feelings inside her body. It was exciting.

Both she and Rachel piled their scrambled eggs onto a piece of toast, stuffed their faces, and raced out the door to school. It actually felt quite natural for some reason, like they'd been doing it forever, but the good feeling ended as she entered English class, and found Frank staring at her as she skirted around him getting to her desk. "So you're my assignment. I wonder what we have to do together, you and I." Claire mulled over in her head. Ms. Letrell was writing several essay questions on the board, her slender body moving like an art form delivering a message with intent and feeling.

"Take a sheet of paper out and write your responses to the questions on the board. You have fifteen minutes to complete this."

Claire answered the questions on Chaucer's Canterbury Tales. She heard a few groans as the time expired, especially the low growl coming from Frank. She passed her paper forward to Jeff, who acknowledged its receipt with a smile, which she returned, feeling her face flush. While Jeff was smiling at her, she got a glimpse of Frank's nearly blank paper as he tucked it into the bottom of the pile. Maybe that was a part of her assignment, to help him with his writing. She'd have to ask him about it, catch him off guard, and maybe even have a civil word with him. Claire smiled inside, knowing she had an upper hand, being an Angel and all. She laughed aloud at her silly thought, turning a few heads towards her. She shrugged her shoulders at them. "My paper really sucked," which got a snicker or two.

Theater class couldn't come too soon in her mind. It was her one and only chance to be with Rachel, except for their lunch break, which she spent most of the time thoroughly enjoying her food – no matter what Arthur had said about the cafeteria food.

She'd liked it so far. She sat next to Rachel in the back of the Theater classroom. "How was your day?" She asked. Rachel didn't say a word. "Are you okay?" Rachel laid her head on the small fold-down surface of her desk.

"No."

"I'll be filling in for Mr. Clark today." Ms. Newman said. "Let's move to the auditorium and we'll get an early start on rehearsal."

"Come on, it'll be better when we get to sing." Claire put her arm around her sister and walked with her from the classroom through a cluttered passage and into the right wing of the stage. There sitting on two stools, were Frank and Linda, chatting and looking happy, and heretofore known as F&L.

"Linda gave me a hard time in the hall outside, pushing me against a locker and telling me we didn't deserve to get the parts we did. I didn't understand what she was getting at. All I know is, she said it in the meanest of voices, like the beast."

"Frank gave me a look in English that wasn't very nice either. Remember, we're the ones in charge here, not them. They followed Ms. Newman to center stage, where she began blocking-out individual parts. Ms. Newman was too busy to notice that Frank and Linda were out of place, standing behind Claire and Rachel, who had gone to their mark on the stage for a scene inside the Coleman home.

"You two scabs don't deserve the parts you were given," Linda whispered from behind them.

She did her best to ignore Linda's snide comment, but Claire couldn't help feeling as if she was doing something wrong, the same way she'd felt in the south of France. Rachel had already turned around to confront her accusers, drawing her 5' 5" frame up into Linda's face the best she could – Linda was 5' 10". Claire grabbed Rachel by the arm and yanked her back a step or two. Linda would be no match for Rachel's powerfully built stature, even though she was five inches taller. Claire placed herself between the two, still holding onto Rachel's arm. Frank had a kind of stupefied look about him like he wasn't there at all. She ignored him.

"What part do you have Linda?" Claire said trying to defuse the mounting tension. Linda glared at her with her icy blue eyes, sending shivers down Claire's back.

"I play the part of Kathy, daughter of William and Catherine Coleman. And we don't like you two in the story." Linda sneered.

Claire stifled her need to laugh at the girl's absurdity. Linda must be so insecure about herself to behave this way. "That's a nice part to have. Rachel and I are the two homeless sisters, Mary and Nancy," Claire said looking at the casting sheet, which also said they were two angels in disguise as homeless sisters, sent to help both Frank and Linda. Claire's eyes widened in surprise. She'd not looked at the casting sheet until now. "Oh, how nice. Your parents are taking us into their home just before Christmas. So you and Frank will be helping us in your home." Claire, being but one inch shorter than Linda, locked eyes with the icy blue stare directed at her, and summoned her most pleasant voice and appearance. "We're part of your family," Frank grunted his displeasure, bringing Ms. Newman over.

"Frank, Linda. You two aren't supposed to be here. You're over there in the living room." She pointed towards left center stage. "Go stand on your marks please."

Claire blocked Rachel's hand as it extended to push Linda away. Linda was looking over her shoulder at them as she and Frank moved across the stage. Rachel waggled her fingers at her, knowing it would probably irritate her. "Really. Must you do that?" Claire said in her thoughts. Rachel's self-righteous smile drifted across the space between them. "Nice face sis."

Ms. Newman had them walk through several scenes, making sure everyone knew their cues, marks, and interactions. Claire was beginning to see how central a part they had assumed from the two absent sisters. No wonder the F&L duo were miffed. And to think, they were real Angels playing angels in the musical – it tickled her insides. She and Rachel did their best to keep up as they walked through the scenes.

An hour and a half later, she was familiar with her blocking and had read all of her lines, enough to be comfortable with them. More practice was in order though. They were leaving with everyone else when Ms. Newman called them over.

"Frank and Linda seem to have an attitude with both of you. I understand why they could make you uncomfortable. They've been good friends with the two sisters who were playing your parts. That and they have a general attitude of aloofness all the time anyway. Ignore it if you possibly can. They'll get used to you. They both like the theater a lot and seem to need it as an outlet. Let's go over your opening duets a couple of times. They set the mood of the story"

Ms. Newman drilled them for thirty minutes, going over the emotions embodied in the lyrics of, What Will I Be and Alone Together, helping them get just the right tonal qualities. After their descent from the heavens, they would be sitting in the snow up against a fence in an alleyway, singing their second duet, Alone Together, while posing as two homeless sisters whose parents had abandoned them just before Christmas. It brought tears to her eyes every time they sang it, making it hard for her to get some of the words out. Claire was beginning to see Arthur's hand in the writing of this musical. It was so like him, reminding her of seeing him for the first time on the ridge path in her little world.

"Are you coming or not," Rachel called from the right wing.

Claire gathered her backpack, not realizing she'd been standing frozen in time after Ms. Newman and the rehearsal pianist had left. She hurried to catch up to her sister, wondering what had gone on in those moments. They were halfway home before Rachel said anything about it.

"What were you doing standing there like a statue?"

"I don't remember. How long was it?"

"Three minutes or so. I don't even think you blinked once the whole time."

"I don't know," she mused. "I really like our opening songs though. They bring a tear to my eye every time."

"I like them too. What did you think about Ms. Newman's explanation of F&L's behavior?"

"I don't know them, but she's probably right about ignoring their rudeness. They'll get over it soon enough." Bosco's big happy cat face was in the front window watching them come up onto the front porch, jumping down from the sofa to greet them with his motor running at full throttle. "Hey Bosco," Claire said picking him up. "Did you miss us?"

"You're home," Arthur called out from the kitchen. "Dinner's ready. Go wash up."

Bosco followed them upstairs, weaving in and out of every step they took. "Crazy cat." Claire brushed him aside with a foot to sneak into the bathroom, leaving him to meow his displeasure on the outside. They raced Bosco downstairs and to the dining room, getting beat-out in the end.

"You're gonna love this lasagna," Arthur set the large glass baking dish on a hot pad next to his place setting, shoeing his inherited pesky cat away with his foot, before sitting down.

Claire's first mouthful was the nearest she'd been to heaven in a long time. The sweetness of the sliced, fresh tomatoes and basil leaves, coupled with the firm texture of layered cheese and thick pasta, took her breath away. "Oh Arthur, this out does anything I've ever experienced – pure heaven." She wound her tongue around the long string of cheese, which draped down her chin. She giggled with delight. Her eye caught Rachel's, who was watching her every move. "What? It's good, don't you agree?" Rachel nodded, amused at her sister's behavior.

"Yes, it's very good. I don't mean to interrupt your ascent to foodie heaven, but I think we have a few unanswered questions. You remember Frank and Linda, our assignments, who we don't have a clue as to what we're supposed to be doing with them."

Claire stiffened in her chair, her neck hair bristling. "I haven't forgotten, Rachel." Claire swallowed her irritated tone, not wanting to engage with her sister when she fell into one of her moods. It seemed they were coming more frequently, these leftovers from the cavern of horrors. "Arthur? As Rachel said, we don't have any idea what our purpose is with F&L. A little help would be of great service to our well-being in dealing with them. Both of them are rude to the Nth degree." Claire set her fork down softly and folded her hands on top of her napkin.

"Well. Sounds like you two had your first run-in with your assignments. F&L you called them? Here's some background on their families. Linda's mom is a professor of political science at American University, and she is a part-time alcoholic. Her father is an orthopedic surgeon, who is seldom home and is ready to divorce his wife. Frank's father, Adam, on the other hand, is home a great deal and is constantly telling Frank how to live his life. He inherited a great deal of money from his parents and socializes with many of the Capitol Hill crowd since he's a DC Councilman. Frank's mom, Evelyn, is a housewife and lets her husband lead in all family matters. Frank and Linda found each other in a seventh-grade theater class and have been fast friends ever since, leaning heavily on their parts in school plays to help them cope with life at home. The three of us have Frank and Linda as an assignment for reasons Sandy never made clear to me. She said we'd figure it out as we got to know them. There you have it. Now, would you two like to fill me in on what's going on with you both? I might be able to help you know."

"Linda called us scabs at rehearsal. What does it mean?" Rachel scowled.

"Yeah, it made me feel like I'd done something very wrong." Claire made a similar face.

"They probably meant you were like the scab workers, who take a union worker's job when they're on strike. Scabs are considered lowlifes, but that's beside the point. What matters is what you say to them. In other words, don't get pulled in by their bad behavior."

"Yeah, Claire complimented Linda on her part in the musical, and I think it pissed her off," Rachel smirked.

"Try to not piss off your assignments. It won't help you much. Ms. Newman probably told you to ignore their rudeness, because they both love the theater, and will get used to the idea of you being in the show. Give them some time to get to know you."

"Thank you for cooking Arthur," Rachel said pushing back from the table. I'm going to take a hot shower and go to bed a little early. I'm very tired."

Claire waited for Rachel to clear her plate and go upstairs, wanting to talk to Arthur alone. "Arthur, today after rehearsal, something happened to me. I lost two or three minutes and was standing like a statue on the stage. I can't remember a thing about it. Do you have any ideas?"

"I'm not sure, but sometimes you can overload the physical brain with an emotional stew, and it will blank-out for a moment. Sleep on it and see what comes to you in the morning."

"Okay." She cleared her plate and loaded the dishwasher, while Arthur put away the leftovers. She gave him a peck on the cheek and went to study in her room

.

DREAMS

Claire nodded off reading The Canterbury Tales and dreamed about her cottage, in the foothills outside Grenoble, in the south of France. Arthur was waiting for her to return with a basket full of the abundant bounty she'd harvested from the surrounding meadows and forest in mid-summer. Their evening meal depended on what she could forage on her long walks, and she'd convinced him she needed to go alone, giving her time to adjust to her physical body. The year was AD 214. Her first assignment as a new member in the Ranks of Angelic Beings was going well, overall. Arthur was her mentor and a new member of the Angelic Senior Ranks, with a long history of helping recruits adjust to their new physical bodies while dealing with the trials of their human assignments. He was quickly becoming a good friend, allowing her greater latitude to learn in her own way, while gently guiding her whenever she faltered. This was her fifth week and she dearly loved living among humans with all of its excitement and unpredictability. Theirs was a small Gallic village during Roman rule, a pristine valley filled with all the busyness of life. Claire often had a euphoric feeling of freedom on her walks in the foothills of the French Alps. It was so beautiful, she'd lose track of time and arrive home late, much to her mentor's displeasure. This evening was no exception.

Claire opened the latch on the wood door of their cottage,

catching Arthur's disapproving gaze. "I'm sorry Arthur. This world is so beautiful and inviting that everywhere I go, I have to stay a little longer. It's never long enough though." Arthur smiled, motioning her to bring the basket.

"What have you brought us today?"

Claire handed him the basket overflowing with herbs and edible flowers, hiding the wild lilies under the basket until the last moment. "These are for you. I found them by a small stream." Her pulse quickened and the palms of her hands tingled as she presented the flowers to Arthur. She liked everything about her mentor, which she supposed was the norm for first-timers. But there was something more to their arrangement, something that wanted to burst out of her, and . . ."

"Claire," Rachel tapped on her bedroom door, waking her. "I wanted to say I'm sorry for being irritated with you earlier. I think I was reacting to Linda's rude comments and treatment of me today. It reminded me of how I felt in the cavern – helpless – and I don't like that feeling. Sorry to wake you."

"Wait, don't go. Stay with me awhile and I'll tell you about the dream I was having when you came in." She drew back the comforter and patted the mattress. Rachel slid between the covers playfully nudging her, setting off a slew of giggles. They pressed their bodies together, lacing their fingers, and jostling to get as close to each other as possible.

"What dream?" Her sister whispered next to her ear.

"In the south of France with Arthur at the cottage. You weren't there, but I know you lived across the valley and came to visit with your mentor Sophia. We would take walks together by the river. Remember?"

"Yes, I remember Claire. And I remember what you did on one of those walks too; something so amazing it was burned into my memory forever. You chose life for that young girl, and because you did, you were punished. Did you know she went on to marry a rich merchant's son, moving far north to Paris? She was happy Claire and loved her husband for all the days of her life. She spoke of you often as her Guardian Angel, always hoping she could thank you for saving her life. She died with your name on her lips. I know, because I was there for all of her life. It's when I first knew for certain that I too, would do the same someday and save a life worthy of a second chance. But, I killed a man in the process of saving a young woman. He was a bad person who deserved his untimely death. Because of my decision, I became one of the Fallen. I knew I had done the right thing as I fell from Grace, but was sorry to lose myself in the process. My last thoughts were of you and the young girl as I descended into the darkness. That was in AD 414, two hundred years after you disappeared."

Claire's heart was pounding in her chest with a heaviness she'd not felt before. The sadness of an Angel falling from Grace is difficult to bear for all. The compassion that an Angel embodies at birth, and exhales with every breath on their journey through life, was their reason for being. Claire had no way of knowing her sister had Fallen, other than the emptiness she'd lived with for all the centuries. Even when she'd entered the cavern where Rachel had fallen, she'd not recognized her sister. "I'm so sorry, Rachel. I have lived alone for so long I've forgotten what it's like to care for someone – for you. I'm still a little lost, but I do know this much, we will never be separated again. Sisters Forever." Claire gazed into Rachel's eyes, melting away any trace of guilt and sadness.

"I'm going to love every day we have together, even if our assignment with the F&L gang is a pain in the butt." Rachel giggled, swinging her legs to the floor. "Good night. Sweet dreams."

Claire hugged her sister's back and then watched as she

walked away. She snuggled down into the comforter, pulling it halfway over her head, ready for a good night's rest. Sleeping in a physical body was certainly different from what she was used to, but it felt good to close her eyes and be enveloped by a quiet restfulness, punctuated with dreams about most anything. She loved the feel of drifting off, trying to linger there as long as she could, before entering the deep sleep her body needed. Her new body jerked several times as she drifted away in sleep.

The wind whistled beneath her wings, carrying her high above the snow-capped peaks, and green valley below. She was home in her own private creation in the Realm. A place she'd fashioned in her mind, to live her life in a way she saw fit. She swooped down to brush the tallest peak, reveling in the freedom of her home, a place where she'd not been disturbed by the thoughts of who and what other Angels thought she should be. "I am free," she sang to the mountaintops, her voice carried by the wind to all corners of her world. She soared higher than she'd ever gone before, where the blackness of a night meets dawn, and stars hang high overhead, pointing the way into the Angelic Realm.

Her valley was small and dark below, so dark she could not find her home. She tarried on high, her wings beating ferociously at the thin air, gradually losing their power of flight. She shivered with fear as she began to fall into the blackness below, tumbling towards the mountain peaks she could not see, crashing into one, and careening down a long slope into the trees far below. When she came to rest in the darkness, she did not know this place in her world. It was strange and dark; unlike anything, she'd created and lived in for the eternity of her self-banishment. The memory of Rachel's cavern of darkness still loomed in her thoughts, but this was different. Her old home was in the Realm. Why then did it suddenly take on the dark and foreboding illusion of Rachel's cavern? One minute free, the next a prisoner in her own world of darkness.

"Arthur, can you help me?" She called out into the darkness. The absolute stillness was deafening, making her dizzy and confused. "I'm here," she called out, again greeted by the silence. She shook the snow from her wings, beating them hard to test the air, rising a few feet and settling back down. She inched her way down the slope in the blackness for a while, sliding on the beads of icy spring snow; just like she'd done many times in the mountain chutes, she'd played in within her world. It was so dark that she bumped into trees and boulders, never knowing what lay ahead or behind, alone in a strange yet familiar place. Eventually, she stopped when the slope reached a plateau, where she stood for a moment, trying to see into the darkness. There was the faintest of shadows beginning to appear ahead, the outline of a pine tree rising in front of her. She stepped carefully in its direction, feeling the way with her feet. Fear was creeping into her thoughts, remembering the stark cliffs in her world, which dominated the landscape. She knew this because she'd soared off them many a time, using their abrupt face and elevation above the valley below as a launching point.

She pulled back abruptly, her foot sliding off into oblivion, catching herself with her back foot on an exposed rock, falling backward onto her wings. She thrashed at the snow with her feet and wings, hauling herself away from the precipice. She stood and shook the snow from her, fixing her gaze on the faint horizon in the distance – the sawtooth edge of a mountain range. She knew this place. It overlooked her valley and hut below, a cliff she'd soared off quite often. But why had the darkness come so unexpectedly, and why had she fallen from the skies she'd soared in so often? She backed away and tripped over a small boulder, further bruising her pride. She would wait here for the coming dawn's light.

"Arthur, you said you'd be listening and there to help at a moment's notice. So, help already. I need you now." Claire wrapped herself in her wings, trying to hide from her fear, and the darkness, which surrounded her. She hummed the song Alone Together, hoping it would help. Sisters alone and homeless, but actually Angels in disguise, and there to help a family in need. She laughed at how much she and Rachel resembled the characters they were playing. "What a great idea Arthur. Thank you for bringing Rachel and me into your world, and into your assignment." Claire continued to hum the words, not understanding his silence.

Claire fell asleep and found herself dreaming about Linda. They were together in a strange setting, almost like a backyard of a large estate. Linda sat cross-legged in the snow, hunched over, and tugging at the sleeve of her bulky sweater. Claire was horrified at the red snow between her legs.

"Stop," she yelled and sprang towards her.

Claire was falling when she came to her senses. She'd run off the cliff trying to reach Linda and stop her from slashing at her wrists again. She beat her wings in desperation as she fell like a stone through the darkness. She woke up when she hit the valley floor filled with pain. Linda's pain. She'd tried to kill herself and failed.

"Huuuuh," she sucked in her breath and sat bolt upright in her bed. She shivered in a cold sweat, glad to be awake and out of the dream. Her labored breathing gradually calmed, knowing that she was home, in bed, and safe. It had all been a dream, everything: the falling, Linda, the darkness, everything. It was at this moment she remembered the blank space in her memory after rehearsal. The one Rachel had asked about, but she was unable to recall anything. It was this dream, down to the last detail. But what did it mean? She lay back, pulling the comforter up around her neck, clutching it tightly with both hands. "Arthur, what does it mean? I don't understand." She again called out to her mentor, but this time she was awake.

"You will," Arthur's voice filled her head. "Be patient and it will all make perfect sense."

Claire fell into a dreamless sleep the remainder of the night, not stirring until morning.

BROKEN HOME

Claire welcomed her school day, with all of its quirky gossip from Lu, and the busy passing periods, where socializing between friends was compressed into a few words in passing. She and Rachel were playing catch up on the teen issues and getting acquainted with high school and all of its craziness, and today, that distraction was a good thing. The further away in time she got from the dream, the better she felt. Today, for the first time, she giggled about her body language speaking quicker and louder than any words ever could, when it came to boys eying her up and down. One look from a shiny-faced boy turned her head before lunch, so much so she'd run into a girl, scattering both their books on the floor. She'd laughed when she replied to the girl, "he made me do it," pointing at the boy who was staring at them. It made her feel giddy and self-conscious at the same time, but she relished the encounter. Her body told her so. She and Rachel both had a good laugh about it all at lunch, and for the first time, they both felt truly happy and free from their past. Lunch period was something of a transcendent experience for them both, feeling like a human being caught up in life, all the while knowing they were really, Angels on assignment.

Claire was surprised when Frank and Linda walked into Theater class. They had skipped the past three days for whatever reasons and Mr. Clark didn't seem to mind, acting like it was normal behavior for the two of them. They sat in the rear of the classroom two rows away and talked softly during most of the class. Mr. Clark ignored them both and proceeded to explain the plot and theme of the Christmas musical, in an effort to help the interested class members understand some of the deeper issues. Although Frank and Linda were talking for much of the class, they did take notes and glance up at Mr. Clark from time to time. After class, Claire went to the auditorium and sat on a stool by a side curtain on stage, and was deep into the lyrics of one of her duets, when she heard Linda talking to herself on the other side of the curtain.

"Is that you Linda?" She asked in a hushed tone.

"Who's that?"

"Claire Tate. Could we talk for just a moment please?"

"I'm busy."

"It's about the incident in your backyard last winter," Claire said so softly she barely heard herself, but loud enough to cause Linda to gasp. "I'm sorry; I just wanted to help if I can." She whispered a little louder to be sure Linda could hear her.

"I don't know what you're talking about."

Claire took a chance, dropped her script on the stage and swiveled around on her stool, her knees parting the curtain. "I'm sorry," she apologized again. "I only thought . . ." Claire stopped herself short, seeing that Linda was not okay about anything that even hinted at what she'd done. Linda's face was the color of death as Claire's hand shot out and touched her shoulder, doing her very Angelic best to give Linda a little Angel Light. Claire fumbled badly with something she'd not used in a very long time. The power surged through her uncontrolled. Linda's script slid from her hands and she nearly fell off her stool, as she turned to face her tormentor. Linda's face was riddled with the painful memory and fought desperately to control what she could not. She drew her face into a tight scowl, with only her eyes betraying her; they were

77

pleading for help. Tears welled up from the utter despair she'd stuffed down as deep as she possibly could. Claire's gift had found its mark.

"I'm sorry. I caused you pain," Claire focused all of her heartfelt compassion for the young teen, who had driven herself into a state of deep depression over her mother's drinking and her father's indifference. Claire's lack of control sent a second surge of power through Linda, who was fighting back hard against the will of this person who knew her darkest secret. Linda's eyes were riveted on hers, not blinking or releasing the tears on the verge of spill overboard.

"What do you think you know?" Linda snapped.

"Nothing. Only that you're hurting and I want to help if you'd let me." Claire said as quietly as possible, trying her best not to piss off an already angry individual. She retracted her hand and lowered her gaze. "Sorry," she whispered.

"You should be." Linda snapped.

The whole thing ended when Linda turned away, signaling she could go no further at this time. Claire turned back around letting the curtain separate them once again. Her heart was pounding and her palms were hot and sweaty. She wiped the tear from her cheek. "So much for Angel Power," she mumbled. She' had made a connection with Linda though. The door was open a crack, making it easier the next time if there ever was a next time. Linda had a hard shell encasing her, probably from all the years of living in a dysfunctional home. Her parents fed her and housed her, but had starved her emotionally for who knows how long. Claire was beginning to see how tough this assignment was going to be; and, she'd not even gotten to know Frank yet. Who knew what lurked inside of him.

Ms. Newman breezed in with an arm full of music, dropping it on the piano bench, and conferred with Walter, the rehearsal pianist. Claire overheard Ms. Newman thanking him for bringing his expertise to her production. He was a retired Theater Professor from American University, who loved giving his time and talent to his alma mater. His Parkinson's disease was plain for all to see, and on some days, she'd noticed that playing was infinitely more difficult for him, but he always seemed to manage. "So much heartache to endure living in this world. How do people cope?"

"Hey, are you gonna sing with me or just prattle on for the rest of rehearsal?" Rachel elbowed her in the side.

"Yes, I'm ready." She said eying Linda talking with Frank across the stage. "Those two have a lot of problems."

"Yeah, they do." Rachel echoed. "More than we know."

On the walk home, she told Rachel all about her failed attempt to help Linda and the dream she'd had that led her to engage with Linda. Her sister never said a word about it.

ARTHUR'S RULES

Walking through the door into Arthur's home, her home now, Claire sensed he'd been listening, and knew all about her troubles with her assignment. She knew because he'd brought home pizza to start the healing process and his smile of understanding for his young charges who'd had a hard day at school. Eating dinner consisted of stuffing down three large pieces in quick succession, while Arthur watched quietly, nibbling on his one piece – all that she and Rachel had left him. After the feeding frenzy, he let out a hearty laugh, breaking the silence and a few other things as well – like her sullenness.

"Guess we were a little out of control, huh." Claire stifled a giggle. "I didn't have much to eat for the last eighteen hundred years. That's my excuse." Arthur was clearly taken with his two young, fresh out of jail, teen Angels. He was enjoying himself way more than he probably should have, but he was proud of them both. She and Rachel cleaned up the kitchen and joined Arthur on the sofa, sitting shoulder to shoulder, getting as close as possible to their mentor. Claire was learning about physical touch and the magic it could work in communicating thoughts and feelings.

"Let's talk about your day, shall we? Claire, you start please." Arthur patted both their knees.

"It started yesterday after rehearsal. Rachel said I blanked out for three minutes, none of which I can remember, until today. Well, as it turns out, the blank space was foreknowledge of the dreams I had that night. First, I dreamed of you and me in the south of France and our cottage outside of Grenoble, which I told Rachel about last night. Secondly, I dreamed about my home where you found me, only this time it had become a dark place. I fell from the sky into the darkness and slid down a mountain to a cliff, which I fell over in the dark. I called out to you several times to no avail. Then I had another dream within the dream about Linda and her attempt on her life. She'd slashed her wrists in her backyard last winter. Then I woke up and told you I didn't understand the dreams. You said to have patience. Today I spoke with Linda very briefly about her attempt on her life, and of course, she denied it all, but what I saw on her face was that nothing about it is resolved. So my conclusion is, Rachel and I are to help her with the traumatic incident in whatever way is best for her. But while talking with her, I tried to use a little of my powers and found them lacking in many ways. Linda didn't really react too well to my attempts at helping her, which leaves me confused as to how to help her. Through all the drama in my dreams, you never did help me when I called out to you."

"You were teaching yourself Claire and there was nothing for me to do. I am glad you dreamed of France though; I still look back fondly on those days together. As far as falling into the darkness of your old home of eighteen hundred years, perhaps you are seeing for the first time just how alone you really were, trapped in a darkness of your own making. The dream within a dream was you remembering those blank spaces after rehearsal. Linda is a very troubled young lady who needs our help. Sandy placed us all here, each with something unique to offer. By helping Frank, Linda, and their parents, we also help ourselves overcome our past, myself included. This is one of the most interesting assignments I've been on in a long time, and we get to work it out together as a family."

Arthur gathered his girls in his arms and just for fun, he flashed them with love, filling the living room with a warm soft glow. The feeling of safety in his arms was a compelling force she'd not had since they were together in France. He was right about her old home though; there was darkness there, a lot of it. But what to do with it, was the question. "Turn a light on," Arthur said in her thoughts, chuckling. "Yeah. Why didn't I think of that?" Claire nestled deeper into his arms, feeling much better about herself and the work that lay ahead with Frank and Linda.

"Arthur," Rachel said wiping a tear from her cheek. "What about the hopelessness I still feel. It follows me wherever I go and I can't seem to shake it off. The anger I felt for Linda today was overpowering and very uncomfortable. I'm still thinking through my helpless state of mind from the cavern. It just comes on so strong, inundating me with its darkness, making me feel trapped in the cavern all over again. Arthur, I'm scared."

"I know Rachel. Sandy told me you might continue to suffer from its deathly pall. You have been strong these first few days of your assignment. Try to believe in yourself and it will get easier for you. Remember that you are an Angel with a mission, and nothing will stand in your way – except you."

"I'm trying, really I am."

"What about our Angelic powers? When will they be restored to us?" Claire asked. "Rachel could certainly use a dose of them at her low points. My first attempts were kinda pathetic, like having no power at all. Even a human could have done it better than I did with Linda."

"There will be no more talk of weakness in this household and no more whining about being helpless. We will have order in my home and that order is of the Realm. You have a job to do and you will succeed if you believe in yourself." Arthur stood and turned to face them.

"Rule Number One"
"What goes around comes around. If you portray weakness,
then that is what comes back to you. If you give light,
then light is what returns to you."
"Rule Number Two"
"Obey Rule Number One."

The seconds ticked by in silence. Claire wanted to say something, anything, but she was mute for the time being. She knew he was right. You have to believe in yourself, or you're lost. She knew first hand, because she'd been lost for a long time thinking she was happy; when really, she wasn't the slightest bit happy in her faraway home in the Realm. "Arthur?" She laid a hand on his arm. "Is what you said true for humans as well?"

"You'll see Claire when you deal with Frank and Linda's issues. Your first encounter did give you a little hope. Didn't it?"

"Yes. But . . ."

"No buts about it. You're either in or you're out in the belief department. Go prove it to yourself. Both of you. Any questions? No. Well then, it's off to your rooms to study. Tomorrow's Friday, and many teachers like to surprise their students with a quiz on the week's material. Besides,
you both look sleepy from all the pizza." Arthur chuckled.

GETTING TO KNOW YOU

Arthur was right about the quizzes; Claire had two back to back, in English and Western Civilization, neither of which she'd prepared for in the slightest. She heard Rachel groan from her Spanish class, obviously unprepared for the vocabulary quiz. "We're quite the pair," she giggled in her thoughts. "School is hard work. If we're going to pass this semester, we'd better study a lot more." Walking into Mr. Boswell's Applied Science class, she stopped to read the answer to the question for the week, a regular thing with Mr. Boswell. The question was: name the solution represented by, "what do you call a crow sitting on a stick?" His use of a metaphor and his sense of humor had left Claire in the dark. The answer he'd posted was a caustic solution. She asked Lu what it meant, and even then, it took her a moment to get his meaning.

Mr. Boswell began class and was deep into an explanation of St. Elmo's Fire when she heard Rachel arguing with Frank in her head. She closed her eyes and saw them in the hallway leading to the Theater auditorium where his hulking form smothered her sister against the lockers.

"Sorry, I gotta go," She blurted out, knocking her stool a few feet into the aisle. "Sorry," her words disappeared through the doorway. When she was turning the corner into the long hallway leading to the Theater room, she heard their heated argument go silent after a loud metallic thud. She ran full tilt down the hall, to find Frank pinning Rachel up against the metal lockers, with her feet six inches off the floor.

"Stop!" She screamed, closing the final few feet in a rage of hormones, which only a physical body could produce. She flung herself at Frank, in all her anger and fear; and in midair, she was suspended in slow motion above the floor and on a collision course. His khaki shirt smelled of sweat as it met her face. How strange it felt to want to inflict pain on another. She wanted to hurt him more than anything else. The surreal moment ended after he'd brushed her aside and she'd hit the floor sprawling like a pinwheel in the wind. She'd knocked him loose from Rachel enough to allow her to break free.

He swatted her away like a gnat and stared at her, amused. His smirk of defiance was akin to the ugly scowl he'd given her on her second day in English class when forced by Ms. Letrell to apologize for tripping her. Frank was two steps away from her and could have easily grabbed them both to do his ill will, but instead, he took a step back and turned to leave for whatever reasons. It was just as well because she was on the verge of violently hurling her lunch.

"You okay," Rachel touched her shoulder.

"Not really. Help me up before I vomit." Claire said clutching her stomach, trying to stop the inevitable. Rachel helped her to stand.

"How did you know?"

"I heard you loud and clear and when I felt your fear, I ran out of Science class. Are you going to report him?"

"No," Rachel said lowering her head, and banged her fist against the lockers. "I started it with a derogatory comment about Linda; his girlfriend by the way. We argued and he slammed me

85

against the lockers. I wasn't afraid until his hand started closing around my throat. That's probably when you heard me. I was pretty scared. He had a strange, otherworldly look to him like he didn't even know what he was doing to me – making me fear for my life."

Claire hugged her sister, both of them shaking from the adrenalin in their system. They sat down and leaned against the lockers across from the Theater classroom, while their bodies calmed and their heads cleared. This was when Claire realized she could hear everything in Rachel's head – every thought and feeling.

Later in Theater class, she was calm enough to notice it didn't come and go but was continuous with both of their thoughts in her head. It was weird to be inside of her sister's head moment by moment. It faded into the background noise of lecture and questions in Theater class and by the time rehearsal came, it was gone. So to, were Frank and Linda. Neither of them showed for class or rehearsal.

Dinner was a quiet affair, which Arthur seemed fine with. Claire didn't want to talk about her day, especially the incident with Frank, or about her hearing Rachel's thoughts. She went straight to her room after dinner, saying she was tired and wanted to lie down for a while.

Claire struggled to wake up when her sister's deafening screams filled her head. Instead, she found herself in the dark cavern of the blue beast, which was clutching Rachel and clawing at her, ripping her clothes away, leaving her raw flesh exposed. Rachel's screams drove Claire to near madness, but they weren't her sister's screams any longer, they were her screams. The sheer terror coming from her sister was consuming her and enveloping her in darkness and dragging her on its death march into blackness.

"Claire," Arthur yelled. "Snap out of it."

Her eyes slammed open, feeling the pain of Arthur's slap on

her face. She was drenched in an ice cold sweat and mute. She was shivering with terror and flopping about, her arms and legs half paralyzed. Rachel's beast was alive and well inside of her head. Her heart sank when Arthur left, moving quickly out the door, and didn't reappear for what seemed an eternity. When he returned with Rachel in his arms, she felt a sense of relief flood her, warming her and allowing her to breathe calmly and deeply. He laid Rachel beside her in bed, covering them both with the comforter, sitting next to her to watch over them both.

"Ar...thur," Claire's whimper dissolved into quiet sobs. "I'm afraid." He stroked her head, looking much older to her.

"I know. It will get better. Wait it out. Somehow, you two merged inside of Rachel's nightmare. The beast's cavern I'm guessing. I couldn't reach you, but I did Rachel, calming her terror with Sandy's help. It'll be okay."

"Oh Arthur, I had no control over myself. It pulled me in and was swallowing me into the darkness. The blackness had claws . . ." She started to sob again, her whole body heaving uncontrollably. He scooped her up from the bed and wrapped her in his wings, rocking her, and whispered in her ear: "I love you." Over and over until she fell limp in the sanctuary of his Angel wings and lost consciousness.

She didn't wake until the next morning and had little memory of what had happened, but knew something had because Rachel was lying next to her in bed still asleep. Bosco was lying at the end of the bed, purring softly, lending his calmness to her fragile sanity.

"Claire," Arthur said from the chair next to her bed. "How do you feel?"

"Better, I think." She gazed into his clear steel-blue eyes, catching her breath as his peace of mind washed over her. "I don't remember much, except I was really scared and you helped me. What happened?"

"In a minute. First, you need to get yourself grounded in your physical body. Just think about where you are and what you're doing here in our home. You had school yesterday, dinner last night, and then came up to your room and laid down to rest."

"Yes. But after I laid down it gets fuzzy. That's a funny word – fuzzy. You held me and it felt warm and fuzzy."

"Yes. I wrapped you in my wings. I needed to return to my Angelic body to help you. Do you remember any more?"

"I fell into Rachel's mind I think." She cringed as the wave of fear from last night laid hold of her again. She blinked back the tears, wondering if she'd ever be free of it. She was back in the beast's dark cavern in its clutches, and it was raping her with its claws. Her fearful gaze met Arthur's and his aura of light grew, encompassing her, and filling her mind with peace. She drew in a halting breath and continued. "That's when I screamed in the terror of . . . no, her terror of being swallowed by the blackness. I didn't exist. I was Rachel and I couldn't even feel myself."

"Yes, exactly right," Arthur said. "You were possessed by the beast in Rachel's memory. And it's just as real as when we were there to rescue her from the darkness. Do you know how this merger happened?"

"No. But I started to notice it right as Frank had pinned her to a locker at school when her thoughts and feelings were mine too. We didn't tell you at dinner. I guess we should have."

"Yes, perhaps so. We can finish this later. For now, I want you to rest. It will help Rachel as well. You shocked her system by being inside of her, essentially producing twice the terror within her memories of Falling from Grace. When she wakes, then we can talk more about what happened."

Claire snuggled closer to her sister and closed her eyes, falling asleep quickly into a dreamless rest. She didn't wake until noon, getting up to use the bathroom, being careful not to disturb Rachel. When she returned, Rachel was sobbing softly, her eyes still filled with the fear from the night before. Claire tucked herself in next to her sister and caressed her cheek, her own hand trembling with the memory of the cavern. "I'm so sorry Rachel. I didn't mean to cause you pain. It just happened. Sandy and Arthur helped us both last night. Do you remember them helping?" Rachel nodded. "It's over now. Try not to think about it." Claire called out to Arthur in her thoughts, telling him they were awake.

Tears were streaming around Claire's lips and rolling off of her jaw and down her neck, as cool embraces of the pain they'd felt while merged in the darkness. She felt guilty, like she was somehow the cause of Rachel's torment, even though she knew that was not true. The connection between her and Rachel was deep within them, but its memory remained just out of reach. She was sure of one thing though; she'd lost control and suffered greatly, while locked in Rachel's dream of the beast, needing the help of Arthur and Sandy to break free. She felt Arthur's presence in her heart and his touch of warmth calmed her. Her eyes met Rachel's with a clarity and strength of their love. "We'll be okay," she murmured, feeling her sister's soft breath on her. "Arthur will help us understand."

"Yes. We will talk about these things, but not now. You need to rest."

Arthur's words carried her into a deep sleep with Rachel. They were dreaming together as one and drifting above a peaceful green valley glistening from a refreshing rain. They slept a long time.

SISTERS FOREVER

Claire yawned and opened her eyes, finding Rachel still next to her at four in the afternoon. They'd slept the day away, taking that long to heal the open wound of terror. Arthur said they would talk more about it later, but she'd prefer it just to be over with. "Rachel, you awake?" Claire whispered in her ear. "Wake up sis."

"Uhhh, not yet." The sleepy voice croaked.

"Wake up, it's late afternoon." She tickled her in the ribs under her arm. Rachel pulled away and rolled over. Claire dug for pay dirt, tickling her sister's most vulnerable spots, both of them squirming under the covers.

"Ok, ok, ok," Rachel said, rolling out of bed.

Rachel snatched the comforter and wrapped herself in it to walk to the bathroom, blowing her sister a raspberry as she disappeared out the door. Claire slid out of bed, pulling on yesterday's clothes from the pile on the floor, hopping twice while trying to pull on her jeans.

"You girls awake finally." Arthur's distant voice wound its way up the stairs.

"Yes," she yelled from the end of the bed where she'd hopped to while trying to get her other foot through the pant leg. She giggled at what she'd almost done – landed on the floor. She tucked herself in and went to use the bathroom.

Rachel was showering and humming one of their songs, Sisters Forever. She poked her head around the shower curtain. "You're feeling better I see."

"Much. I'm hungry too." Rachel said.

"I'll go help Arthur with dinner," Claire ran a comb through her hair, snagging on knots, and traded it for a brush, which worked better. She was learning, she told herself. After all, it was only day six on her assignment. "See ya downstairs," she said, with a cloud of steamy vapor following her out. She liked everything about having a body, especially when it was time to eat. Arthur was cooking and the aromas drifting up the staircase were enticing.

"There you are," Arthur smiled from the open refrigerator. "Want to help?"

"Smells good. What is it?" Arthur closed the fridge door and handed her a head of lettuce.

"Chili, the hot kind." He grinned. "You can shred some lettuce for the green salad. The rest is done."

While she was helping her mentor, she was thinking aloud in her thoughts about what had happened, wondering if her and Rachel's little mishap was solved, or if it would return. She was asking Arthur this way because she didn't want to hear the words spoken. Her body was still a little shaky from the shock she'd given it. She was learning to deal with it the best she could, and so far, her track record was a bit sketchy at best, but getting better.

"Claire, I can't possibly know. What you did with Rachel caught me off guard. I don't remember encountering anything quite like it before. But that's beside the point." He said turning to face her with a ladle in his hand. "What's important here is how you proceed, even if what happened remains a burden to you both. Works, my dear Claire, are everything. Personally, I don't think you're through with what happened, its way to complex to just evaporate with a single dose of Angel Dust, figuratively speaking."

Arthur returned to stirring the pot of chili. "Oh," she said and continued cutting the lettuce. "So, you gonna be there to help in round two?" Claire spoke the words, feeling bolder.

"If you need me."

"Well, if we're both lost, how could we ever call for help when we're consumed by darkness?"

"It's only dark because you make it so." He turned and smiled.

"Right. So you're saying it's our fault if we fall into it again?"

"That's not what I said, Claire. I said you're in charge of your mind, not the other way 'round. Listen, let's set this aside until after dinner, so we can enjoy the food. Okay?"

"Sure." They dished up three large bowls of his chili and carried them to the dining room table to eat. He'd even lit some candles and dressed the table with some Thanksgiving decorations: a fold-out turkey, some colorful gourds, and a family of cardboard Pilgrims in native attire. Claire liked how Arthur adapted himself to the assignment, assuming many of the characteristics of the time period and cultural setting. He's blended. Claire laughed at her pun because it was Arthur's style.

"Very funny," he chuckled.

Rachel sauntered into the dining room and sat down, looking far better than a half hour ago. They enjoyed Arthur's four-alarm chili, emptying the fridge of milk in the process. It was a welcome distraction and gave them all something earthy to talk about. She got a good laugh out of Bosco's quick retreat from the offer of some hot chili. She could have sworn he had an indignant look while doing an abrupt about-face and hopping away, after he'd gotten a whiff of their spicy dinner.

After doing dishes, they sat on the living room sofa at

Arthur's request. He made a point of petting Bosco for several minutes, getting his motor up and running, and causing him to twist and turn in Arthur's lap. He finally stretched and curled up in a tight ball, running his motor so loud she thought the neighbors could have heard.

"Sandy and I had a long talk while you two were sleeping off the shock of your encounter with Rachel's dark memory of the cavern, and yours Claire, of scattering yourself into nothingness, afraid you'd never find yourself again. You did these things together, merging your souls as sister Angels. You see Claire when you saved that girl you set up a chain of events in both of your lives: your feelings of guilt for having broken Angelic Law, and Rachel's wanting to save a life but succumbing to human emotions and taking a life to save one, two hundred years later. You merged souls at the moment of Rachel's Fall from Grace but had to go in different directions. One fell straight into Absolute Darkness to have her life sucked out by a beast, and the other locked away in a world of her own making to live out life alone; both suffering separately, yet both suffering together in merged souls, neither understanding what was happening or being able to control the outcome. This is not the way it's supposed to happen with Angels. Why you two did this is a bit of a mystery, and even Sandy is mystified by it all. The Higher-Ups were no help, remaining silent on the matter – it's a lesson for mentors and students to figure out. My feeling is that you merged with Rachel out of love . . . and guilt. You gave her part of yourself to try to save her from being forever lost in the darkness. How, is the mystery, because you were lost yourself, wandering the Realm for nearly two hundred years, and hiding from anyone of us who came looking. You two merged right before you created your world, Claire. Am I making any sense?" Arthur paused. "Perhaps it's all a testament to the enduring power of love."

Claire nodded, wiping away a tear and feeling guilty about hurting another living being, let alone her sister. Her insides were churning, but not as bad as last night. "I'm sorry," she said, her gaze sinking into her lap. Arthur extended his wings, having switched to his Angelic body. He enfolded both of them, drawing them close, having perhaps anticipated their needs for more than just a pat on the knee and a kind word. She thought he was right. She was slipping into her old ways and having to fight off her need to run away again because she'd hurt the ones she loved. Arthur's love for her was the only thing she had to hang onto, and she so dearly wanted to not run, not banish herself again. Why did all this have to be so hard?

"Good question Claire." He said. "What do you suppose the answer is?"

He jostled her with his wing, trying to shake some sense into her. "I don't know," she whispered. "I really have no idea."

"Then we have some work to do. Both of you. Rachel, you haven't said anything yet."

Claire giggled as Rachel peeked out from between Arthur's feathers with a pixyish face.

"I don't know either," she said sheepishly. "But after last night, I think you and I should find out what's happening between us. I love being your sister, but I harbor a darkness deep down, which is dangerous I think, especially after seeing it in action. It sucked us in with such force, we'd still be lost if it weren't for Arthur and Sandy helping us. I love you both too much to be the cause any more suffering."

"Come with me," Arthur said gathering them up in his arm.

Claire felt herself fall away from the physical body and crossed over to her Angelic one for whatever Arthur had in mind. The same had happened to Rachel, and they were both in tow with Arthur leading them to an unknown destination, crossing what felt like a long expanse of time, to a place that was old, dark, and musty. They were standing on a cobblestone street at night, between wooden buildings, the half-moon casting dark shadows on the dirty gray stones. In a side alley, there were dark silhouettes of two people engaged in a scuffle, one on top of the other, muffled screams coming from the one underneath. Another dark shape came running from between the buildings and raised a roundish object high above, striking the oppressor in the head three times in quick succession. The sound was a dull, hollow crack, with no cries from the one struck. The oppressor fell on top of the one beneath, causing more screams. The third person helped roll the oppressor off and sat next to the victim, placing an arm around their shoulder.

"I hate you," Rachel was screaming at the scene. "May you burn in Hell for all eternity," she screamed repeatedly, slowly falling to her knees.

"Rachel," Claire called out. "Oh Rachel, what have you done?" She knelt beside her sister, who was wailing and banging her head against the stone street. "Arthur, why are you doing this to her? Stop it I beg you. Stop it." Claire wrapped her wings around her sister, who was vanishing right before her eyes, as was the person who had struck the oppressor. "Nooo," she cried. "Stop this Arthur. You're punishing her all over again." Claire fell on the stone street, sobbing, her sister gone, and her wings bent in anguish against the stone. "Nooo," she cried softly until she could no longer bear the pain. How long she lay in that dark lonely place she didn't know, but the pain eventually subsided and she felt Arthur's hand upon her head.

"Why," she murmured. "I don't understand why."

"Because it is as it must be for you to save your sister. It's up to you Claire because you're the one who blames herself for what happened sixteen hundred years ago in Paris. It's up to you to save yourself from those many years of lies and oblivion in the misbegotten world of your making. Release her, forgive her, call out her name, and you shall be free."

Arthur's words were so gentle she barely heard them, and yet, she obeyed her mentor's request. She spoke her words as a prayer to the part of herself engulfed in pain. Softly, the words fell from her lips and into the night's darkness, the night her sister Fell from Grace, and the night their two souls merged as one.

"No longer will I accept death's empty call, nor tarry for one more moment out of the light. I am but one who has fallen among many, all, imposing darkness on ourselves. Rachel hear me, I didn't know how to help you. I couldn't even help myself. Let me walk with you again. You are my sister and I love you more than life itself. Forgive me for stumbling and failing you. I love you." Claire fell into Arthur's arms, spent and listless. And when she awoke from what she thought was another dream, she was back on the sofa in Arthur's living room.

"What did you do to us?" Claire's distraught and questioning eyes pleaded with Arthur for understanding. "The pain was unlike anything I've ever felt."

"Not so," he said. "It is what the two of you endured for all of those sixteen hundred years. You just didn't know it. All I did was to help you see your jumping off point into a lifetime of suffering, one done together I might add. Now you see it for what it really is. A choice you both made, but now you have seen a better way. I'm sorry for your pain, but you have taken the first step to free yourselves. Sandy told me you'd probably have to experience it again in order to let it go, but at least you're prepared now."

Arthur rose from between them, his wings gently nudging them together. She and Rachel were back in their physical bodies again, drenched with sweat and shivering. Claire wrapped her arms around her sister, sorry for all the pain they had endured together, wanting absolution from her mentor, but knowing it was up to her to let go of her pain. "I'm sorry, I didn't mean for us to suffer apart." Rachel sank into her arms with a ferocity that spoke of the eons of sorrow.

"So am I," Rachel whispered in her sister's bosom. "So am I."

A DAY OF REST

Claire wanted to sleep in, but Arthur came upstairs and woke them at 7:30 a.m. She groaned, rolling over and covering her head with a pillow.

"Come on sleepy head," he said tickling her.

She squirmed and mumbled something unintelligible into the pillow. "I doe wanngehp".

"I'll be back in five minutes," he said.

The sound of the shower running in the bathroom kept her in bed awhile longer – Rachel liked long hot steamy showers. It was hard to ignore the aroma of French toast drifting in through the doorway though, so when Arthur returned to say breakfast was ready, so was she. She waited for him to leave and then got dressed, avoiding the full-length mirror on the door. She already knew what pillow-hair looked like.

"Smells really good Arthur," she said sitting down at the kitchen counter. "Why did you wake us so early?" She scratched Bosco's head, while he squirmed in her lap.

"We're going to the 9 a.m. Sunday service at St. Columba's Episcopal Church. They have a great choir. You'll see," he said, delivering a plate piled high with French toast.

"Okay. We're going to church. It's been awhile for me." Arthur smiled at her implied eighteen hundred years, "awhile." Rachel had quietly sat down beside her, bringing the smells of shampoo and conditioner with her.

"Did you say church?" Rachel's sleepy eyes met Arthur's.

"Yes and a good morning to you both. After that, I have another surprise. The Redskins are playing the Cowboys at 10 a.m. We'll be a little late, but we get to walk into a packed stadium of eighty thousand hopped-up fans. It's a rush you won't ever forget. I caught one in the 60's." Arthur grinned. "Now eat up, we don't want to be late for church."

Claire thought he had something up his sleeve, taking them to church and a football game. She and Rachel didn't even know what football was all about, or what a real stadium looked like. But, he was the mentor and they were the students. She was just glad to be feeling a lot more normal after last night's wild ride.

They were out the door at 8:45 a.m. and walking the five blocks to St. Columba. They sat down in the back pews a few minutes before the service began and listened to the choir and the seven musicians who accompanied them.

"Do you recognize any of the choir members?" Arthur asked.

"I can't really see them. Quite a few of them look like they're in high school though." Claire said craning her neck to see above the heads in front of them.

"Front row, third from the left. And back row, far right." Arthur said.

She and Rachel stared for a while before recognizing Linda and Frank. "Oh, our assignments. How nice to see them on our day off." Claire said sarcastically.

"Pay attention please," Arthur said nudging her in the side.

They sat and listened to John Rutter's four-part harmony of, For the Beauty of the Earth, one of the most lyrical songs Claire had ever heard. She wished they were closer so they could see Frank and Linda's expressions. The choir's voices reverberated off the sanctuary's vaulted ceiling and made them sound like the choir of Angels, who'd given them a send-off to find Rachel. The cello, viola, guitar, bass, and a large horn, maybe a French horn, melded in with the choir of twenty-some members. It was simply beautiful, lifting her out of any remnants of last night's epic battle within herself. Even Rachel's face was as soft and ethereal as the music.

The song never left her thoughts for the remainder of the service, and she found herself humming it on the way home. Her image of Frank and Linda transformed after seeing them away from school and participating in something they both appeared to love. There was so much she didn't know about Frank and Linda, so many unknowns.

They boarded the DC Metro a few blocks from home, greeted by a car full of boisterous Redskins fans. She hung onto Arthur with one hand and a vertical pole with the other, all the way to their stop.

They followed the herd of people on the mile walk, and upon arriving at the stadium, she was beginning to get the picture of how important sporting events like this one were to people. But she was totally unprepared for the impact of eighty thousand-something cheering fans when they finally emerged from a short tunnel and into the stadium. After living in the silence of her own private world for so many centuries, the people gathered at this sporting event taught her something about strength in sheer numbers. She covered her ears with her hands, but the intensity was still overpowering. Claire started to laugh she felt so good, and ignoring the noise level, she uncovered her ears and drank in the emotions thick in the air.

"Arthur, this is wonderful. We should do this every weekend." She yelled above the crowd, her arms in the air, reaching high like the intensity in the stadium. He wrapped his arms around them both and led them to their seats, just in front of a bank of large video screens at both ends of the field. Arthur sat between them so he could easily answer their questions. Stunned by the cheering crowd, she forgot about all of her questions. Arthur broke the silence first.

"You know, Frank played football his first two years at Woodrow Wilson, but after an injury, he had to give it up at the end of his sophomore year – something about his knees. He comes to the Redskins games with his father, who, being a DC Councilman, has a seat in one of the suites you see behind those glass fronts. He's probably here today." Arthur pointed it out to her.

"Really," Rachel said.

Claire saw the look in her sister's eyes, the same one she'd had after her confrontation with Frank. "You want something to drink." She asked her, leaning across Arthur.

"Sure. Something hot, please."

Arthur started to get up, but she caught the top his shoulder with her hand. "I want to get it, but I don't have any money." She smiled, holding out her hand. He gave her a wad of bills from his jacket pocket. "Where am I going?"

"Go back the way we came. We passed a food stand on the way." He said.

"Right, I remember." She climbed passed all the legs in her aisle, leaning on a few shoulders in the row in front of them, and excusing herself half a dozen times. She went right to the stand and purchased three hot chocolates, paying with a twenty-dollar bill. She was getting her change when she heard a familiar voice behind her.

"Hey, Claire."

She turned, knowing who it was. "Oh, hi Frank." She stuffed her change into her jacket pocket and got out of the way of the person behind her. "You just get here from church?" The expected quizzical look found its way onto his face. "I saw you in church. That was a beautiful song the choir sang." His face is almost serene, she thought, staring into his bluish gray eyes.

"Yeah, it is." He said. "What are you doing here? You like football?"

"Don't know yet. It's my first time. It's exciting to be in the crowd – and loud." She smiled, but immediately drew back, remembering what Frank was like at school. Clearly, she needed to maintain the upper hand for the moment. Frank looked like he was caught off guard and fumbling his usual macho image, seeing the girl who had knocked him loose from her cousin. They were the new girls at school, the ones with dead mothers, and, the ones who were closing in on their prey. Claire's coy smile changed his face even more, adding the hint of a smile to Frank Richardson's face. She bit her lip at her choice of the word – prey. "Where are you sitting?" She asked.

"My dad has seats in one of the suites. I had to get out of there. Get some air."

"Oh. It's warm in there I'll bet. Well, I need to get these back before they're cold chocolates instead of hot." Claire turned away before he could say anything more and walked away. She found her way back through the masses, taking her seat and handing out the hot chocolates, and gave Arthur his change. They were still hot, but it didn't take long at all to consume hers. Its sweet richness warmed her through and through, adding to the excitement of the adventure. "Arthur, was Frank a good football player?" She asked close to his ear.

"Yes, he was."

She nodded, knowing Arthur had overheard her speaking with Frank. So maybe, that's why he took us to church and the game. To which, he nodded. She turned her attention to the play on the field for the first time. The team with the stars on their helmets was approaching the metal "H" post on their end of the field. One of their team members had the ball tucked under his arm and was zigzagging his way towards her, quite deftly she thought until abruptly knocked sideways and slammed into the grass by two

Redskin players. She winced at the sounds of the collision, the brutality of it all. Arthur leaned into her, telling her what was happening, and explaining their possible strategy – run, pass, field goal. They wound up scoring what he called a touchdown, and then a point after, placing the number 7 on their side of the scoreboard.

"That's a bad thing for the Redskins in case you're wondering." He said.

She nodded but was thinking about Frank again and his state of mind when he and Rachel had their confrontation, especially the anger he was expressing, like what was happening on the field. This morning she'd seen a different side of him, both in the service and at the concession stand. She'd learned a lot about him in just a few minutes this Sunday morning. She watched the play on the field, catching on to this violent game called football. Sometimes she heard the players grunting in their contacts in-between the deafening cheers of fans. It wasn't until late in the first quarter, when someone was injured on the field, limping off with the aid of two others. Maybe that's how Frank got hurt. They sat far enough away to insulate them from the sounds of the violent contacts – players caught in vulnerable positions by the opposing players. Except for those times, she was enjoying the excitement of the game and the energy of the fans.

Late in the fourth quarter though, and close to the end of the game, a pass play was broken up by the Cowboys, and the intended receiver had hit the ground hard after being blindsided by the defense. It was at the far end of the field, so she was looking at the video screen's picture of the play. The Redskins player was not moving at all, and three men from their bench had rushed out to him. The feeling in the pit of her stomach was sickening. She had no explanation for it, but it was causing her pain, and she couldn't do anything about it. She looked to Arthur for help, also seeing that Rachel didn't look very good either.

"Watch the screen and say a prayer for the player." He said. "It's all part of the game."

A few moments later, the player started to move his arms and then sat up with the three trainers around him. "So, he's alright?" She asked him. He pointed to the field, where a cart had arrived, and the player was loaded and then driven off the field and into a tunnel. The discomfort in her midsection was subsiding, but still there. The fans were all largely quiet until he got into the cart and was taken from the field. Then, they applauded him all the way into the tunnel.

"It's part of the reason we're here," Arthur said. "I wanted you to see all the different kinds of human behavior, everything from kindness to the absolute violence on the field. This is an important part of what humans are all about. What you felt in the pit of your stomach was fear coming from the fans; a fear that the player on the field was seriously hurt and cheering for him as a hero when they knew he was alright. Humans are a complicated lot, but then so are we."

He was right of course, Angels were a complicated lot, and she and her sister were prime examples. "Thank you for this Arthur, no words could ever have imparted what I've felt sitting in this stadium – the raw emotions of humans peppered with compassion." He patted both their knees, standing as the final seconds ticked off the scoreboard clock. The Redskins had lost this day, but she had won a deeper understanding of what it meant to be human, which would serve her well in her assignment.

The mile walk to the Metro seemed longer and more strenuous, with all the excitement and emotions of the day catching up with her. Even amid all the aggression and pain on the field, she was still glad to have seen and felt it all. Because now, she knew the human race on a deeper level, that spoke of humanities capacity for kindness and caring, even while immersed in a physically brutal game. She'd seen Frank in a different light this day, something she was sure Arthur had intended for her to experience, being the wise and all-knowing mentor he was. She giggled at the last part, knowing he'd heard.

"Yeah right," he inserted in her thoughts, elbowing her side. "All knowing? Ha." Their ride home in the packed Metro cars was comforting to her, the closeness, the physical contact of strangers, the possibility of meeting someone who you might know for the rest of your life, all defining characteristics of the human experience. She would cherish this day for a long time.

ACTING OUT

M s. Letrell was a reasonable person, willing to give a student the benefit of her doubt, but Frank left her little wiggle room this morning, causing her to lash out at him in an uncharacteristic way, catching Claire by surprise. The petite Ms. Letrell stood toe to toe with Frank Richards, barking orders at him like the quarterbacks in yesterday's game. His smug face, standing in defiance of her, only caused her further irritation. This all took place before the bell rang and in front of the entire class at 7:45 a.m. Claire hadn't heard what the cause was, but she was thinking he must have made some sort of snide comment when he walked past her desk on the way to his, just a short ten feet away in the front row. She was in back talking with Jeff, who had somehow weaseled out of her that she'd attended the Redskins' game. He was jabbering on about it when the sound and the fury began up front.

"Frank Richard," Ms. Letrell said through clenched teeth. "You will be suspended if you don't retract your ill-advised remark and apologize to me right now."

Claire heard that loud and clear. Frank must have said something derogatory to her. He was stiff as a board with her face only inches from his chest, him being six foot five, and she at five foot three. If it weren't such a serious matter, she might have laughed at the absurdity of their size difference.

"I'm waiting, Frank."

Claire couldn't hear him mumble his apology, but it must have been sufficient, because he got to sit at his desk, and Ms. Letrell returned to hers, taking a minute or two after the bell rang to regain her composure. She had to hand it to her teacher, giving a young upstart a tongue-lashing in full earshot of a classroom full of students. Gumption, plain and simple. Jeff had turned around, rolling his eyes at Frank's risky confrontation. She paid him no mind, focusing on Frank, who was obviously uncomfortable in his seat. Class passed quickly and when the bell rang, she quickly gathered her things and chased after Frank, who had bolted from the classroom, like it was on fire.

She caught up to him a hundred feet down the hall, pulling alongside him, as if it was the most natural thing in the world. "Hey Frank, I got a question about the musical." She said a little out of breath and having to take three steps to his two. She looked up at him, his face drawn into a deep frown, his lips pressed hard together. The thought of her petite teacher coming face to chest with one such as this scared her a little, but the hall was full of witnesses to ward off any threats of aggression. He took two more strides and then grabbed her sleeve, jerking her back.

"What!" He snapped.

She saw the looks on the students around her, faces filled with fear, all stopping in mid-stride to distance themselves from the impending confrontation. She didn't care. Frank was just a teenager; she was one in charge here, even though he was twice her size. She grabbed him by the by the same arm he was holding her with, barely able to hold on it was so bulky. "Frank, are you mad about the Redskins losing?"

"No," he said yanking his arm away and glared back at her with the same defiant face he'd given Ms. Letrell.

"What then?"

"Who do you think you are, wanting to know my business?

You're nobody, and even if I knew you, it still wouldn't be any of your business. So what's the question about the musical?"

"Gotcha," she whispered to herself. "Oh, I was wondering how you and Linda were going to play the scene where you two find us huddled in the alley. It would help me and Rachel define our parts, and it would set up our place in your family in the following scene. That's all." Claire smiled, knowing he'd be interested – if not now, then later.

"Could we talk about this during class? I'm in a hurry here."

"Sure. And I did enjoy the game yesterday, even though we lost to those pesky Cowboys. See ya later." She walked away quickly, not wanting to hear his answer. At least she'd gotten his attention away from what happened in English. He came really close to being suspended, but Ms. Letrell seemed a very forgiving lady, even for the likes of him.

The rest of the morning was pretty normal. When she met Rachel for lunch in the atrium, her sister had on the same sourpuss face as at the football game, so she definitely wasn't going to say anything about talking with Frank after English.

"You're awfully quiet Claire. Something wrong?" Rachel finally broke their mutual silence.

"I was a little unsure if you even wanted to talk with me. Same question to you. I'm fine. Are you?"

"Not really. More dreams about the cavern. I can't seem to get it out of my mind. It's like it's got a mind of its own. At least it wasn't as bad last night."

"Maybe all the violence we witnessed at the football game yesterday had something to do with that. I know I got upset about it. I really don't understand why people like a sport where players get hurt all the time. I glad it wasn't as bad for you though, the dream, I mean." Claire tried to hear her sister's thoughts and feelings but came up empty.

"No, the game was not the cause; at least I don't think it was.

Claire, it was difficult waking up from that dark place, and then jumping headfirst into a physical body again, probably didn't help much either. I appreciate all of your help, but I'm going to have to work it out for myself. You and Arthur have done all you can, and now it's up to me to leave it behind. A lot has happened during the past week, so I guess I'm not doing so badly, considering where I came from. I still can't wrap my head around what I did to myself. Maybe I never will."

"At least we get to sing together. I look forward to it every day. And no matter what happens during the day, singing with you cheers me right up." Claire reached across the small table they were seated at and took her sister's hand in hers. "Sisters Forever, eh?" Rachel set her carton of milk down and grasped Claire's hand.

"Yes. Sisters Forever and heaven help those who get in our way." She laughed. "You know, Frank and Linda."

"Right," Claire nodded her approval, seeing Rachel's frown lines disappear. "Oh by the way, please don't get upset with me in Theater class, because I have to talk to Frank. I think I'm finding a way through his thick hide." Rachel's face darkened at the mention of his name. "Sorry. Just wanted to give you fair warning."

"Give him hell Claire," Rachel glared.

"Sure will." She finished her lunch early, leaving to talk with Lu in Applied Science. They had left a conversation hanging on Thursday, about boys – important gossip. She hurried off to meet Lu, who was always early to every class she could. She'd called herself an "excessive, compulsive, overachiever," on their first meeting, saying it was, "an inherited trait from her father's side of the family." In any case, Lu was filling her in on Frank and Linda's 'extended friendship', she'd called it. Rumor was, they were doing it. Claire, of course, had to ask her what that meant. Lu had laughed so hard she turned beet red. Claire, being embarrassed, of course, did the same. That had cemented their bond of friendship, so now, Lu was burning her ears with gossip every chance she got.

"Hi Lu," she sat next to her at the lab table. Lu was busting out at the seams with something. So, Claire leaned in, planting her ear inches away from Lu's lips, ready for her dose of gossip. Actually, she had learned more about high school from Lu than everyone else she'd come into contact with.

"The word is, Linda's pregnant," Lu whispered.

Claire drew back, frowning in disbelief.

"That's right. You heard me."

Claire held her hand up to stop Lu from launching into more gossip, rumors, and the like. She was stunned, her thoughts racing in circles of disbelief, trying her best to process Lu's words, "Linda's Pregnant!" This was just too much for her to deal with in the few minutes before class began. She patted Lu on the knee, thanked her, and turned away, pretending to shuffle some papers, opening her science notebook, and making meaningless notes about this wild rumor. Her train of thought was interrupted by Mr. Boswell wheeling in his, "cart of special effects experiments," as he called it, and proceeded to set it up on his table up front. It was the last thing she remembered about Science class because she was thinking about what she was going to say to Frank in Theater, hopefully, aside from Linda.

Frank and Linda were in their seats when Claire walked in, her head still spinning with the rumor. She breezed past them and sat in the back of the classroom, thinking she'd have to wait until rehearsal for the chance to speak with Frank, and even then, she'd probably have to finagle Linda away from his side – they were joined at the hip most of the time.

Right after class, she approached them both, saying she needed a moment of his time to go over their characters' interactions. Linda cooperated and let her take Frank aside for a minute before rehearsal started. She walked to center stage and asked him to block out his movements in the alley. As he did, she struck up her intended conversation as quietly and inoffensive as she could.

"You surprised me yesterday at the game. I never thought . .."

"Skip the small talk. What's your question?" He interrupted her.

"Okay. When you spoke to me at the snack bar, you seemed upset. I was just wondering if seeing me there was the cause."

"No. Actually, you were a good distraction. It was tight quarters in the suite. I had to get some air like I said yesterday."

"Frank, I'll be honest with you. I'm a pretty good judge of character and can read people's mental states with a degree of depth. I'd say that someone in the suite pissed you off and you had to escape their presence. Tell me if I'm right or wrong." Claire folded her arms across her chest, a posture she'd seen Linda use on Frank. She knew she was right, she could see it written all over his face.

"Go on," he said looking challenged by her.

"If my intuition serves me right, it was your father." She dropped her arms to her sides, looking more vulnerable. Frank's face got some added color to it and his eyes darted away from hers.

"Good guess. Ms. Newman's here now." He said pointing. "You think you're pretty good at this, don't you?" He said walking away.

"Well, that went okay for a first step," she mumbled to herself, walking over to where Rachel was in the left wing.

"How did it go?"

"Not bad. He's almost human." She giggled with her sister about their assignment. "I think his father rides him pretty hard, not that he'd admit to it. I saw it in his eyes at the game yesterday, when I was getting our hot chocolates. He surprised me from behind. I think he was actually glad to see someone his own age. His father's suite at the stadium is probably full of people in power, like his dad."

"You're way too nice Claire. If I had my way, I'd pop him one in the you-know-where." Rachel motioned her intent.

"Down girl. Be nice to the human." Claire said with a hint of sarcasm. "We're supposed to help him, not send him to the hospital." She stifled a giggle.

Ms. Newman walked them through their first scene together, giving them suggestions to use, and then left them to rehearse their opening scene in the alley, moving on to other cast members. Claire appreciated being given a measure of freedom with her character, making her draw upon experiences and emotions to breathe life into her portrayal. It was no wonder Frank and Linda liked theater; they could act out their stuff through their parts.

Linda and Frank's characters would find the two homeless sisters in the alley while walking the family dog on a cold snowy night. She and Rachel would be huddled against a fence, dressed in tattered clothing, trying to make it through the night without freezing to death. They were supposed to be angels in disguise, there to help this family get back together. Billy and Kathy were the troubled teens in the family.

"Are we going to do this or what?" Linda sneered.

Claire held Rachel back from engaging with Linda, hauling her to their place on the stage where they'd be for the scene. They sat and waited for Frank and Linda to begin.

Do It For Love
Act I Scene two
(Billy and Kathy Coleman are walking their
dog on a winter's night)
Billy
"Hurry up and do your business Angel." (Billy hated that name. Their mother,
Catherine had named the dog.)
Kathy
"Don't jerk on her leash like that." (Kathy grabs his coat sleeve

to stop him.

They continue further down the alley)

Kathy

"Billy! Look! Over there." (She points to a fence where two
bodies are leaning

against the fence, drifts piling up on them.)
(Billy and Kathy hurry over to them and
Billy nudges one of them with his boot.)

Billy

"Two good for nothing homeless bums. Maybe they're dead."

Mary

"Uhhhh." (The homeless girl groans)
(Kathy squats down next to them, removing her glove
and touching them with the back of her hand.)

Kathy

"God Billy! She as cold as ice! What are we going to do?"

Billy

"Call the cops" (He gets his phone out and starts to dial.)

Kathy

"Wait! We need to get them warm now. The cops could be half
an hour.

Help me get them up."

(Together, Billy and Kathy get the two homeless girls
to their feet and start walking them to their house.)

Billy

(Billy dials his cell phone.)

"Mom, meet me at the back door. We found two half-frozen
people."

Frank and Linda smiled at each other, pleased with the way
they've addressed their parts in the scene. Claire rolled her eyes at
the irony of the musical and who's playing who. "Great Frank. Let
us freeze, eh. Thanks for the rescue Linda. I can see who our ally
is going to be."

Claire and Rachel looked at each other in amazement, knowing Arthur had set this scene and written the dialogue for Ms. Newman and Mr. Clark. They both had to try hard not to laugh, with doubtful results.

"What's so funny?" Frank asked.

"We are," Claire said wiping the smile off her face. "You two are ready to bite our heads off at the first opportunity, and here we are in our parts, and you're helping us. Funny, don't you think?"

"I suppose so," Frank responded with a smirk.

"Do we have time for the next scene inside our home?" Linda asked.

"Maybe." Claire shrugged her shoulders. "We could start it at least."

Ms. Newman clapped her hands from the front of the stage, getting everyone's attention, and saying that the remaining time was for song rehearsal. It was fine with Claire; she wanted to sing with Rachel to wipe away all the mixed emotions of the day. She'd see Frank tomorrow in English.

THE CONVERSATION

Frank surprised her in the hallway as she was about to enter Ms. Letrell's English class. He was leaning against the lockers on the opposite wall, almost as if he'd been waiting for her. Class didn't start for a couple of minutes, so Claire went over to see what he had to say.

"Good morning," he mumbled. "You said something yesterday, and I thought about it last night. There was no way you could know it was my father who caused me to leave the suite. And there's no way you could just guess it either. I thought about what you said, about your intuition, and your ability to read people. So, tell me what you think he said to me. . . I mean, you might be a good guesser, but you'll never get this right."

Frank folded his arms and crossed one leg over the other, while leaning against the lockers, an arrogant stance if ever there was one. She stifled her need to laugh. Should she tell him or not? She hedged her bet a little, not wanting to be self-righteous about the whole thing.

"Frank. Your father has it in his mind you should take after him like most fathers think their sons should do. He's a DC Councilman and a lawyer, so he probably was talking, no, bragging to his lawyer buddies, and whoever else was there, that you're going to Harvard Law School." Claire paused to examine Frank's body language of, a straight face and restless feet. "Well, what do you think? Am I right or what?" A grin crept across his face.

"It's Georgetown, not Harvard."

The bell rang, breaking up their first conversation. As they entered the classroom, he opened the door for her, letting her pass underneath his arm. Ms. Letrell was watching the whole thing. Claire thought she was proud of her, getting the arrogant big lug to hold the door for her. Their entrance was almost a parade, demanding the attention of everyone in the classroom, making her feel special, excepted, and perhaps now able to command a higher social status, maybe even seen as someone to talk with, or even date. She'd not even been kissed yet. While the heady high school thoughts of status danced in her head, she tripped over the desk at the head of her row, moving it several inches to the surprise of Judy, the one seated there. "Sorry," she whispered and continued to her seat with a hot face. She wasn't very good at this teen thing, being a transplant in an unfamiliar body and setting, but she must be doing okay – no one laughed at her, out loud anyway.

Paying little attention, she hadn't heard one word of what Ms. Letrell had said. She was too busy plotting her next move with Frank. She figured that in order not to lose her window of opportunity with him, she needed to continue the conversation as soon as possible. When the bell rang, she launched herself towards the door, beating all but two students into the hall. Frank was one of them.

So, what do you want to do after high school?" She asked having jogged up alongside him. He smiled down at her.

"Why don't you tell me? You're the one with psychic powers, supposedly." He chuckled, slowing his pace.

"Okay. After high school, you're going to Juilliard and then onto Hollywood to become a big star and make a lot of money." She grinned. By the looks of him, he was enjoying their little hallway crystal ball session.

"Not really," he shook his head. "But please, go on, amaze me some more with your stories."

"Right. You know those angels in the musical; you know me and Rachel. Well, we're gonna get you an audition for the Off-Broadway production of that very same musical. It's going to be your ticket to the big Broadway production of it and the Hollywood picture several years later." She giggled at the nonsense dribbling out of her mouth. "But even more importantly, you and Linda will be, MARRIED, move to Malibu and live a life of fame and fortune." She'd dropped the big "M" bomb on him, causing an assortment of expressions: from horror to pleasure, shock to acceptance, but most importantly, a flushed face. "Gotcha," she mouthed. They traveled several more steps down the hall before he closed his mouth and gathered his wits enough to cough out a nervous laugh.

"Where do you get these outrageous thoughts?"

He made an abrupt left turn down another hall and quickened his step, leaving her standing in the hall and watching him disappear into the crowd. "That may not have been the best thing to say," she mumbled, turning around and headed for her next class. "Not the best thing at all." She wouldn't see him until Theater class, and it was probably a good thing, giving her some time to think about what she was doing, besides just plowing her way into a ditch.

She joined Rachel at lunch, as usual, sitting around a large planter, letting out a long sigh from a busy morning. "Hey, how you doing?" Rachel looked as tired as she felt.

"Dandy, just dandy." Rachel sneered. "Linda crapped all over me again, telling me all about her woes, especially her parents being a pain in the ass."

"Oh. Look on the other side; she actually carried on a

conversation with you. Now there's something to talk about."
Claire moved closer to her sister, touching shoulders with her.
"Frank and I had a conversation in the hall, before and after
English class. And, he held the door open for me. You should have
seen the look on Ms. Letrell's face. Of course, then I tripped on a
desk, not paying the least bit of attention. But, miracles of
miracles, no one laughed. I guess they were too stunned by Frank's
errant behavior."

"How nice for you. I'll trade you a load of Linda's stuff for
some of Frank's"

Rachel's face drooped more with each word, giving Claire the
hint she needed. She recognized her sister's sullen look that didn't
have a thing to do with Linda unloading on her. "Hard night?"
The minute the words slipped between her lips she regretted
having said them.

"Not that it's any of your business."

"Well, sorreeey." Claire pressed down on her sister's shoulder
to prevent her from getting up and leaving. "You know, you're no
fun to be around either. You've been a sourpuss on and off for
days now. How about we call a truce. We both came from a bad
situation, straight into this place. It's not been easy for me either,
so sister, a little less sparring would be helpful to us both." Claire
removed her hand. Rachel eyed her warily, not something Claire
was used to seeing from her.

"I didn't sleep much last night, and what I did get was filled
with that damn beast and its cavern. It won't let me alone, no
matter how hard I try, and no matter what you or Arthur has
done. It's relentless, Claire, and it's wearing me down and giving
me headaches."

Rachel rubbed her temples, hiding her fearful eyes. Claire
could feel it in the pit of her stomach, the upside down, everything
is all wrong feeling. "I'm sorry. Maybe when we get to rehearsal,
you'll feel a little better. I know I do."

Unfortunately, lunch period was over, and there were still two more periods to go before rehearsals started. They said their good-byes, going their separate ways. She stopped by Arthur's classroom and left him a note, saying they all needed to talk tonight about Rachel's problem breaking free of her past. She had to run to Applied Science to get there on time, just stepping into the room as the bell rang. She took her place next to Lu, who looked excited to share something juicy, the words barely kept captive until Mr. Boswell's attention turned to setting up an electricity demonstration. Lu curled her fingers for her to come closer.

"It's official," she whispered into Claire's ear. "Linda has morning sickness."

Lu pulled back with an exclamation mark on her face, mouth wide open, eyebrows raised, and arms forming a goal post. So, Linda's definitely pregnant. Her parents would disown her, and Frank's dad would kick his butt. And Rachel thought she had problems. F&L had by far, won the prize for being screw-ups, major offenders of parental headaches suffered unto them by their children. Trouble was, it was her problem too, and Rachel's and Arthur's. Plenty to go around. "Who told you?" She whispered in Lu's ear.

"Jamie. She overheard her in the girl's room and then ducked out just as Linda emerged from the stall. There was no one else in there but them."

Great, Claire thought. Now the whole school's going to know by the end of the day. Social media strikes again. Only this time, it was going to hurt someone. "Have you tweeted it yet?" Lu made a face at her, the kind that meant she had. By the time rehearsal started, someone was bound to slip up and comment to Linda. Misery, misery, misery, was what awaited poor Linda. Mr. Boswell cleared his throat, looking at the two of them. She straightened up on her stool and smiled an apologetic smile at him. She made a mental note to ask Arthur for a cell phone to keep up with the latest news of her peers.

Frank was not in Theater class, so she assumed Linda had already told him. She didn't expect to see either one of them at rehearsal, and in fact, she didn't think they'd be in school tomorrow either, maybe for the rest of the week. She told Rachel everything she'd heard from Lu, watching a light go on in her head. "It's probably why Linda unloaded on you this morning, sensing that someone had seen her barfing in the girl's room early this morning, and then not going home sick."

"What are we going to do?" Rachel asked.

"What can we do at this point? We're not friends yet in their eyes." Claire said shrugging her shoulders. "We should speak to Arthur about it tonight. I left him a note after lunch."

"Oh, good thinking."

Mr. Clark was helping Ms. Newman, by going over their songs. He took them to a practice room and spent the entire hour helping them with voice inflections and their characters' portrayal of emotions to the audience. He worked them hard, leaving her breathless at the end of the hour, but it was a good thing, bringing her closer to her sister, and helping Rachel step out of her problems for the hour. Walking home though, was a different story. The feeling didn't last for Rachel, returning to her sullen mood by the time they got home.

The house smelled like pizza, giving them a pause from their problems. She waited to spring their stuff on Arthur until the last piece of pizza was finding its way into Rachel's mouth. "Let the indigestion commence," she said loudly in her thoughts – loud enough to get Arthur's attention.

"Arthur," she began. "Rachel and I have some things we could use your help with. First, Rachel's still affected by those memories. Secondly, I've been unable to help her much at all." Claire left her face poised in question, knowing Arthur would take over.

"Would you explain further," he asked. "Those memories?"

"The nightmares are still there. Last night I couldn't sleep at all. Every time I closed my eyes, I found myself with the beast. It won't let me go, Arthur. It's relentless in its pursuit. It's getting so that I don't even want to go to bed, I'm so afraid of what might happen."

"I conferred with Sandy about this and she said we needed to return to the originating incident again to resolve the issue. Now I know what you're going to say about revisiting Paris, but it will be different the second time and third if need be. A lot of what you're experiencing is enhanced by your physical mind's inability to rid itself of memories, merely shelving them in an out-of-the-way place and ignoring them. But in your case Rachel, your connection to the incident and aftermath is a real thing and resides on a deeper level of your being. It inundates your physical mind, causing a fear reaction in your body, which in turn amplifies the fears in your physical brain. In other words, your brain is no match for what you have opened it to.

So, enough with the psychoanalysis. Are you ready for the conversation of your life?"

In a brilliant flash, Arthur changed into his Angelic form, filling the room with his stature and presence of mind. Standing at seven foot, his wings spread to twelve feet, and connected to the Angelic Realm, he exuded confidence to her and Rachel, gathering them in his wings and changing their form to their Angel bodies. They departed the living room in a flash of light and an odd sound like a champagne cork popping. Claire's parting thought was one of, what the neighbors would say if they were walking by. She was new to this life and everything was cause for excitement, except maybe where they were headed.

"Remember who you are and you won't be waylaid by the power you both gave this event in your lives."

The wet cobblestone streets were the same as before and the dark buildings cast ominous shadows in the moonlight. There, in between the buildings was the cast of characters: a young woman being stripped of her dignity, of her very soul by a caped invader, a rapist culling his herd; and the young Rachel, guardian of the young woman, her angel of protection in human form, taking revenge on the evil that was accosting the purity of a young life, striking three blows with a fist-sized cobble stone she'd pickup; striking with all the rage of the evil doer, becoming what he was, shackling herself to darkness for time everlasting. All this played out before them, the observers, while separated from the acts of violence.

"Arthur, I don't feel anything. Why is .. ?" At that very moment, Claire found herself lying on the damp stone street next to Rachel, her sister of old, and the evildoer lying dead in the street. The scene was surreal, not existing for her, merely a distant memory to which she had no connection. It was then, she fell into Rachel, headlong into the anguish of a soul who had killed herself, through an act of violence. She was overcome by the power it held over her sister, yet she stood above it all, observing while feeling her heart wrenched from her body, her mind tormented by the blackness appearing out of thin air. She was falling into the darkest pit of death, of aloneness so fetid; she retched from its revolting odor. It pressed down upon her with a ferocity that could only accompany the twisted torture of the death of a soul; a death where every last ounce of life was squeezed from her being and relegated into the nothingness, yet still conscious in the utter darkness of her dead soul.

"Arthur, are you saying Rachel and I lived like this for all those centuries: she in the darkest of caverns, captive of the beast; and myself living within a lie, alone in self-inflicted punishment for not saving the one I loved, a kindred spirit, sisters forever bound up in darkness of our own making?"

"All you have seen and experienced lives within your being and shapes who you think you are, and what you are. Return to your sister-of-old and help her through her pain, give her the hope she needs to free you both. Live within the lie no more. Now go."

Claire did as she was told, returning to her sister-of-old and the Rachel who'd come with her to this place in time. She stood for a moment, observing the two, one with wings, one without in physical form, both Angels, both in pain. There wasn't anything she knew to do or say, but to offer her life, so they may live as one, free from pain and darkness. She was immediately drawn back into them by the quickness of spirit, that which sustains and stands firm and strong within all life; the kernel of light that grows within the soul of all life. They were together at last, all three of them bound together in their one soul; standing strong and lithe within her thoughts and ready to soar again. But the Rachel-of-old fell away from her, slipping through her fingers, her body limp and without life. Claire tried to cry out to her, but the words simply vanished into the darkness swallowing her sister once again. The other Rachel, bound to old, a rope secure about her neck, did follow, ripped from Claire's grasp by unseen forces, shredding her lifeless wings. And to her horror, she too fell into the darkness, bound in like kind, overpowered by the darkness that still breathed within her. "Arthur," she cried weakly. "Help us please."

The room was cold and nothing about it seemed like home. Her sister was draped across her lap, limp and barely breathing. Was this real? Was she home in Arthur's house? Where was he, and why didn't he help them? There was a whooshing sound accompanied by a brilliant flash of light in the living room, which brought back the feeling of aliveness to her. She awakened from some dark slumber; a fitful dream that defied belief. She felt warm now. Arthur settled in his chair beside the sofa and changed back to his human form, helping her ease back into reality. They were home at last. Rachel stirred, struggling to move off Claire. "We're back," Claire said softly to her sister, breathing a sigh of relief to be home again. "Arthur, I failed again. Will I ever succeed?"

"Patients, young one. You must give yourself time to heal. Eighteen hundred years is a long time to live within a lie. But, you will heal in time. You learned something about yourselves and your past. You spoke to each other, even though it was a one-way conversation. You were heard. And that is cause for celebration. We all should rest now."

Arthur walked his girls, his charges, up to her room, tucking them in together, to be close and feel the warmth of a sister's love." Claire closed her eyes and fell into a dreamless sleep.

GO TIGERS

Empty was the only word that could describe how she felt, like a hollow shell. It was six o'clock and still dark outside on this early November morning. She groaned rolling over to face Rachel in the bed. So peaceful, she thought, with nothing of the night before showing on her face. She had failed again last night; failed to overcome the darkness. It had swallowed both her and her sister, and the Angel, Rachel of old. Arthur had said it might take several attempts before they conquered their fears of what they'd done to themselves. Arthur had no magic wand to wave over their heads, relieving them of their past transgressions. They'd chosen their paths and had to deal with fallout the best they could. Arthur had made that abundantly clear. Rachel stirred, turning away from her, pulling the covers over her head.

"Stop thinking about it," Rachel mumbled. "You're in my head again. Go back to sleep."

Claire rolled over, retreating to the edge of the bed, one arm and her knee draped over the side. "Sorry," she murmured and let herself slide out of bed, landing on her knees, her head still lying on the bed. She sighed, thinking of the day ahead. It had none of this nonsense in its schedule, just plain old high school classes, and the cacophony of hoots and hollers between classes, all mixed in with the rivers of conversations in the hallways. It was an experience in and of itself. She smiled at the image of Frank leaning against the lockers – so smug. She dressed in whatever she found on the floor next to the bed and went downstairs to make some hot tea and stare out the kitchen window into the backyard, a sanctuary of someone's making.

She had ten minutes to herself before Arthur stirred and began his morning rituals; yawning loudly at least twice before rolling out of his futon. He joined her in the kitchen, making coffee for himself, something he'd grown accustomed to throughout his many assignments. They sat together sipping their tea and coffee, enjoying the peace of an early morning.

"You sleep okay?"

"Yes, thank you. How's the futon? "You know, you could have put us together in Rachel's room."

"I thought you'd need the space since you both haven't had a roommate for a while, and the blue beast doesn't count. You did well last night, taking another step in your freedom from the past. We'll keep at it in our spare time." He grinned.

"You're funny Mr. Arthur. You should have a part in the musical at school. Dr. Arthur's School of Laughs for Fallen Angels. We breakum, you fixum." Claire giggled. "You did a nice job with the musical you know. How did you get Ms. Newman and Mr. Clark to sign off on the changes you proposed?" She raised an eyebrow at him.

"Very funny. I'll hang my shingle over the classroom door. As far as how I wove your assignment into the musical, arranging for you to play opposite Frank and Linda, it's a secret for me to know and you to find out."

"You certainly are in your element, aren't you? I do have a real question, and it's about our assignment. What is Frank's relationship with his father? He and I met at the Redskins game after he'd left his father's suite to get away from him. Anything would be helpful."

"There's a JV football game Frank might attend after school

today. Try talking with him some more. If I tell you something about him, it wouldn't have the same meaning if he did. Besides, you should get to know him better when he's away from Linda. Well, I'm going to use my bathroom before you two take it over this morning."

He left his empty mug on the counter and went upstairs. "Another football game, eh." She said. She fixed a pan of scrambled eggs and got the toaster out, ready for them when they congregated briefly before running out the door with food in hand. She'd come to like scrambled eggs on toast, on the fly.

On the way to school, she told Rachel what she'd be doing after rehearsal, inviting her to come if she wanted. Rachel gave her a funny sort of look when she said she'd be talking with Frank at an after-school game. Her morning was quiet and subdued, a pleasant surprise. She found Rachel in the atrium and joined her for lunch. She was quiet while they ate, and was getting ready to dump her trash and return the tray, when Rachel grabbed her arm, pulling her back into her seat.

"Did you hear anything new about Linda?

"Not really, but I'm sure Lu will fill me in before Science class. Why, did you?" Rachel shook her head, letting go of her arm. "I'll see you in Theater." Claire bused her tray and went to class a little early. She wanted to give Lu a chance to spread more gossip, but more importantly, she needed to ask her what usually happened in cases like this. Claire had no clue about such things. Lu was late, so they didn't get a chance to talk right away, but Lu found the right time to lean in and do her thing. Claire held her tongue through Lu's bursts of tabloid shorts.

"I have a question for you. What usually happens to the pregnant girl?" Claire whispered in Lu's ear, avoiding Mr. Boswell's roving eyes. Lu shrugged her shoulders. Claire leaned in again. "First time for this?" Lu nodded.

"Something you wanted to share with the class." Mr. Boswell's gaze locked onto Claire.

Claire shook her head, her face heating up with embarrassment. "No thank you."

"Then perhaps you could tell us about the magnetic field lines, which surround an electrical current."

"Probably not," she said making the class laugh.

"Please pay attention Miss Claire Tate; you'll discover that science is important in our daily lives."

"Yes, sir." Claire tried to make herself invisible, but sitting on a stool at a lab table made it next to impossible. Class droned on and she tried her best to listen to Mr. Boswell, to no avail. All she could think of was what would happen to Linda. Being sixteen and pregnant wouldn't be easy. How would she tell her parents? And what would Frank do? Would he stand by her?

Frank wasn't at Theater class again, which was not a good thing in her mind. If he wasn't with Linda, then he must be beating his head against some locker in an empty hallway, wondering why him. Poor guy.

"Hey," Rachel nudged her. "What's the matter? You look worried."

"About Linda. She's going to have to tell her parents soon. I feel like everything is crashing down around her and she probably feels the same way we did last night – out of control and falling into a dark chasm."

"Her choice, right?"

"Yes, but think about what you just said Rachel and then remember when we made our choices. There were consequences, whether they were self-imposed, or the rules of the Angelic Realm. Now think about why we're here." Claire paused as a light went off in her head, having just told herself something important about their assignment and their past. "Frank and Linda's little problem has consequences, just like ours did long ago. By helping them, we help ourselves with our problems. Thanks for saying that really unsympathetic remark; it's what we both needed to hear."

"Really Claire? You're comparing us to them? Maybe you're in worse shape than I am."

"No, it's all bound up together. You'll see." The bell rang, releasing them to test her hunch if Linda and Frank were at rehearsal. They walked quickly into the theater auditorium, scanning the stage for the two. Walking down the aisle, she heard the soft sobs of a girl somewhere in the auditorium. When she got halfway to the stage, she saw Linda hunched down in a seat, her hands covering her face. Claire stepped into the row of seats and sat next to Linda as quietly as she could. Linda leaned forward to get up, but Claire held her down with a gently laid hand on her shoulder. She placed a finger to her lips and offered her hand. Linda began to cry openly, for all the cast and crew milling around on the stage to see and hear. She tried to think of what to say, knowing that Linda was vulnerable in this state of mind. Claire laid her head on her shoulder and whispered so softly, even she had a hard time hearing herself.

"Linda, how can we help you?"

Slowly, Linda wiped her tears and wet nose with the back of her hand, and looked at Claire, not with a look of disbelief that someone she didn't really care about was trying to help, but with haunting eyes seeking a place of rest. Linda was stripped bare of any caring what people thought; she only wanted to know everything was going to be alright. She wanted to be loved. Tears spilled from her eyes and ran down her cheeks, falling into her lap, and reminded Claire of how she really felt deep down every day of her exile; trapped and alone, with no way out.

"I'm going to say this," Claire whispered, "and it will no doubt come out all wrong, but you have to hear this. We all love you and if you let us help, you'll never feel alone. We're here for you Linda, always." Claire motioned to the cast on stage to come down, including Ms. Newman, who had just come from backstage. Claire let Ms. Newman take her seat, knowing Linda looked up to her in many ways. She was a widow with a young daughter, and she was a dedicated theater and music coach, who Linda had known since the eighth grade. Claire watched, as the cast members gathered around Linda, letting her know they cared and were there for her.

She stood in the aisle with her arm around her sister, perhaps seeing for the first time since she'd arrived at this place, the real strength of people; what keeps them going on their path. They have each other to lean on if they're willing; a strength she couldn't match, even if she did have her powers. "Arthur you crafty old Angel, you knew this would happen." And his response was classic Angel fare, the quiet strength of silence.

Claire told Ms. Newman that she and Rachel couldn't stay for rehearsal and left. Rachel went straight home, while she stopped by the JV game and waited for Frank, but he never showed. No surprise. She walked home alone thinking about what had happened, mostly about how many friends Linda had on the cast. She was seeing a different side of Linda, one that spoke well of her. But she still didn't know how to help her – not a clue. "I'll ask Arthur, he'll know. He knows everything."

"And what makes you think I know the answer to everything?" Arthur said with his hands on his hips, when she walked in the front door.

Claire took one look at him and broke out laughing – he'd heard her. "Sorry, but you're the parent and you're supposed to know everything. Right?" He laughed with her. "We left rehearsal after we found Linda crying in the auditorium. I sat down and tried to comfort her. I told her I loved her. It seemed to help Linda, but not like the cast and Ms. Newman did. They really supported her and made her feel wanted. They connected with Linda and did a better job than I ever could."

"Don't think so, but if you say so, I guess it makes it so." Arthur smiled at his young charge.

"Nice. Did you save that just for me?" She knew exactly what he was saying to her. He was showing the young rookie Angel what is and isn't the truth, and he'd made her laugh at herself, which was a good thing. Rachel came bounding down the stairs and into the kitchen.

"Did you tell her yet?"

"Tell me what?"

"Frank ran away with Linda after she left rehearsal." Rachel said.

Claire stared at Arthur in disbelief. "But she seemed better ..."

"They'll probably call their parents tonight I should think, telling them they need to think it through on their own. They both have credit cards, so money isn't a problem. The problem is whether one of their parents goes ballistic about it and calls the police. Then it will be a mess to reckon with. Not our call though." Arthur said.

"I feel sorry for her," Claire sat at the kitchen counter, leaning her elbows on it, and holding her head in her hands. "This is getting complicated. What are we supposed to do? I'm at a loss."

"Right now, let's eat dinner," Arthur said picking up a cell phone.

Claire's eyes bugged out when he pushed a phone across the counter to each of them. "Really? Thanks, Arthur." She jumped up, hurried around the counter, and gave him a kiss and a hug. "Now we'll know all the gossip first hand."

"I was afraid of that." He said making a call.

"Hello, yes I'd like to order . . . oh, no thanks,
but I would like a large vegetarian, and hold the artichokes
please.
Arthur . . . my number? . . . Just a second . .
It's 435-9880. Fifteen minutes, okay. Bye."

131

His eyes darted between the two of them, making them both giggle. "Your very first cell phone?" Claire covered her mouth to keep from laughing at her mentor's funny face.

"Hey, just because I'm old-fashioned doesn't mean I can't learn something new."

They laughed and made small talk about nothing important for a change, while they waited for the pizza to be delivered.

UPROAR

Claire got Lu Mitzer's cell number from her the first day of school and wrote it at the top of the back page of her notebook. So far, it was the only one. Lu would know what was going on, because she was connected to practically the entire junior class and had sources for the others, except for the seniors, they were a tough nut to crack though. Lu was proud of her little network of gossip spies. Claire sent her a text, knowing she'd be busy gathering everything about Frank and Linda's little adventure.

"What's up with F&L? cm Claire"

They'd hit it off pretty well in Science class; at least she hoped it was the case. Ten minutes before the pizza arrived she got a text from Lu.

"4 sure it's serious police called
cu in 10 must have told M&D"

"The police were called by one of their parents. My friend Lu said she'd call in ten minutes or so. What can the police do?"

"Not sure," Arthur said. "Your friend Lu might have heard where they are though. You should ask her."

"Okay," Claire said. She was thinking of the consequences to Frank and Linda if the police descended on them at the motel because one of the parents was mad at them and wanted to teach them a lesson. Claire knew about the Angels sent to track her

down, making her hide deeper and deeper in the Realm, finally
scattering herself to the wind. She never knew if they'd found her
and merely let her hideout of her own free will. There were many
questions never answered when she was picked up by Sandy's
Search and Rescue Crew – Arthur.

The pizza arrived the same time Lu called her, sending Claire
up to her bedroom to talk in private. Lu told her she'd hadn't
heard much of anything yet, just a lot of gossip about the two.
Claire asked Lu to call her if she heard anything about their
location, even in the middle of the night. She went back
downstairs and sat between her sister and her mentor at the
kitchen counter, her head feeling a bit fuzzy about everything.
"Lu didn't know anything yet," she said getting a piece of pizza. "I
told her to call me whenever she learned anything, no matter the
time." She took a huge bite, stuffing her cheeks, wanting to know
something, anything. She'd felt a connection with Linda in
rehearsal as if Linda could trust her. As she slid another piece onto
her plate, she realized she was hurting deep inside, not because of
what Linda and Frank were going through, but more along the
lines of her unresolved issues. She wiped a tear out of each eye with
her paper napkin, which had little cherubs on it, another subtle
hint from Arthur.

"What's the matter, Claire?" Rachel asked. "Are you worried
about Linda?"

Claire nodded quickly as the waterworks turned on,
completely out of her control. "I guess so," fell from her lips
between the tears. Arthur slid his stool closer and wrapped his arm
around her shoulders. She'd lied to her sister so easily she didn't
even think of it as a lie.

"It's okay to grieve about what you did to yourself." He
whispered in her ear.

Her heart ached so much it made her suck her breath in. She
grabbed a fist full his shirt to keep from falling off her stool.

"Would someone tell me why it hurts so much?" Rachel laid her head against her, holding her hand between hers. Claire couldn't hold back the tide of pent-up emotion that she'd locked away for so long. She fell limp into Arthur's lap, blacking out for a moment, and then felt the sure and strong hands of her mentor gather her up into his arms and carry her away. When she opened her eyes, she was on the sofa and no longer crying. "Tell me, Arthur. I need to understand. What did I do to myself?" She barely heard her own words, but Arthur had heard her thoughts, which were crying out for help.

"When you saved the young girl's life in the south of France, you took away the opportunity for a young man to redeem himself, by doing what you stole from him. He needed to save the girl in order to save himself from certain destruction. He'd been thinking of taking his own life for some time before the incident. He lived for several more years, but spent them in absolute misery, dying a painful death of loneliness and despair. Had he saved the little girl, he might have recovered his soul and lived a happy and fulfilling life. You didn't know that of course, but all the same, you assumed all of his despair and grief without knowing it, and along with your own shame of breaking Angelic Law, you drove yourself into a self-inflicted banishment, covering it over with the self-deception of a world you created far away from everything. I can't think of a greater punishment, except when you piled on a mountain of guilt with Rachel's Fall from Grace. You thought it was all your fault because she watched you save that girl, which she emulated by saving the woman, but killed her attacker in the process. Linda, in her own way, is suffering like you with her guilt and shame of trying to end her life, and now adding to it the unwanted pregnancy, she thinks it will tear her family apart even further. Then you go and open yourself to her and all of her pain, guilt, shame, and few other odds-and-ends. I can't imagine how you could feel any worse off than you do right now."

Arthur's words were crushing her heart, but at the same time, they offered a reprieve from her self-imposed punishments. Which one was stronger depended solely on her choosing. She vacillated, having known pain for so long. She lay on the sofa feeling only the rise and fall of her breathing, listening intently for Arthur's voice, knowing he was allowing her the freedom of choice, as he must do. Poor Arthur, Had she made him suffer for all those centuries? He was sitting beside her, waiting patiently for her to decide. She could almost hear him waiting for his student, his charge, to turn the wheel of her misdirected ship, and sail towards her purpose in life, that of an Angel fulfilling its legacy. Surely, there were more difficult things under heaven than this. Why then was she having such a hard time choosing? It made no sense. She moved her legs and let them fall to the floor while pushing up on an elbow with Arthur and Rachel's help. Together they got her sat up. "Such a fuss over one so small," she mulled in her fuzzy thoughts, knowing the hard part still lay before her. She had to choose her path.

Her cell phone rang back in the kitchen where it lay on the counter, next to the empty pizza box. "Would you get it," she croaked out through her dry mouth. Rachel got up and hurried to answer what was probably Lu's call.

"Hello, this is Rachel. Just a second, I'll get her."

Her sister handed the phone to her.

"Hi Lu," she said trying to sound normal.

"Oh? Nothing yet? Thanks for the heads up. Bye."

She laid the phone on the coffee table. "Nothing yet," she said hanging her head.

"What just happened to you, Claire?" Rachel asked.

"Maybe Arthur could explain it better." She said looking at him. He always appeared so calm and collected, even when things were falling apart around him.

"Yes, I'd be happy to explain it to you. Did you hear everything I said to Claire?"

"Not really. I was moving in and out of my own stuff – something about it being a mistake to save the girl? And the tragedy it caused another?"

"Yes. This is why we must be careful about intervening in human affairs, it can have unforeseen consequences much of the time."

Arthur laid it all out again for both of them, and it was good that he did because she had needed to hear it a second time, and probably a third in the future. Both she and her sister had a much clearer understanding of the originating event that led to her self-banishment and her sister's Fall into the abyss. She was tired, very tired, and full of pizza. "I think I should go to bed early. I'm really all wore out, but I feel better about a lot of things." Arthur walked her upstairs and tucked her in after she used the bathroom and changed into her PJs. She nestled down under the sheets, pulling the comforter up tight around her chin. "Thank you, Arthur. I owe you my life many times over."

"Shh," he said softly. "You rest now. I'll set your phone on the table here. Wake me if Lu has news if you would please. Good night."

"Good night." Her words, spoken so quietly, they carried her away into sleep, with their last sounds but a distant hushed lullaby.

She was dreaming of school when her cell phone rang, sounding like the passing bell from English class in her dream, and interrupting a conversation with Jeff.

"Hi Lu," she murmured half asleep. "They did! When?"

Claire was wide-awake after Lu told her where Frank and Linda were staying, and that the police would probably be involved, given the state of affairs with both their families. It was after 2 a.m. and Rachel was sleeping next to her, so she slid out of bed without disturbing her, and dressed in jeans and sweatshirt. She crept downstairs as quietly as they would allow, doing her best to step over the creaky ones. She donned her winter coat and stocking hat, borrowing Arthur's gloves, and silently closed the front door behind her. She took Arthur's old fifteen-speed bike to ride the three-quarter miles to the Days Inn on Connecticut Avenue, where Frank and Linda had a room. When she arrived, the police and Frank's parents were already in the lobby, getting the night manager to unlock the door for them. She stayed behind some low bushes a hundred feet or so from the front door, not wanting to be seen by Adam and Evelyn Richards. She had a clear view of the entrance and waited for a few minutes before the police exited the elevator with Frank and Linda. A lady officer escorted Frank and Linda out of the lobby, with her partner following behind, and unhappy looking parents bringing up the rear. The two police officers loaded them into the backseat of their patrol car and drove off, with Adam and Evelyn following them. She jumped back on the bike and tried to keep up, as they headed south on Wisconsin Ave. The substation wasn't too far, which was a good thing for her because she nearly lost sight of them right before they turned on a side street to enter the parking lot. When she leaned her bike against the rack close to the front doors, she was breathing hard and had started to sweat inside her down jacket. She cautiously approached the entryway to the DC Metro Police Substation and hesitated, her stomach doing flip-flops. She paced around outside for a few minutes trying to calm herself before she walked in and approached the officer behind the counter.

"I'm a good friend of Linda and Frank, who just came in a few minutes ago. I not family, but I was wondering if I could ask about them." Claire's eyes met his questioning gaze. She was shivering inside her parka, thinking she was probably doing something wrong and had to force herself to stand her ground against his arresting gaze.

"Unless you're family, I can't tell you anything about it. You can have a seat and speak to them when they leave." Officer Lewis told her.

When she sat down, her fingers laced together in a tight ball, and the only thought racing around inside of her head was that she'd made a mistake by coming. "What's the matter with me?" She growled at herself.

"Everything alright over there?" Officer Lewis said.

She shook her head yes, her eyes meeting his. She forced herself to smile; it was pathetic at best. A moment later, she heard Frank's voice yelling from somewhere beyond the counter. There was another male voice yelling back at him, so she assumed it was his father. It quieted for a moment and then resumed, only growing louder. Now there were female voices as well, and they seemed to be moving towards her. A door opened and the two officers who had picked up Frank and Linda, emerged with Linda, Frank and his parents, and Linda's parents; who must have arrived while Claire was racing to keep up with the patrol car. Linda had been crying and looked ten years older. Everything about Frank had defiance written all over it. Mr. Richards and Dr. Connor signed a sheet on a clipboard and left with their teens in tow. Claire lowered her head trying to hide in plain sight, feeling stupid and exposed on the bench seat. She watched them get into their cars and drive off before she left the station and rode home.

Arthur was snoring away in his study as she hung up his parka and tiptoed up the stairs, avoiding the noisy ones. She slid under the covers still dressed and took more than an hour to fall asleep, with all the early morning's commotion playing out in her head over and over.

RACHEL'S CANDOR

Claire woke up at 5 a.m. thinking about the night before and what it meant to her and Rachel. Their assignment had taken on new aspects, encompassing a far greater number of people. Now there were two families on a collision course. There were decisions to make, some of them would be made in haste, causing a backlash, and most assuredly, a rift could divide parent and child for the rest of their lives. But where did she and Rachel fit into this picture? Their assignment grew from two to six people because the parents would dictate a great deal of what would happen between Frank and Linda, no matter what the two teens wanted. Claire didn't expect to hear anything about the incident because she was the lone witness. Certainly, Frank and Linda would never speak of it. Somehow, Claire had to figure out a way to help Linda. She was hoping their brief moment of connection would help, but her doubts and lack of experience told her the odds were against her. She knew she was young and inexperienced, but her eighteen hundred years of solitude had to count for something in the ways of the world – patience maybe? She reluctantly rolled out of bed a little before six o'clock and showered early, and went downstairs to make some tea.

"You're up early," Arthur said leaning over a cup of coffee. "Couldn't sleep in?"

"No. I was awake at five thinking about Linda and Frank." She set the kettle to boil.

"So, was it cold last night?"

The shock wave roared down her spine and sent her reeling, knowing he'd seen her leave. "Not so much. My jacket is quite warm." She answered after a long pause.

"Tell me about it. Maybe I can help."

Her eyes roamed the kitchen floor as if she'd find anything of use there. "Sure. I got a call from Lu at 2 a.m. and found out where they were and that the police were called to intervene. I rode over to the Days Inn and watched from outside as Frank and Linda were taken to the substation down on Idaho Ave. I rode there and waited. They came out arguing with their parents, and I left and came home. I woke up thinking about it all." Claire filled her mug with hot water, dropped in a bag of black tea and sat across from Arthur.

"You were busy last night. What did you learn?" Arthur said refilling his cup.

"Life is complicated, isn't it? For two so young, they have some life-changing decisions to make, if they get to make them."

"Complicated might be an understatement in their case. Both their families have ongoing issues, which have affected the children for years. Now, it's all come to a head, as the saying goes. Are you going to try and talk to either of them today?"

"Don't know. Will they even be in school today?"

"You'll see. How about an early breakfast? You go wake your sister and I'll fix banana pancakes."

She woke her sister, saying that Arthur was fixing breakfast and had something to say to them before they left for school. Rachel looked well rested for a change, which made Claire happy. They went down together and were greeted by the sweet aroma of banana and vanilla pancakes.

"There's a stack of pancakes under the plate," he said pointing.

Arthur finished cooking the batter, flipping the last one on his plate, and joined them at the counter. They ate in silence, except for the clatter of their forks scooping up generous bites of syrup-laden cake. Claire pushed back from the counter and patted her belly. "Thanks for breakfast, it was really good.

"Fill Rachel in," he said motioning with his fork full of pancake.

Claire told her sister what had happened with Frank and Linda the night before. Rachel did say a word and didn't even look curious – she just chewed.

"I believe you both have a better idea of what your assignment is now that the cats out of the bag and both families are involved. What I wanted to tell you before you dive into the pool of consequences, gossip, hurt feelings, and general life-altering decisions, was that both Frank and Linda may not want to talk about it. They both have a deep emotional needs to seek out help, but it's hard for either one of them to accept it from anyone, except for you two. You may not realize it, but Frank and Linda admire you both and might be willing to talk to you today. But don't be hurt or feel they hate you if they are insulting you and yelling before they quiet down and listen. Be patient and listen for clues, open doors, or out-right challenges to your credibility as peers, because they need to talk to someone. It'll be an education on human behavior."

She nodded, acknowledging his wisdom on such matters. She slid off her stool to clean up, patting her full belly, and thanking him again for breakfast.

Halfway to school, Rachel finally commented on the morning's news report.

"Ballsy Claire. Were you scared?"

"Kinda, but I kept my distance to be on the safe side."

"I would have liked to have seen their faces coming out of the police station."

"They were scared. I could feel it."

"See you for lunch." Rachel said going her way.

Claire sat down at her desk in English class and was the only one in the room; she was fifteen minutes early. She wrote Frank a short note like she'd thought about in bed this morning.

"I need to talk to you both. It's important.

Claire

She got a piece of tape from Ms. Letrell's desk and taped it to his seat. Waiting for class to begin seemed to take a long time, with each student drifting in, sitting in silence until Ms. Letrell came in, and started her lesson plan for the day. Frank was last to enter, sitting down on the note she'd placed there. She didn't hear one word of the day's lesson. Her head was somewhere else, pounding on the doors of reason, trying to make sense of the feelings racing through it and the jumble of thoughts. It was a craziness that unnerved her; listening to her head swim in a soup of hormones and memories of her past. When the bell rang, Frank got up quickly and turned to look at her. She pointed at his desk hoping he'd see the note. He looked at her oddly like she was from another planet. He saw it and tore it from the seat, leaving without a backward glance. She was the last one out of the room, drifting by Ms. Letrell's desk, feeling her eyes following her. She breathed a little easier out in the hallway and started to walk to her next class.

"What do you want?" Frank said pulling her aside.

She froze in front of him, startled and forgetting what it was she wanted to say. He looked tired from the night before and like Linda, quite a bit older.

"Could we talk before rehearsal? I think I have something important to say to you both." Claire rubbed her face, trying to grasp what she'd just said. What a dumb thing to say, she thought.

"Yeah, I guess so."

Frank released her arm and walked away. "I think I have something to say," she muttered, shaking her head. She ambled on to her next class, still half in a daze, not really waking up fully until she met Rachel for lunch.

"Wow, what a morning." She said sitting down next to Rachel on the edge of the large planter. "I've been in a daze most of the time."

"Oh."

"I made a big deal out of telling Frank I thought I had something to say to them both. How lame is that? Not sure what I'm going to say yet, but I guess it must be important."

"I've been thinking about what Arthur told us this morning, about us having what those two need. So, I was thinking about how we could convey, um, knowledge to them, not that we're experts or anything. We're just a couple of rookie Angels fresh out of a dark hole, trying to find ourselves. So what right do we have to tell someone how or what to do? And . . ." Claire's thoughts simply ran away from her. "Stupid," she mumbled.

"And what? And we don't have a clue?" Rachel laughed.

Claire smacked her on the back, nearly knocking her lunch tray off her lap. "Nice. That helps me a lot. I'll keep your advice in mind when I talk to them before rehearsal." Her sister kept laughing at her and gradually she began to feel better, even snickering when she left to face Lu.

Lu was strangely silent through Science class, only saying hi. Claire was thankful because she didn't need any more info on the subject of Frank and Linda. She wandered into Theater class a little late, having gone to the girl's room to splash some cold water on her face. She sat with Rachel, ignoring Frank, and paid little attention to Mr. Clark's lesson. She still didn't know what she was going to say. When class ended with a joke that Mr. Clark had told, garnering laughter from his students, she was panicking about meeting Frank and Linda. Rachel walked with her trying to calm her fears, but when she saw the F&L gang waiting for her backstage in a corner full of props, her knees got rubbery and wanted to fold under her. Rachel stepped out ahead of her and marched right up to them.

"Listen up you two," Rachel said in an authoritative voice. "If you think you have problems you ain't seen the likes of real problems like ours. Two angels sent to help both you and your parents just before Christmas. And what do you know of us? We just came out of the depths of our own private hell to help you with your tiny little insignificant problem of bringing a new life to the world. Well, here's a news flash, we don't know what we're doing, so don't listen to anything we have to say. Got it? Good. Now give your friendly rookie angel a hug so that we can get on with whatever we're going to get on with." Rachel held her arms out to them both.

Claire was stunned by her sister's candor and her allusion to their parts in the musical as a way to deliver their message of, "Angel Help Found Here." Frank and Linda looked about the same, not knowing what to say. Rachel was just standing there with open arms, waiting for her hug. "That's my sis," Claire mumbled, enjoying the moment. Linda tittered first, accompanied by amazement in her eyes, a laugh following along quite naturally, soon spreading to Frank and the two rookie Angels. Laughter's a mystifying feeling, spreading without borders into everyone within earshot. All it took was one to light the fire. The how's of it, she wasn't at all clear about, but the proof was right in front of her. She and her sister made two friends that day, and that was a good thing.

MEMORIES

Rachel had done the impossible and made friends with Linda and Frank. They were still laughing about it when they opened the front door to find Bosco waiting for them. He began circling in and out between their legs, stopping to stretch his body as far up their legs as possible, his paw touching Rachel's waist and her mid-thigh. Apparently, he was tuned into and entertained by their laughter

"Meow, meow," he kept saying.

Bosco cornered Claire and continued his incessant greeting, while Rachel escaped to the kitchen. Claire followed, running through the living room to the kitchen, managing not to trip. "What's with him I wonder?" Her sister shrugged her shoulders. "Is Arthur home?"

"Yeah, you know you ran right past him. He's on the sofa."

She returned to the living room and found him sprawled on the sofa under a homemade quilt he'd bought at a flea market, complete with holes, rips, and missing stitching. "Hi," she said leaning over the back of the sofa speaking to what she thought was his head. There was a muffled reply, saying something about a hard day at school. She pulled a corner of the quilt back to reveal his face. It was a nice face she thought, bending a little further to kiss his forehead. He mustered the trace of a smile. "What happened?" Claire leaned on the sofa with her elbows, holding her face in her hands.

"Eminent disaster headed our way. Ms. Rickels, the school social worker, told me about her meeting with the Connors and Richards because she thought you two might be able to help Frank and Linda with their problem. It seems Councilman Richards wants Linda to abort the baby for both their sakes. His wife Evelyn, wants Linda to keep it and even offered to help by caring for their baby, so they can finish school and go on to college. Linda's mother, Sharon, said abortion was an option or adoption. Dr. Connor said they made their choice and they can deal with it by raising the child. An argument ensued and Councilman Richards tried to bully everyone else, including Ms. Rickels. She said it was the most hostile fifteen minutes she'd ever experienced, which is why she spoke to me about you two maybe helping Frank and Linda deal with their parents. You know, act as their sounding board, since you're all together in Theater and the Musical. Sounds to me like there's a war brewing. Anyway, that was my day, at least the end of it anyway. Did you two get a chance to speak with Frank and Linda?"

Arthur emerged from his cocoon and sat up. "Yes. Rachel did all the talking though because I was tongue-tied. Rachel made us two new friends, so I'll let her tell what happened." She called her sister in from the kitchen to tell the tale and perhaps cheer Arthur up a bit. They sat on the sofa, with Bosco in Arthur's lap, and laughed together at Rachel's gift for humor.

"Pretty good, don't you think?" Rachel's shy smile brightened the room considerably.

"Incredible," Arthur slapped his knee. "What made you say that?"

"I dunno," Rachel shrugged. "Maybe an Angel made me say it?" She giggled.

Arthur roared with laughter. "Maybe an Angel made you say it. You're good Rachel. You opened the door to those two and you gave them the strength to face their situation. Betty was right about you both, you'll be a big help to Frank and Linda."

Bosco arched his back and hopped into Rachel's lap, sitting on her legs with his body stretched out, his paws on her shoulders, his face right in hers. He licked her cheek, purring softly, then rubbed his whiskers and side of his head there, marking her with his scent. "What's he doing?" Claire asked. Rachel held his head with both hands, her thumbs stroking his whiskers and the side of his jaw.

He meowed softly.

"Claiming her as his own." Arthur patted Bosco's head. "I'm going to fix dinner."

Later that evening, Claire had a strange feeling about what Bosco had tried to convey from the moment they'd entered the house like he knew something and was reacting to what they were feeling. She was lying in bed with the lights out watching the shadows of tree branches dance on her ceiling and walls, from the streetlights out front. She'd already dozed off several times after having gorged herself on apple pie ala mode. Arthur had brought home several pies for Thanksgiving, and they'd gotten a head start on them tonight. Bosco pushed the door open and jumped on the foot of her bed, meowing. She swept her leg across the bed to brush him off, but he hopped over it twice, still meowing. She sat up and patted him on his head before he jumped down and meowed from the doorway. She followed him down the hall and into Rachel's room where he stopped meowing. Rachel was tossing and turning, and murmuring words.

"Rachel," Claire shook her sister's damp shoulder gently. "Wake up. You're dreaming." She sat on the side of the bed and pulled back the covers. "Rachel, wake up. What were you dreaming about?"

"Cla . . aire?" Rachel said sleepily and opened her eyes. "I was back in Paris walking to . . to . . you know, where I saved that woman. Is it late?"

"Not really. It's a little past eleven o clock. Bosco brought me here. Are you alright now?"

"Yeah. It wasn't so bad this time. Will you lay with me for a while?"

Claire slipped under the sweat-dampened covers. She snuggled up to her sister and it wasn't long before they were both asleep, both dreaming about school and rehearsals. They woke several times looking at each other, knowing they'd had the same dream; then falling asleep to begin all over again. They were locked into each other's thoughts and memories, all the centuries of history together; each bound within their own private guilt and shame, one a Fallen Angel, one a runaway, each lost in their togetherness. Until. . . They were falling into the darkness of empty cobblestone streets – Rachel's entry into her dark prison of sixteen hundred years. Claire was helpless to resist what seemed inevitable; their descent into a destiny shared by each.

"This way," a voice said in the distance.

They strained to see in the blackest of night, stumbling on the uneven cobblestones. "There," Claire pointed to a light in a faraway window; one candle setting ablaze a picture of quiet and hopeful peace, framed by the lace curtains of the second story window. "We can go this way," she whispered, hearing the heavy breathing of the beast coming across the veiled divide. The darkness of the cavern lay just ahead in memory, waiting to swallow them in its cavernous despair.

"This way," the voice repeated.

They moved quickly across the distance; the candle's glow holding back the darkness until Claire saw the way. A safe haven lay within the memory of her world. She surged ahead, her sister in tow. "This way. I know a place."

They left the dark streets behind, entering her valley, with the sun warming them on the path up the ridge where she'd picked wildflowers. They walked side by side in perfect unison, absorbing the breathtaking beauty of her world, breathing in the mountain air scented with exotic flowers, unlike any on the world of humans. Claire led them to her secret hiding place at the base of the tallest mountain. There, tucked behind an immense slab of rock that had slid into place from above, was her cave, where she'd come to be alone, away from the illusion of beauty in her world. Her cave was not always a place she wanted to be in, but it was so interwoven into her being, that she could not exist without it lonely envelopment. It was the place where she hid away from her pain and regret. Together they entered her sanctuary, parting the curtain of shrubs and vines, which grew from the cracks in the rocks. They sat just inside the entrance with their backs to the opening, waiting for the interior to reveal itself in the sparse light.

"There!" Rachel pointed to the figures on the walls and ceiling of the cave. "We drew those a long time ago. I remember them because you stole me away from my descent into darkness just before I was claimed by the beast. We had but a brief moment before I disappeared. You handed me a soft chalky stone and told me to draw a remembrance. I drew you trying to save me. It was the last memory I had outside of the darkness of the cavern before I was swallowed whole by it, and imprisoned by the beast as it slowly drained the life from me. Oh, Claire, the pain, and anguish inflicted on my soul was so great, I blacked-out, and have only fleeting memories of its moans and growls as it fed on me."

Their hands reached out to touch the drawing of an Angel's outstretched hand, its wings stretched wide and struggling to keep another Angel from falling into the darkness. They wept together until night fell in her world, and then awoke in Rachel's bed, from the dream that wasn't a dream at all.

"Take me there. I need to be there a while longer." Rachel whispered.

They closed their eyes awakening in her cave. Claire started a small fire near the mouth of the cave, huddling in its warmth beside her sister. "This is not a happy place for me," Claire said drawing her sister close. "I came here to suffer your loss and increase mine. Not often, but enough to not forget our parting. My suffering is out of guilt for leading you astray, even though I had no way of knowing it at the time. I was too young and inexperienced. It was my burden to bear though, and is so even now; just as yours is the memory of falling into darkness for all eternity." Claire opened her eyes and gazed at her sister. "So much pain in our lives for such a long time. It was good we had those few moments together. It's what kept us both alive in our prisons." Claire caressed her sister's face, glad they were finally free and back together. "We should rest now. We have a new life to return to that needs us rested and able to help Frank and Linda." They fell asleep staring into each other's eyes, knowing their love ran deeper than any ocean.

THANKSGIVING DAY

Arthur woke them early, drawing them both out of a scene in the musical. Claire was reluctant to leave – they were singing together.

"Good morning. Happy Thanksgiving." Arthur opened their blinds to let in the muted light of a cloudy day.

"Thanksgiving?" They both mumbled, rolling over together. They giggled after he'd gone downstairs, remembering they had four days off from school and promptly fell asleep a while longer. Claire was first up, making tea and toast for them. Rachel joined her and they talked about their journeys together, while Arthur listened. "I'm not used to this mind merging stuff yet." Claire filled their cups again. "It difficult for me to know my feelings from yours, that's how close I feel to you. When you drew us on the cave wall, I knew I'd see you again someday. I'd felt it all those centuries in my heart, even though I failed to believe it in my mind. I always wanted to believe that nothing could take you away from me, not all the years of aloneness, or the darkness which held us for so long. I wasn't strong enough to believe it I guess. When Arthur came for me and found me on the same path you and I walked on last night, I was returning from a long stay in the cave, sore afraid we were both lost forever. Seeing him startled me so much I fainted. Arthur coaxed me back to life and then we came for you."

"Hearing your voice in my dark place was the most powerful experience of my life. I was being given a second chance. I'll never be able to repay you and Arthur. Never." Rachel's hand trembled in hers.

"We should do something around the house, it'll help clear the cobwebs from your heads," Arthur suggested. "I'll start in my study."

"Okay," Claire hopped off her stool, to begin with the dishes. They moved upstairs next and an hour later they finished in the living room around 11 a.m. just about the same time the doorbell rang. They looked at each other, still connected to each other's feelings, shrugging their shoulders. Claire plopped herself down on the sofa, while Rachel went to see who it was.

"What a surprise Linda," Rachel said. "Please, come in."

Rachel and Linda appeared in the archway, which led into the living room. Linda looked like her morning sickness was in full swing, and even her hair was not fully brushed out to its normal sleekness and draped in fullness over her shoulders. Linda was a pretty girl, five inches taller than Rachel, with burnished blond hair and powdery blue eyes. The former cheerleader body was still intact, lanky yet stout, with well-formed musculature. Claire stifled a giggle over her choice of the words. "So what brings you here on this Thanksgiving morning?" Claire adjusted her position on the sofa to see their guest seated across from her in Arthur's recliner. Linda was fighting back tears.

"Rachel and I are upset over what happened to you and Frank two nights ago. We thought it unfair and it made an already difficult situation, worse." Claire found herself genuinely sympathetic to Linda's plight. Linda's eyes widened that anyone could know what happened to her. "I'm sorry I startled you. I only know because I sneaked out of the house and rode over to where you were staying with Frank. When I got there, the police were escorting you out of the motel with Frank's parents looking on. I wanted to tell you how much Rachel and I care about you and to offer our help if you want it." Now the tears were running and Linda couldn't do a thing about stopping them.

"Tell us why you're here Linda." Rachel leaned over to take her hand.

"Linda, we want you to know we support you, no matter what other people have said. After all, we're your guardian angels, like Rachel said the other day." Claire said with a hopeful smile. Linda's eyes glazed over for a second as if she was reliving something. Her face grew serious when she focused on Claire.

"My parents are fighting again and so are Frank's. My mom was drinking this morning. She wants me to have an abortion. My dad says we should accept the consequence. Frank's parents are split too. I don't know what I should do, and neither does Frank. We never got the chance to really discuss this the other night, because our parents called the police, and we were hauled down to the station, where our parents argued the whole time before taking us home. I've never been so angry at them. But, what am I going to do?" Linda sank deep into the overstuffed recliner, wiping her nose and eyes on her sleeve.

"Are you and Frank going to be able to talk alone about what you want for yourselves? I mean, isn't that what's important, not what your parents think is right? Did the school social worker call you yet? I'm sure she can help you make your decision. How can we help?" Claire could feel Linda's head spinning out of control with all the uncertainty, but still, in order for Linda to get a handle on any of this, she needed to decide something, even if it was only temporary. Claire chided herself, because who was she to tell someone else how to make decisions. She'd literally taken forever to not make up her mind, hiding from herself in her made-up world. "I'm sorry. I didn't mean to ask any of those questions except the last one. How can we help?"

"I don't really understand why, but I feel I can trust you both.

I didn't know that until yesterday. What happened in the auditorium touched me deeply and it scared me, but it's why I trust you."

Claire got up and knelt in front of Linda, taking both of her hands in hers and bowed her head, saying a silent prayer, but mostly imparting a little Angel dust on her, feeling her body tremble in response. "Sometimes we need to trust ourselves over what others tell us. I think this is one of those times, Linda. You know what is best for you deep in your heart. Have faith in yourself." Claire rose, pulling Linda up from the chair and into a hug. "Thank you for trusting us. Have you talked with Frank today?" Linda shook her head.

Claire stepped aside with Rachel, while Linda made her call. "If she asks us to go with her like I know she will, then things could get complicated if any parents show up. Are you all right with that?" Claire said in a hushed voice.

"Does Frank feel the same way Linda does about us? He may not want us there."

"I don't know." Claire cut her thought off when Linda was done talking. "Did you get a hold of him?"

"He stayed home too. He spoke with his mother before she left to volunteer at her church's free Thanksgiving dinner for the homeless and families who can't afford one. She'd been doing damage control all morning after her husband had spoken harshly to Frank and walked out in a huff. He's home alone now. Would you come with me? I really could use your support."

Claire looked knowingly at Rachel, who nodded. "Yes. We'll come, but you're the one who's going to do all the talking. Okay?" Linda nodded.

"My car's out front if you want a ride. I can bring you back when we're done."

Linda drove them over to Frank's home about twelve blocks away, close to American University. It was a large two-story older home, with ivy growing on the brick and large oak trees throughout the yard. There were no other cars in the drive when they parked, so Claire felt better about being there. Frank reluctantly let them, whispering with Linda before he took them upstairs to his room. It overlooked the backyard, with large branches of an oak tree just outside his window. Frank and Linda sat on his bed and she and Rachel opened two folding chairs stacked by his computer desk. Frank wasn't looking especially comfortable with their presence, eying them warily until Linda again whispered something to him, which seemed to calm him. Claire was wondering why they had tagged along, feeling very much out of place in Frank's bedroom. She wasn't sure she trusted him just yet, especially after what happened to Rachel in the hallway, and his aloofness with her in English class.

"First things first," Frank's sullen eyes fell on Rachel. "I apologize for my aggressiveness with you in the hallway. I overreacted to what you said and the way you said it. I am sorry. Now, please tell me why you are here." Frank unfolded his arms and rubbed his forehead with both hands.

"Thank you, Frank," Rachel said folding her arms. "I'm sorry for the derogatory comment about Linda."

"But it will be a cold day in hell when I trust you," Rachel thought very loudly for her sister to hear.

Claire knew this man. It was his father speaking. Apologizing without totally meaning what he said. Claire thought about what she wanted to say to a young man such as Frank, a bully who had murderous thoughts when he had Rachel pinned to the lockers. "Frank," she began. "It is not in my nature to tell an outright lie to someone, not even to someone like you. You have to remember that I saw the anger on your face. You scared us both. You were clearly not in control of yourself. If I had not shown up when I did, who knows what would have happened. Your display of rage will always be foremost on our minds, and no amount of feigned apologizes can ever take back what you intended to do to Rachel. Your hand was on her throat. Such actions can never be taken back with an apology; Rachel could have pressed charges against you, using the marks on her neck as proof. We wouldn't be having this conversation if she had because you'd be in jail or out on bail with a restraining order. I would be lying if I told you I could forgive you. I tell you this so you know where I stand. You asked why we were here. We're here at Linda's request, and that's the only reason we're here, unless there's something you have to say to us." Linda looked scared from what Claire could see. Was she afraid of Frank? Did he force her to have sex? Claire was risking a lot, but if she and Rachel were ever to be of any use to Frank and Linda, the truth had to come out into the open right here and now. Frank was fidgeting with one of the knots on the cotton bedspread.

"Please don't do this," Linda's voice quavered with fear.

Claire was betting on Frank being a better man than his angry self-image. And he did love Linda from all indications, but he harbored a secret, which only he could reveal. Linda was incapable of admitting she'd let Frank force himself on her. She'd kept the secret locked away inside, afraid to even hear the words mentioned. "The word is RAPE," Claire yelled in her thoughts, watching her sister stiffen in her chair, ready to attack. There were plenty of objects in Frank's room to take the cobblestone's place, ready to crack open a head, needing only a hand to thrust it into action. Even she was getting nervous, the longer Frank waited to speak. The same angry face she'd seen in the hallway was returning, flashing on and off, as he struggled to contain his anger.

"FRANK!" Rachel bellowed.

Everyone in the room jumped with Rachel's wake-up command. "It's time to change Frank," Claire said in her thoughts. "Time to choose between who you want to be and who you were." She was a little scared because this man could easily hurt all three of them, and they could do little to stop him. Dare she risk more? There was a reason behind Frank's actions, a reason so obvious he couldn't see it for what it is.

"Frank," she whispered softly in her thoughts. "Forgive your father. Don't repeat what he did to you. Forgive yourself. Tell Linda you love her and ask for forgiveness. It's the only way, Frank. Try." She hesitated to reach out to him, waiting for him to initiate the gesture. "Come on Frank. Don't think, just say it." Claire could feel her sister's murderous thoughts ready to replay her past. "This is why we're here Rachel. It's for us too, as much as it's for them."

"Frank," Linda murmured her voice no longer fearful. "I know you're sorry it happened. I love you. You know I love you no matter what."

Claire would never have thought Linda had it in her to say those words aloud. She felt like cheering, it moved her so much. Linda was fraught with pain and yet love was overpowering her pain. It was all it took for Frank to break wide open. Claire had never seen a man so broken by the pain he'd inflicted on the one he loved. Claire was so taken with the moment when Frank realized the awful truth about himself, knowing he'd caused immeasurable pain to the one he loves and was being forgiven by Linda – she let out an ANGELIC WHOOP. A burst of brilliant light flooded the room for the briefest second, and she'd not even realized what she'd done until it was all over. Claire clamped her hand over her mouth, elated, yet worried she'd let the cat out of the bag for sure. She'd leaked again. She was fortunate though because Linda and Frank were locked in a ferocious hug with their eyes squeezed shut, completely unaware of what had happened. "Pretty good for Thanksgiving Day," she whispered, grinning at her sister.

SINS OF THE FATHER

Claire was light as a feather in the after-glow of her zapping Frank and Linda with her Angelic body's aura. She'd waited eighteen hundred years to have such an experience, but it was well worth the wait in her mind. Rachel was looking happy about it too, especially after her near miss with a one-way ticket back into the cavern.

"It was scary and exciting all mixed together," Rachel commented in her sister's mind. "You had me worried . . no, I had me worried. I was losing control . . but you stayed calm . . and we made it. It's done. I mean, look at those two wrapped in each other's arms."

As Rachel yammered on in her head, the pit of Claire's stomach sank. She felt the uneasiness of a bad-tempered person in the house. The muted footsteps coming up the stairs foretold of a family member closing in on an event in their home. Claire's stomach hurt like it had the last time something bad was about to happen.

"Frank!" A loud rapping on the door accompanied the gruff voice. "Coming in."

Claire and Rachel's little celebration turned south and disappeared as the door open abruptly, revealing Adam Richards, who filled the open doorway with his stature. Frank was small compared to his father. The look on his father's face was telling her that things were not okey-dokey, and her thoughts of being close to completion with her assignment were far from right. Adam looked at Claire and Rachel with demanding eyes, wanting to know who these two strangers were in his home, and what they were doing.

Claire took the initiative and leaped out of her chair, putting on a happy face. "Hi Mr. Richards, Happy Thanksgiving, I'm Claire and this is my cousin Rachel. We're here talking about the musical we're in with your son and Linda." Claire cringed inside as she regurgitated another not so truthful statement. But, at least it stopped the giant of a man from advancing his agenda, for the moment. His face softened, almost revealing a wry smile.

"Happy Thanksgiving," he grumbled, immediately turning his attention to his son and pregnant girlfriend. "Frank, we need to talk. In private. Now."

Claire and her sister had won the battle, but the war was still up for grabs. Daddy ruled the house with a firm hand and things were always done his way, according to the look on his face.

"Sure," Frank said letting Linda go and standing up to obey. "Ah, excuse me, guys."

Frank had been a pushover compared with what his father brought to the table; a DC Councilman who was as big as a linebacker and had an ego to match. "Way to go Arthur. I don't suppose you and Sandy could have picked an easier assignment for us. This is our first one in over eighteen hundred years, after all." Claire yelled in her thoughts, mumbling on until she realized she needed to hear what dear old Dad had to say to his son. "Linda, I gotta pee." She pointed towards the door. "Which way?"

"Just beyond the stairs, there's a powder room," Linda said and then corrected herself. "No, wait. that's downstairs. Frank's bathroom is across from the top of the stairs."

"Thanks," she said and motioned to her sister to stay with

Linda. She walked towards the stairs, listening for Frank or his father's voice. Not hearing them, she started downstairs to what she thought was a library or office. Every third step there were ominous creaks, definitely not cooperating with her need for stealth. When she reached the bottom of the stairs, she tiptoed towards their voices coming through a partially open door. Being more than a hundred years old, the floors were also booby-trapped with creaks and other ear-pricking noises. She found one loud one just outside the room, which sent a shiver down her spine. She knocked and peeked into the room. "I'm sorry to interrupt. I was looking for a bathroom." She said trying to appear innocent of spying on them. Mr. Richards didn't take kindly to her intrusion, looking her direction with contempt.

"Go back the way you came. There's a door under the stairs." He said in a dismissive tone.

"Thanks." She said as he slammed the door behind her. Her tail feathers were afire with the look he'd given her as she hurried away, stopping and quickly retracing her steps; only this time she avoided the creaky spot in the floor. She listened to Mr. Richard's searing tone, easily penetrating the heavy wood door.

"After that stunt, you two pulled the other day, I have half a mind to tan your hide. I didn't raise you to make bad decisions. How did you ever think becoming a father at seventeen would enable you to achieve anything of value in life? You're setting yourself up for failure in life, and I won't have it, not for one more second. How do you know you're even the father? I mean how many others has she lain down for?"

Claire's ears were burning bright, heated with contempt for this poor excuse of a man. She had to get control of herself, or she'd miss hearing him while she was shredding his sorry butt in her thoughts – so much like her sister.

"One of them could just as easily be the father of this unborn child. Did you discuss her having an abortion yet? You have a year and a half before Law School at Georgetown begins for you. You need to put your affairs in order and you need to do so now. I know her father would agree with me. I mean he's a surgeon for god's sake. He works with cause and effect every day, leading his patients down a road to healing with a disciplined approach, an application of sound logic and surgical expertise. A baby so early in your life will only make success in your life that much harder, if not impossible. You have to know I'm right about this. You need to handle this situation and get on with your schooling."

Claire hadn't heard one peep out of Frank. She was beginning to get the picture of how much he was bullied by his father. It's any wonder . . . She fled for the door under the stairs, gliding her steps, trying not to make a sound, grasping the door handle and swinging herself through, turning around and stepping back out, just as Mr. Richards was emerging from his office. She lifted her hand in thanks and walked quickly back upstairs, her heart pounding wildly in her chest. Rachel was sitting next to Linda on the bed when she entered the deathly quiet room.

"They're coming," she said returning to her chair. Linda reacted like a startled bird at the sound of her words; her eyes wide with fear and her entire body taught, and primed to flee. "Rachel, I think we're done here. Maybe Linda would give us a ride home?" Linda's eyes darted helter-skelter around the room like she was looking for a way to escape.

"Okay," she blurted out.

Frank's browbeaten face appeared in the doorway, with downcast eyes unable to meet even Linda's. Claire could feel his pain, one that extended all the way back through his childhood. Whatever they'd accomplished before his father had shown up seemed lost now, trampled underfoot by the iron will of Adam Richards. "Come on Rachel, we need to go now. Right now." She said with a tone of urgency, grabbing her sister's hand and leading them down the stairs. The weight of Mr. Richard's ego was pressing on her chest hastening her descent. The three of them must have looked as though there was a fire they were fleeing from, with the way they bounded down the stairs, rushing to the front door and outside where the oppression seemed to lessen. Never had she felt this way around anyone else.

"This is how I felt when the blue beast was sucking the life out of me – for sixteen hundred years. It was a horrible feeling to be consumed by another at their bidding. An eternity of horrors."

There was no doubt in Claire's mind now. She was sure Frank and Linda were both lorded over by their parents, without discussion, without choice, and most assuredly without freedom of thought. Linda's emotional state broadcasted loud and clear as she sped away from the impending doom at Mr. Richard's house; slowing only to let them out at their home. No words were exchanged, no looks, no thanks, there was nothing to be said after being accosted like they had. "Sorry," she said. The word slipped from her lips as she closed the car door and Linda hurried away in search of a safe haven, which was probably not at her home.

Stepping inside Arthur's house, Claire let out an exasperating sigh of relief – she could breathe now. She felt foolish for ever believing they'd accomplished their task, fulfilled their assignment, and would be rewarded by Arthur and Sandy. "Rachel, would you smack me upside the head and knock some sense into me." Rachel just smiled at her, shaking her head, knowing full well what they were up against, having been held captive by one such as this for so long. They had a lot of work ahead of them if they could even hope to accomplish what they were charged with doing.

BIRTHRIGHT

"Teaching about life," Arthur said from the kitchen, "is a birthright for all Angels. You two made a choice at your conception to work with both humans and the lost souls buried in the Depths of Darkness."

"What Arthur?" Claire said from the front hall, as she and Rachel hung up their coats in the closet. She didn't have a clue what he was talking about. They'd just been run over by Frank's father and were still recovering. Claire's questioning gaze met Rachel's. "What about birthright?" She mumbled under her breath. Arthur sat at the kitchen counter fixing a large bowl of salad, holding a long carrot, which he waved at them as they entered.

"Teaching about Life, I said. It's one of the many things Angels do with humans, but then I think you've already figured all that stuff out – birthright, and purpose in Life." He waved the carrot again before dicing it up and placing it in the salad bowl.

"I wanted to talk with you now," he continued, "after your initial interaction with Frank's father; because you will need the information I have to tell you for future dealings with him. You see, Adam's father committed suicide at forty-three when Adam was a sophomore at Georgetown University. It was just before Christmas when Adam's mother discovered her husband was having an affair with one of his firm's law clerks, and it wasn't the first time either. The hard part for Merrick was finding out the young woman was four months pregnant with his child and threatening to tell his wife if he didn't compensate her and provide for the child's future. Merrick's firm was in a bad way after losing two high profile consignment cases, having expended much of its capital reserves on his new house and the cases. He overdosed on his wife's prescription sedatives in his office after everyone had gone home. He was found the next morning by a clerk. Adam took it pretty hard, fell into a depressed state, and only snapped out of when he learned of his father's affair and the demand for compensation by the mistress. Adam flip-flopped from depression to a prolonged state of anger that eventually landed him in the hospital with heart palpitations. Frank wasn't far behind him, taking on many of his emotional burdens, from which he never recovered. Adam never lost his distrust of women and passed some of it on to his son, Frank. Frank dealt with it through sports mostly, taking his anger out on the playing field, and gained a reputation for his fierce aggressiveness as a linebacker, like his father Adam, only Frank got hurt and had to quit football last year. Both he and Linda found themselves together on the stage, where they discovered an outlet for their pent-up emotions. Are you starting to get the bigger picture?"

Both she and Rachel were mesmerized with his dissertation, nodding together, and exchanging glances with each other. "Arthur, why were we selected for such an involved assignment?" Claire frowned. "I mean, we're just out of the frying pan, and now we've been chucked into the fire. Who chose this assignment for us?" She could have sworn a smile was about to write itself on Arthur's face. He pointed his right index finger towards the heavens.

"They did. The Higher Ups. We won the Angelic Lottery, so to speak."

"My, my, aren't we lucky." Rachel planted her hands on her hips. "So, now what?"

"Now I tell you the really important part," Arthur said. "The part where you both get to fulfill your birthright as Angels. We're assigned the task of finding Merrick in the Pit and presenting him with a choice. Does he stay put, or does he forgive himself and leave behind the past? Merrick was raised in the Catholic Church, so he has a pretty good idea of what's happened to him, according to their doctrine."

"You're asking too much of us," Claire said, feeling her sister's fear rising within her.

"Maybe. But They don't think so, or They wouldn't have sent us in the first place. I mean, if you think about it for a minute, it makes perfect sense to have the three of us together again on an assignment of this magnitude. You've just come from such a place, Rachel. And you Claire constructed one to your own likings to live in for all eternity. You're both well equipped to deal with Merrick's final destination, which he created for himself. Besides Claire, you and I are just back from retrieving Rachel from a similar place, and Adam needs to know his father's in a good place. We'll be okay."

"Yes Claire, we'll be okay. All is as it should be." Rachel whispered.

Claire back peddled up against the kitchen wall, feeling the same skin-crawling fear she'd experienced in the dark cavern where they found Rachel – the cavern was thick with it. Her eyes met Rachel's and found, of all things, a peaceful confidence in them. She was confused with her sister's strength; no longer the one afraid of the darkness or of falling again. Her insides were roiling in all the years of lies she'd told herself in her world, with none of it making any sense to her. Her pleading eyes met her mentor's.

"Your sister's right," Arthur said. "Believe it or not, everything you've experienced has prepared you for this assignment. All is as it should be, and the answer as to why lies within you both, and will be discovered when you're ready to hearrrrrrrrrrrrrrrrrrrr . . ."

They were swept out of Arthur's kitchen and deposited in Sandy's living room in a blinding flash; each now adorned in their Angelic bodies, pulsating with light and ready for whatever darkness presented itself. She and her sister beat their wings in unison, causing quite the commotion in the room: knocking over lamps, vases, dry floral arrangements, blowing pillows off the sofas, and fanning the flames in the sunken fireplace at the center of the room. The room went silent with a wave of light that rolled through the canyon, enveloping Sandy's retreat, and making her feel lighter, higher, and more competent as an Angel than she'd ever known was possible. "Be prepared," Arthur's words echoed in her thoughts.

The whole side of Sandy's little retreat that faced the river opened up to the sky and billowing clouds, illuminated from within by a growing source of brilliant yellow-white light. "Uh-oh," she murmured. A sphere of light hurtled towards them with blinding speed, landing just outside the house on the patio. Sandy popped out of nowhere and stood beside the most pleasant-to-look-at being Claire had ever laid eyes on, who appeared neither masculine nor feminine. The being was adorned in the simplest of robes and bowed, offering an outstretched hand. As if by command, the three of them each took the hand of the Being in theirs, and were filled with its loving presence.

"Welcome: Arthur, Claire, and Rachel. Thank you for being outstanding members in the Angelic Ranks, and for the mission, you are about to undertake. No greater love for life can be found than being of service to others. I embrace our Oneness."

Claire just about fainted, as the brilliant figure raised the level of: light, love, happiness, understanding, and just about everything else Claire could fathom, except for maybe the kitchen sink. "Knock my socks off," Rachel giggled in her thoughts. Claire almost burst out laughing as the multicolored knee-socks, which just appeared on their feet, flew off willy-nilly in every direction.

"All is as it should be," the being's voice resounded as it departed.

Claire's whole being expanded as she heard those parting words, leaving her a sense of wellbeing beyond anything she'd ever felt before. "Nice," she whispered

"Congratulations," Sandy stepped inside from the patio. "Arthur, you have things well in hand I see." Sandy smiled and then simply vanished.

"Well, I never."

"You never what Rachel," Claire asked seeing a coy look in her sister's eyes. She knew exactly what her sister meant. "So you're saying we spent eighteen hundred years, give or take a few hundred, preparing for this moment, and it was all over in less than twelve seconds. It was a letdown. Like, is that all there is?" She gave her sister the same coy look. "If you ask me, I kinda like how things happen in the physical realm, almost better than here. Everything happens a lot slower, and with a lot more latitude for interaction; you know, like friendships. You know, hands-on experience." Arthur laughed, nodding and stroking the beard that was no longer there from eighteen hundred years ago when they were all together in the south of France

"You're on to something there, I think." He said scooping them up in one fell swoop.

"Arthur, who was that being?" Claire asked as they left for home. He shrugged his wings.

"Maybe one of those elusive Higher Ups? Dunno." He laughed heartily.

MERRICK

Claire had never seen nor conceived of such undefined desolation. This was Merrick's everlasting place of self-inflicted punishment – a desert of the mind without end. It was hard for her to describe anything about it; it literally defied description, because there were no defining characteristics. "Arthur, how can a place be nothing? It has to be something, doesn't it?"

"This is the outcome of Merrick's suicide: a place where he has taken away everything he was, is and ever will be, gone for all time within his mind, and even whether he had a mind was in question on his departure from the physical realm. You see, to his way of thinking he has canceled himself, and otherwise removed himself from the face of existence. Yet here he is, alive and suffering in his desert of nothingness. He is here because of what his religion taught him: he who takes away by his own hand that which God has given, removes himself to a place of everlasting suffering and anguish. This is Merrick's place, his concept of what he thought his punishment should be. He's been here for forty-two years, but by his reckoning, it's been an eternity, because there is no time in his world. And he believes he's meant to exist in this state forever. Do you see his dilemma? He's a captive in his beliefs about the afterlife. To him, there is no escape from what he has done to deserve this fate. I must warn you both before we descend into his world, his mind is fragile and in a constant state of fear of the nothingness, which fills his world. You'll find out how he thinks and feels in a moment. Remember, we are together, even though by all appearances in his world, we are not. We're going to scare the dickens out of him by just being in his world. You both know what I mean by being utterly alone. It's why we're here gang, we're the specialists in the alone business."

Claire's parting thought was how do you find someone or thing that isn't there. Arthur whisked them from their perch above Merrick's world, planting them squarely in the middle of its nothingness. They were together she knew, but in her mind, she was totally alone in a place full of nothing. She had no sensations, no feelings whatsoever, other than; she knew she was in Merrick's place of suffering. She called out in vain, not even hearing her own words. "Great. What do I do, wander around bumping into nothing, waiting to bump into Merrick – who may not exist anyway? "Try to stay calm, Claire." She said to herself. "Could Rachel hear her? Or was she really all alone in this place?" Claire set about thinking on what Arthur had told them about her and her sister's beginnings, their mission in life. One had fallen; the other had lived a lie, each lost and trying to help the other. How can I use that here? Rachel can't hear me. Arthur's off somewhere in this place and out of touch with us both. Merrick, well he's the guy we're after. Get Merrick. She loved this game, which didn't really exist. No rules, no guides to steer her in the right direction, and no destination. But they did have an assignment – get Merrick.

"Arthur, if you can hear me. I'm leaving. This is hopeless." She yelled very loudly into the nothingness. She picked up what she thought was her foot and started to walk, or at least she thought she was walking. How do you know if you're walking if you can't feel anything and don't know if you have legs to walk with? So, she sat down in Merrick's place and began to empty her mind of everything she knew to be reality. One by one, she shut down her perceptions of the outside world; doing her level best to live in a non-world. She was doing pretty well until she had to lose the part of her mind doing the eliminating.

And then it hit her, Merrick had done the same thing in taking away his life. He had ended his life and his ability to function by killing his physical body and mind. He really believed he'd killed all of himself. Claire smiled to herself, knowing that one could not take away that which did not belong to you – one's spirit or eternal essence. Neither could Merrick – he just thought he could. "Gotcha," she whispered. She'd met the terms of his world and connected with Merrick, disrupting the nothingness in it, and thereby scaring the dickens out of him. Now there was something tangible for him to fear, in her acknowledgment of his presence with the word, "Gotcha." "You're mine now," she thought.

"Uh-oh," she said. "Now I've gone and done it. He can hear me now. I exist in his world. What do I say?" She thought about it as silently as possible, which wasn't too very silent. Merrick was panicked with her every word suddenly existing in his ears. "This is nuts," she yelled. "Merrick, listen to me. My name is Claire and I've come to help you out of this place."

"No-no-no. You can't be real." The echo in her thoughts said.

Merrick's panic rolled over her with such force, she was taken by it, consumed within the life given it by Merrick. She was quickly losing herself in the jumble of Merrick's fear, drawing herself into a panic as well.

"Rachel, Rachel, give me the memory of your Darkness. Cast us down into its depths. Let the beast lay hold of us and suck the life from our very souls." Her words fell empty from her lips because her sister could not hear her. "But I hear me!" She screamed in terror, remembering the fear of the hands clawing at her on the way down into Darkness. Claire screamed so violently she made herself a captive in the cavern of the beast, held in its claws, with the life being drained from her, just as her sister had. She was no more. Her last breath, gagged in desperation, suffocated by the beast, brought a blood-curdling scream from a voice she knew. Merrick.

"Help meeeeeeeeeeeeeeeee." Merrick screamed.

Claire wrenched herself away from her memory of her sister's captivity, throttling it in desperation, choking on the beast's final breath through her, before she was free. Merrick lay at her feet gasping for breath, his body heaving with convulsions from the struggle. They were in his world again, the cavern but a distant memory in her mind. Claire reached down and helped Merrick to his feet, grasping him gently to keep him from bolting. She extended her wings for him to see; his eyes wide with fear.

"My name is Claire and I have come to help you." She spoke in calm yet firm words. "You have nothing to fear from me." Merrick's face was panic-stricken at the sight of an Angel in his world. She held his quivering body in her arms and enfolded him in her wings for a time, letting him accept that she really was there with him. "Rachel, Arthur, give me a few minutes before you come." She said, knowing she could be heard now in Merrick's world – she'd changed it by changing his perception of it. Claire hummed the same song she'd sung to Rachel in the cavern. Merrick responded immediately, sighing within the melody, perhaps the first thing he'd felt since he died and created this life for himself.

"Merrick, do you know my name?" He nodded, a tear forming in his eyes. "I have come with my sister and our mentor. We have come to take you from this place. Do you understand me?" Again, he nodded, the tear now rolling down his cheek. "Good. Their names are Rachel and Arthur, and they're standing right over there." She pointed to them in the distance. "May they approach us?" He nodded again, his eyes growing wide with wonder as Rachel and Arthur appeared to grow larger with every passing second. "They are my friends, so you have nothing to fear from them. When they get here, we're going to leave this place, and we'll be going this way when we do." She pointed to a star in the sky he'd never seen in his place of nothingness. His face glowed as the star grew brighter and the four of them ascended from his world and traveled to the star. Merrick was breathing in gulps of sunlight for the first time in an eternity by his standards.

When they arrived at the star, they moved towards a planet not too far away. It had oceans and continents, all framed by billowing clouds. They descended into Sandy's canyon with the river and her retreat home. Merrick was nodding off to sleep as they entered, spent from his escape. She laid him on the sofa by the fire pit and sat down on the other sofa to await his return to life.

"You have done well," Sandy said appearing by the fire pit. "But you must be going now."

With a wave of her hand, Sandy sent them home on this Thanksgiving Day. Claire had a funny thought as the three of them landed back in Arthur's living room, something perhaps leftover from Merrick's mind. They were the Three Merry Angelic Troopers: Arthur, Claire, and Rachel, the three merry warriors of light, ready for another day at the hands of humans – those whom they loved and served.

MONDAY MONDAY

Claire woke early after a restful three days off. The first day being Thanksgiving, but didn't really count as a restful day because they'd: confronted Frank's father; helped his son and pregnant girlfriend to see what's important in their lives; learned about their birthright; and rescued Frank's grandfather, Merrick, from his desolate world. That's quite a lot to be thankful for, she thought. Arthur had ordered-in pizza to go with his salad, not a traditional after Thanksgiving dinner, but they'd never gotten around to cooking a turkey. She hadn't heard a peep from Linda or Frank, so maybe they were okay after the dust had settled from the family confrontations, not that they'd call her anyway. Claire knew little of such things, being new to the game, and having to rely solely on Arthur's knowledge of human affairs. However, she did know without question, he'd do what was right for both her and Rachel. It was relatively warm on this Monday morning, the start of another week on their assignment: Frank, Linda, Adam, Merrick, and whoever else wound up on the growing list of participants. Claire spoke quietly in her thoughts with Rachel on their way to school.

"Right you are," Rachel raised her voice and stopped in the middle of the street. "And the list keeps growing." She spread her arms wide.

They smiled at each other and went to their first class. Claire entered her English class a few minutes early and deliberately sauntered by Frank on her way to her desk. He didn't even look at her, simply staring straight ahead. He had to of seen her. Maybe the long weekend wasn't so kind to him. The only way to find out was to confront him after class – which she did.

"Frank," she ran to catch up. "Frank Richards, you stop right there," Claire yelled above the boisterous crowded hallway. Several people turned their heads to see what would happen. But, he never even slowed down. If anything, he sped up, bulling his way through the masses. She'd had her answer alright – everything wasn't alright.

She waited for her sister at lunch just past the cashier stand, but she never came. The sun was bright in the atrium and more crowded than usual, as she looked for a place to sit. A hand grabbed a fist full of her sweatshirt from behind and pulled her several steps backwards.

"Hey," she yelped. "Let go of me." She back peddled as fast as she could to keep up. Somehow, she managed to save her lunch, but the top of the hamburger bun had flipped over and was staring back at her with two round pickle eyes coated in ketchup and mayo. She whirled around to face the rude and aggressive person, with only her tray separating them. "Frank!" She growled through gritted teeth. "What the . . ." Claire bit her lip on the words she wanted to say – not words an Angel would ever use. His drew her even closer, his angry face just inches from hers.

"You caused me a lot of grief the other day. My father pushed me around and yelled at me for an hour after you left. It was the worst day of my life and all because you came over with Linda. None of this would have happened if you'd not .. ." Frank suddenly fell silent.

She looked into his broken angry face and was afraid for the man he'd become if his father had his way with him. His contorted grimace spoke worlds about the constant pain present in his family, something she could do little about unless Frank chose to stand up to his father. She felt sorry for him in a way because she too had suffered under an oppressive hand, but in her case, it was her own. "Frank," she said softly. "Please let go of me. We can talk somewhere else if you like. Just not here." She said turning to look at the gawking students who were crowding 'round. His hand fell away from her and the weight of what he was doing in front of his classmates took hold. He backed up a step, looking at her in disbelief like she was some kind of witch casting a spell over him. He turned and careened through the onlookers as they parted a way for him. Truly, she'd never seen such a broken human before.

She sat down on the edge of a planter, which held a tall ficus tree. Things were not going well for her this Monday morning and she wondered if it would ever get any better. The crowd was dispersing, disappointed nothing had happened, at least nothing too dramatic. She drew in deep, halting breaths, trying to regain her composure, but found it difficult to shake off the broken spirit of Frank Richards.

"Claire." Rachel sat beside her. "Are you alright? Frank walked right by me and it took me several seconds to register it was him; he looked so different, so old and angry. What happened?"

Claire looked into her sister's eyes unable to answer. She did not know how to explain what she'd seen in Frank's face. It was as if all of his problems had fallen on top of her and were suffocating her belief in anything right, and true, and good. This was not his face, not himself. It was something else, someone else. Not Frank. "Arthur," she called out. "I need your help."

"Not so loud," Rachel said sitting beside her. "We can talk

to Arthur tonight."

"No. I need to know something now." Claire's weak voice tried to reach out to her mentor. "I need to know how to help Frank free himself from whatever veil of pain he's shrouded in. Arthur, why aren't you answering?" Claire's lunch tray slid from her lap onto the floor, sending her orange rolling across the floor until it struck a foot and sent flying across the atrium. Rachel was holding her now and keeping her from falling to the floor herself. She was teetering on the brink, ready to black out. It was Frank's veil covering her, his pain and anguish awash in her thoughts, stripping her of any semblance of being an Angel on assignment. "Arthur," she whispered in her mind, feeling her sister's tight embrace.

"The pain is not yours Claire, neither is it Frank's." Arthur's words found a home in her mind. "It's his father's pain that hangs over him. Frank suffers because his father suffers and doesn't know what happened to his grandfather. Adam suffers from the memory of Merrick's death and has all of his life. He fears for his father's soul in the afterlife, and is also afraid of punishment for his own sins with his son."

Claire jerked upright, breaking free from Rachel's arms, and gasped for breath. She was free of the heavy shroud of fear Frank had around him. "I'm such an idiot," she mumbled to herself. Rachel's eyes told her how frightened she was by what she'd witnessed. "I'm sorry Rachel. I didn't know what to do, so I just stood there and took on all of Frank's baggage and all of his family's too. I'm ashamed to call myself an Angel. I didn't help him by falling into the same pit he's trapped in. At least he could walk away from it. I could only manage to weakly call Arthur for help. I really don't understand my behavior at all. I mean, didn't we just rescue Merrick? And then I turn right around and nearly faint from fear of what Frank deposited in my lap. Go figure." Claire's head sank into her sister's shoulder for comfort. "Thank you for being with me, both of you." She whispered squeezing her eyes shut from the prying eyes of students nearby.

"Well sister," Rachel shook her by the shoulders. "You rescued my sorry butt from a worse place than Merrick ever dreamed possible. I think it's different when we're dealing with living people, they have so much to deal with, so many facets, and secrets they don't even reveal to themselves, let alone anyone else. It's no wonder we're having such a hard time dealing with their stuff. It does tend to make our problems appear, not trivial or easy, but maybe a little less complicated than Frank's. Wait, that didn't come out right." Rachel frowned.

"Sounds good to me," Claire sat upright glad to be with her sister. She eyed the students staring gazes, daring them to look her in the eye, and throwing them a contrite little smile. Her stomach growled reminding her she had a body, which needed food. She looked down at the mess in front of her. "I guess my lunch has seen better days," she looked at her burger upside down on the floor, and next to it, the fruit cup on its side. She laughed. "Did you see which way my orange went?" They laughed together, picking up the tray and assorted lunch items from the floor. Claire opened her carton of milk and drank it hungrily. She went back through the lunch line for a sandwich to eat on the way to her Applied Science class. She needed something to keep her stomach from growling all afternoon.

Lu was waiting for her, nearly falling from her stool when Claire sat down next to her friend. Must be some ear-bending gossip anxiously awaiting her, she thought. "Shoot," she smiled in anticipation.

"Well," Lu began by scooting her stool closer. "Linda went home from Frank's on Thanksgiving crying and distraught. So much so, that her mother called the Richardson's right away to ask what had happened. You and Rachel were mentioned as the cause. It's all I could hear of the conversation between Linda and her close friend, Amy."

Lu pulled back to look at her reaction. Claire nodded. "Yes, that's right. We were the instigators." She strung Lu along, knowing she'd wait as long as she had to for the details. Claire didn't have an answer for her friend, and probably never would. Lu's gossip column had no rights to family secrets. She turned away and stared straight ahead, waiting for Mr. Boswell to finish writing on the blackboard, in no mood to engage with Lu any further.

Claire spent the rest of the afternoon thinking about her centuries of seclusion, alone and hiding out from the rest of her Angelic Clan. It had not been so long ago that she too was a fugitive from her own secrets, and unable to view herself with any degree of openness. Even though she'd cloistered herself in loneliness for so long, she'd never forgotten who she'd started out as; a young passionate Angel ready to set the world on fire with her love for life. And look where it got her – out of the pot and into the fire – Frank and Linda's fire. She barely acknowledged Rachel in Theater class, sitting down oblivious to anything except what was going on inside her own head. Class went on without her, leaving her staring blankly out into space; so wrapped up in herself she'd not even noticed Frank's absent from class, or that Mr. Clark was standing beside her speaking to her.

"Claire Tate, would you like to tell us where you are? Claire?"

"Claire!" Rachel yelled in her thoughts. "Wake up!"

Claire snapped out of her stupor to see everyone in the class waiting for her to answer. "What Mr. Clark? I'm sorry, I didn't hear you."

"Yes, I gathered as much. I asked if you could identify with your character's shortcomings in the Musical."

"Shortcomings? I don't understand. I didn't know she had any such thing."

"Class. What do you think? Does Claire's character have any faults?"

"Yes," Rachel said raising her hand. "She doesn't pay attention in class."

The class laughed, easing the tension inside of her. "Very funny," she responded. "Well Mr. Clark, Mary, and Nancy come from a failed home, abandoned by their parent's, because of drug use. So I'd have to say that my character Mary, who is the eldest, blames herself for not being able to take care of her younger sister. They wind up in an alley, shivering against the cold, with no place to go; until Billy and Kathy come along and Kathy takes pity on them. But, since they are really angels in disguise, how could they possibly have character flaws? I mean angels after all. Actually, I think their character flaws are the very way in which the author intended these two sister angels to assist the Coleman family. The only way the two angels in disguise can help the Coleman family is to allow themselves to be helped first by the Coleman's. Which raises the question of whose problem is in greater need of resolution. The answer, of course, is both. The resolution of this problematic family lies in their mutual forgiveness, not in the angels saving their assigned parties. And the resolution of the two angel's problem lies in getting their character flaws mended. Now every good cook knows that a recipe must be executed in the proper order so, the two angels must first lose their powers in order to regain them and complete their assignment. This dictates the character flaws of the two angels: one that stems from having failed before in their assignments, and the other being their attitude towards authority, causing them to lose their powers. So, it's the human family who winds up saving the two young and inexperienced angels; thereby helping them overcome their character flaws, which in turn allow the angels to complete their assignment and bring this family together again. Hence the title – Do It For Love. Without love, nothing would have been resolved." Claire let out a long sigh, thinking what she'd just said was nothing but double-talk, her own confused mind hard at work. She shrugged her shoulders and hung her head, feeling vulnerable and backed into a corner, wondering in the back of her mind if anyone suspected . . . Mr. Clark's voice interrupted her thought.

"Very good Claire. Did you come to those conclusions by yourself, or did the co-author help you?"

Claire's embarrassment was there for all to see, her face flushed and her ears were burning, all because she was hiding the truth about her and Rachel – two Angels on assignment who'd failed before. She fumbled for the thoughts and words to answer him, seeing for the first time how much the musical applied to her and Rachel. "No, he didn't Mr. Clark." The words fell into her lap, unheard by most of the class. "He would never tell us how to interpret our parts. He believes that in order to learn something, you have to experience it, make decisions about it, and then live with your choices." She raised her head and put on a weak smile.

"Class. What do you think? Is Claire right?"

It was strange no one asked a question or said anything either for or against her explanation. When she finally worked up the courage to look around the room, every face was painted with awe and wonder, like she'd struck a chord within them, which made them think about life, their life.

"Exactly right Ms. Tate," he said. "Class is over and I believe some of you have rehearsal now. I'll see you tomorrow."

Claire took a few minutes to collect her wits. She was ready for this day to be over with, but that's not the way things worked in this world. Every minute of every day has its place, and nothing can make it speed up, pass by, or simply go away. This assignment was getting harder and more complicated with every day, and today was an especially difficult one, this first Monday after Thanksgiving.

"Are you alright Claire," Mr. Clark asked.

"Oh, I suppose so." She answered walking slowly towards the door. "It's been a tough day for me I guess."

"Well, keep your chin up. You're young and have your whole life ahead of you. I appreciate your in-depth answer to my question. It shows me how much the world is going to benefit from your presence. Have a good rehearsal, Claire."

She stopped at the door, a tear streaming down her cheek, feeling the love her teacher had for his students. She turned around and their eyes met, sending chills down her back. "Thank you, Mr. Clark. I'll try to." She ambled out the door and down the cluttered passageway to the auditorium, wiping the tear from her cheek. She entered just off stage right, where Rachel was waiting for her by the curtains in the wings. She was talking with Evan and Liz, who played the parents of Billy and Kathy, Frank and Linda's characters. She stood a few feet away to collect her wits.

"Hi Claire," Liz said quietly. "We were just talking about your answer to Mr. Clark's question. I can't believe how smart you are. You made me see things about my character and myself I'd never thought about before. And do you know the mystery author? Mr. Clark and Ms. Newman never said much about it, other than there was another writer who had helped them."

Claire nodded and smiled. "He's quite a guy." Rachel stifled a giggle and actually so did she. "He's helped us both to reach deeper inside ourselves for meaning with our characters, but never once did he tell us what to think. He'd rather see us frustrated and working hard for meaning, than just telling us what he knew. He said we would change the nature of the Musical with our characterization of what he wrote. Everyone affects the lives of others with their presence or absence thereof." Claire was explaining it to herself by saying the words aloud. Arthur really was a pro at helping his charges, by letting them work things out for themselves – up to a point of course. "Thanks, Arthur," she mouthed.

"Well, I'd sure like to meet this person," Liz said.

Evan hadn't said a word, and Claire wondered if he even understood what was being said. He was a boyish seventeen, with the peach fuzz still on his face. Maybe he really didn't understand, or maybe he was the silent type who'd never say anyway. Did he have a part in their assignment too? "Really Claire, this is high school after all." Rachel said in her thoughts. Claire shrugged off her sister's comment and decided to find out.

"Evan, what do you think about all this?" Claire smiled a shy smile at the boy. He was turning a little red in the face and his eyes were downcast.

"Come on Evan," Liz slid an arm around his back. "Tell them what we've talked about."

Claire pricked up her ears, more curious now than before. "If you two know something that will help Rachel and me, please my all means, share. We're family after all – we're your adopted kids you brought in out of the cold."

"Well, okay." Evan shuffled his feet, his eyes still glued to the stage floor. "What if it were really true, I mean, if you two really were angels sent to intervene and assist. I mean, it could be true. And the way you two sing together, well it makes it all the more believable. The other two girls who were supposed to play the parts weren't half as good as you two, I mean, not even close to what you bring to the musical. The first time I heard you guys sing a duet; I had goosebumps all over. So, you kinda make it all seem real, I mean, you really are like angels."

Evan gathered his eyes up off the floor and brought his gaze straight into Claire's, sending shivers down her back. Did he know? How could he? The boy is a dreamer and a lot deeper than he lets on. He could know in his heart. She bit her lip hard, looking to return to reality, and not the fantasy born of inexperience she was conjuring up. "Thank you, Evan. That's the nicest thing anyone has said to me in a long time." And it was true too. She eyed Rachel, wondering if she was going to say something.

"Yes it is, isn't it." Rachel winked at her.

Ms. Newman was walking down the aisle in the auditorium, calling her cast to assemble center stage. Claire hadn't noticed the cast and stagehands were milling around on stage, as she pushed aside the curtain and joined them. Ms. Newman launched her bottom up on the front of the stage and swung her legs around, extending a hand to the nearest boy.

"Well, come on. Don't be shy. Stand me up."

One of the stagehands got her stood up with a grunt. Claire thought it odd she would do such a thing. The stairs were less than ten steps away.

That's what you're going to have to do to pull this musical off. Offer a hand when anyone needs it, whether it's requested or not. If someone misses an important mark and you're right there, then walk them to their mark and make it seem like part of the action. Forgotten line – whisper the first three words if you're close-by. They'll remember the rest. People, we have twelve more rehearsals until performance night. Remember that this involves the orchestra and choir, and we haven't even gotten together with them yet. Work together and rehearse at home. Today we're going to do a walk-through with sets and lights, so the stage and lighting crews can work out any kinks. Places please."

Claire and Rachel ran across the stage to the left wing, where they'd be lifted by a small platform into the heavens, for them to hold counsel with the angels in charge. Kind of a side-play woven into the musical. It was also where they'd make their entrance into the main set, at center stage, where they were in a snowy alleyway. Claire and Rachel would be outfitted with wings for their entrance and would descend on a hydraulic lift with stars and moving clouds in the night sky behind them. She thought it very dramatic, but it had yet to be tested with lighting effects on the scrim curtain, which either hid things from the audience or was used for projected images. It occupied a small corner of the stage, but was an important part of both Acts, delivering a narrative, which defined the theme of the musical.

"Frank and Linda aren't here yet are they?" Claire whispered to Rachel. Her sister pointed to the opposite wing, where they were talking with Liz and Evan, partially hidden by the leg curtains. "Right you are." Linda was looking there way, having all the appearances of a scared animal ready to bolt to safety. Claire half-raised her hand in a greeting, wondering if Linda could shake off the remnants of all the ragged emotions left over from the confrontation at Frank's house on Thanksgiving Day.

A stagehand attached a safety belt around her waist and handed her a three-foot lanyard to hook onto the back of the four-foot square platform they'd be ascending and descending on. With their wings attached, it left them little room to stand without bumping each other off the platform. When she'd extend her wings to their full nine-foot width, she would have to step to the front of the platform to give her the space to do so. Rachel would only partially extend her wings, lest they get tangled up in each others. The platform did have a waist-high grab bar they'd hook onto at the back, and a one-foot extension on each side to lean against for balance. Their two sets of wings were also held by a hook on the bar, allowing them to step up under the padded frame and attached celestial garment, which would sit on their shoulders. Every time they needed to hear from the angels in charge, they had to leave the main set and return to the platform, slip into their angel costume, and ascend to a position in the heavens nine feet above the stage floor. Two stagehands helped them into their wings, reminding them they'd have to hook on before they stood up under the costume because it would be difficult after with the garment getting in the way.

The auditorium darkened, the main curtain drawn, and the set for Act I was in place. Their little corner of the universe remained dark until the opening music began, whereupon it would be faded-in gradually, with the platform already raised to nine feet above the stage. The butterflies in her midsection were fluttering all over the place; she was so excited to begin the first full walk-through. "Here we go," she said in a hushed voice as the platform began to lift.

"Yeah, you know we're headed home," Rachel giggled elbowing her.

Claire's eyes were twinkling – she knew it – because she could feel her Angelic Self stirring within. Now that would be something to talk about if she inadvertently switched bodies.

"Yeah, you know, as Angels we'd be fired for life if the tabloids got wind of it," Rachel whispered sarcastically.

The platform bumped to a stop and the heavens shone all around them, stars and drifting clouds shrouding a half moon, and their mini-spots fading in to bathe them within a soft halo. The rehearsal pianist played ten measures of the opening music, which would accompany them for their duet, What Will I Be. It was a melancholy song, to begin with, and then rose to a crescendo. It happened right after the angels in charge spoke to them about their assigned family, and reminded them of the rules governing angels interacting with humans. The choir and orchestra carried the same melody, rising and falling to accent the importance of their mission while they descended to the snowy alleyway and the opening of Act One on the main set.

Claire stepped forward to extend her wings, finding she'd put on Rachel's costume by mistake – her wings only extended halfway – so she couldn't beat her wings on the descent. Out of the corner of her eye, she watched as Rachel extended her wings the full nine feet, but didn't have room to move them much. Maybe the stagehand had hooked them on the wrong side. In any case, they ducked out from under them when they touched down on the stage floor, stepping carefully from behind the scrim curtain, which was now dark.

They waited for the nighttime scene in the alleyway to fade-in with snow gently falling behind a stage width scrim that was side lit. This was their entrance into the world, sprawled against a fence and partially covered in a snowdrift. From this position, they would sing another duet, Alone Together. Again, the pianist played only a few measures before Frank and Linda showed up with the dog, finding them half frozen to death in the alley. The first few lines made it out okay, but Linda's voice was cracking with emotion.

When Linda knelt beside them, reaching out to touch her face, Claire saw for the first time that Linda was in distress. Everything pent up inside her about the pregnancy, the word getting out, and the confrontation at Frank's house with his father, all came rushing out as Linda's hand brushed Claire's face. Claire looked into her eyes, finding all the pain she was enduring and saw it was about to spill out of her.

Linda collapsed into Claire's shoulder, distraught, able to suffer no more. Claire's eyes immediately filled with tears, the emotions of her physical body rushing to take over. She turned and wrapped her arms around Linda, holding herself back from doing anything stupid, like she wanted to do. They were quickly sobbing in unison, Claire's breast rising and falling with Linda's. She was quickly losing control of herself. She could feel it about to overpower her when all the stage's strobe lights winked on at full intensity for a brief flash. All she could feel though, was Linda's pain, her overwhelming pain, taking control of her fully, and washing over her with tidal force.

It was quite dark now, with voices shouting from the wings, Ms. Newman's being one of them. Claire was still holding Linda in her arms, although Linda was much calmer now, staring at this homeless girl in the snow who was cradling her in her arms. When their eyes met, Claire knew something had happened that shouldn't have. She had done something to Linda because it was written all over her face, the incredulous look of wonder someone has when . . .

"Yeah sis, you leaked." Rachel chimed in her head. "Do something now, or Linda's gonna know for sure."

"What did you do?" Linda barely whispered.

"I didn't do anything, except jump a mile when the lights flashed. You did too. It scared the posies out of me. Maybe that's what you felt." Claire blurted out the words, hoping to cover her tracks. She'd leaked alright – big time. She let go of Linda when Ms. Newman came sailing across the stage, sliding to a stop beside all of them.

"Linda, are you alright? I'm sorry about the lighting glitch. I think it was my fault; something I did on the control computer messed with the lighting program. You sure you're alright?"

Ms. Newman bent over and placed a hand on Linda's shoulder, as Claire rolled aside and got to her feet, dusting off the fake snow. "I think maybe it was my fault. We had a little incident on Thanksgiving Day that upset us all. Sorry." She

189

backed away a step or two, rattling her brain for why she'd done something so stupid, and done it in front of the cast and crew.

"I think only Linda noticed, you knucklehead." Rachel's voice said in her thoughts. "You only did it to her. Only she could feel anything. Never mind the slight flash of: "Golly, My Angelic Bonehead Sister Zapped the Human with Just a Dash of Angelic Light; which just happened to get lost in the stage lighting mishap. Great timing though." Rachel's words rang in her head, leaving Claire to reflect on what she'd done and possibly revealed to Linda.

Linda's eyes never left hers as she passed by with Ms. Newman. They were still questioning and wondering about this person she was looking at, and what she had felt while in her arms. This was the second time it had happened between them.

"Come on sis. Let's get a drink of water." Rachel grabbed her arm. "It is Monday after all. Isn't there supposed to be something weird about Mondays anyway?"

LECTURE NOTES

Arthur didn't say much at first, but then he always was the strong and silent type. Claire had managed to finish the walk-through without tripping over her own two feet before Arthur had said anything. On the walk home, he'd thanked her for regaining her composure and finishing the day without further incident. Never mind that Linda had seen the light – literally – and felt an angelic presence take away all of her emotional pain, leaving only a shell of a memory, forever changing her perception of – are there Angels among us. No big deal. Nothing out of the ordinary there. She'd responded to Arthur's kind words, the same way she always did when she'd screwed up – which seemed to be on the newly acquired habits list – she'd said she was sorry. It won't happen again – at least not until the next time. By the time they got home, Claire had run the whole scenario a couple of hundred times, and the trench she'd dug with it was long and deep.

"Well, you know what they always say about those ruts, trenches, or whatever they're called." Rachel grinned as she held the front door for her sister. "A rut is just a grave with both ends knocked out."

"Thanks for those encouraging words." She wiped her shoes on the entry rug and hung up her coat, listening all the while, to Arthur chuckling to himself in the kitchen. "Not funny," she yelled on her way up the stairs to her room. "No, but your sister's comment is apropos, don't you think." Arthur's words went off like a bomb in her head. She was headed for bed for a little sulking and didn't need the peanut gallery's running commentary going off in her head before dinner, which reminded her she'd spilled her lunch and the meager half a cheese sandwich she'd gone back for was long gone. The caged animals in her midsection were restless and loud as she lay staring at the ceiling. They got the better of her after a few minutes, sending her thumping down the stairs to the kitchen and into the open arms of her mentor.

"Thought you were going to sulk for a while?" He patted her back.

Arthur wiggled his bare feet under hers and walked with her feet on top of his to the stove, where he stirred some sort of sauce in a pan. "Yeah, yeah, yeah. Make fun of me. It's okay, I deserve it." Claire wiggled free of his arms to set the dining room table for what smelled like a really good dinner. "So, was it you who messed with the lighting, saving my sorry little Angel butt?" She called out from the dining room.

"Why, it must have been someone else; maybe your friendly neighborhood Angel on Duty.

Yes, guilty as charged," Arthur chuckled. "I decided to keep a close watch on you when you were waffling between bodies a few moments before. You broadcast your intentions you know. Nothing happened that wasn't meant to happen though. You'll see, it's all part of the plan a little later on. You did no harm, Claire. Believe me."

"Sure felt like it did. You didn't see the look in her eyes. She knew darn well something had happened to her. And, it's the second time too."

"Be patient. You'll see how it all fits together. But for now, let's try to avoid such things. It would be better for all of us if you laid-off pulling anything else out of your Angel Bag of Tricks for a while. Okay?"

"Yeah. You're only supposed to be a pretend angel in the musical." Rachel wrapped her arms around her sister's waist, jostling her a bit.

"Thanks. I'll try to remember." They strolled back into the kitchen arm in arm, humming their Sisters Forever duet. Nothing in the universe could make her feel better like her sister could and probably never would. "Can we help you with dinner?"

"You can dump the egg noodles in now. Chicken's done and sauce is ready, so it's noodle time. I'll get the cheesy breadsticks warmed and then we can eat. After dinner, we'll talk some more about your day."

Their conversation at dinner stayed focused on how they were enjoying their time together. Arthur said he was most pleased with their progress on the small things in their everyday activities. Rachel's most pleasant experience thus far was with the come-on from the boys vying for her attention, which made her feel warm inside. Claire agreed, boys were definitely important to high school girls, because her body said so, doing acrobatics from time to time with the attention she'd received. Even Arthur admitted to succumbing to such feelings with several young teachers, not the least of who was Ms. Newman, who was part of his assignment. They also admitted to each other they'd been embarrassed by how their body had made them feel, sometimes having to step away from a person to take a deep breath. Dinner was over too soon for Claire's liking, wanting to prolong it just a little bit longer, as always.

They settled in the living room to talk shop after the dishes were done, with Arthur taking charge. Claire prepared herself for the promised lecture about Angel Etiquette with humans. She squished herself as deep as possible into the pillows on the sofa, pulling an afghan from the thrift store up around her to lessen the blows of reality headed her way.

"Claire, I believe you learned something valuable today in your interaction with Linda. Tell me what you think it was." Arthur leaned back in his recliner.

"I learned how vulnerable I am to Linda's need for attention and to her emotional Armageddon, when she leaps off some cliff, hoping someone will come to her rescue. I was literally sucked into it when she touched my face. It was as if a hurricane of need descended on me, sweeping me off the ground, and carrying me away. I didn't really try to help her intentionally; she, in all of her pain, merely made a withdrawal from my Angelic body, taking what it needed. I felt as though I had no control, no will to resist what was so easily given by me. And when she looked me in the eyes afterward, it was as if she was looking right through me, seeing me for what I am. I felt naked and powerless against her will. I don't think she did it intentionally, but it doesn't change the fact that I need to learn to control myself, and remain in charge of my faculties." The same feeling was beginning again like she was losing control to another's will. She looked at her sister, thinking she might be feeling the same way.

"Rachel cannot answer that for you, Claire, because she experiences it differently. Rachel, why don't you tell her what you're feeling."

"The difference is, you give in to Linda's needs, on whatever level they come from, just like you gave into your need to disappear yourself deep into the Angelic Realm when you ran away. I didn't run away. I was taken away, thrown out of the Realm, because of my actions. I didn't give in to the beast. It consumed me against my will. I fought it until I could fight no more, and only then did I give up, knowing I was powerless against its will, just as the person I killed was powerless against my will. I feel what you feel Claire, but I do not give into it like you do; I fight and try to retain control. But, what happened today scared me, because I knew you were at a loss to resist the will of a human; just like the little girl who called out to you to save her. You knew you were breaking the rules then, just as you know you are now. The difference between us is, you saved a life, but I took one to save another. Big difference. The rage I felt is still overpowering at times, like in Frank's room a few days ago. I still don't understand why I'm being given a second chance after having Fallen from Grace. I thought it was a one-way ticket into the depths of darkness. You'll never know how grateful I was to see the two of you in that hell hole." Rachel wiped away a tear.

"What happened today comes as no surprise to me." Arthur leaned in closer to Claire. "It's the same thing you've done for an eternity, and always playing out the same way. You give away your will, your consciousness as an Angel, to whoever is in need. And I might add, you do it at the drop of a hat. Compassion you have. Discernment, well, it takes a backseat. Claire, humans will always have needs, which they pine for help with. Can you tell me if you are capable of meeting all their needs?"

"No. I know I can't. But . . ."

"No buts about it Claire. You have to learn how to help and when it's appropriate, not just haphazardly plow headfirst into the affairs of humans. Do you see how this affects free will? You wouldn't want to take it away would you?"

"No. But how do I keep myself from . . ." Claire fell right back into everything that Linda had brought to rehearsal, and she was helpless to stop any of it. She was being sucked into this black hole of Linda's need, right back into all the pain and suffering Linda carried around with her. Claire's head was spinning out of control when she left the living room, getting sucked right through the back of the sofa and into the face looming in front of her. Linda's face. This was the moment when Claire learned that Linda's mother had lost a child when Linda was six. Linda had fallen into the same dark depression her mother had succumbed to ten years ago, and had never really been able to climb out of the hole she'd dug for herself. Little Linda at six had given herself to her mother, not wanting to see her sick and alone in her grief. Linda's father was resigned after a year and months of therapy together, withdrawing into his work as an orthopedic surgeon, unable to help his wife who'd taken to drinking herself to sleep many nights, just so she could teach the next day. Claire had fallen into the same deep hole the six-year-old Linda had fallen into trying to help her mother. She reached out to the young Linda, taking her hand and doing an about face, she walked away from the dark hole and back towards the glimmer of a life in the distance. Claire popped back into the living room and opened her eyes, and for the first time, she saw her life in a new light, understanding her need to help, no matter the cost to her. It was too easy. Why hadn't she seen this before? Why had she spent eighteen hundred years trying to understand the most simple of concepts? "Arthur. It can't be this simple. Can it?"

"Why not? Does simple violate some Universal Law? Look again Claire."

When she tried to get it back, it was too late; it had gone from her mind. Her simple revelation, the epiphany, had flown the coup – until the next time. "It's gone, Arthur. I don't understand." For the life of her, she couldn't see the words any longer; gone too was the feeling they'd brought with them.

"Don't try so hard Claire. Think simple. Think four letters." Arthur smiled warmly.

"I love you Claire, more than words can say." Rachel snuggled next to her on the sofa. "It's the only thing I know for sure in my life."

"I love you too. The hope of seeing you again through all those years alone was the only thing that kept me going. And, I didn't even know you yet, not really know you." She couldn't get any closer to her sister than she was right now, practically tripping over the love she felt for her. Rachel had given her what she couldn't seem to find on her own. Now she knew what she had to do with Linda. Love her like she did her sister. The rest would follow along.

WORDS TO LIVE BY

Arthur had given Claire a lot to think about the night before, her sister too. He'd reminded them both that love trumps all in this universe – no exceptions. But, it came with a mixed bag of troubles, at least for her anyway. Arthur had always been beyond patient with her foibles, but she thought she'd crossed the line because she'd flashed Linda twice. Claire worried she'd blown her cover and shown Linda she was a real Angel, not just the teen playing a part in a musical.

"Hey Claire," Jeff said.

His shy hopeful eyes met hers for a fraction of a second, flushing his cheeks. She smiled and sat down, not wanting to engage. She looked past him to the front of the room, where Frank's seat was still empty, and Ms. Letrell was writing on the board. All during the previous day's rehearsal, he never once actually looked at her, except when the lights flashed and went out. She'd seen him staring at her out of the corner of her eye. After that, he'd made it his business to avoid eye contact with her, even when his part required him to pay attention to her. As she recalled, he'd stared at Rachel instead, who was usually right beside her.

"You know, Frank Richards, if you're not careful your whole life will look just like this." She said, her eyes fixed on his empty desk. "The habits you form now will persist throughout your entire life." Ms. Letrell waved a hesitant Frank into the classroom interrupting her mini-lecture.

"I apologize for being late. I was talking with my mother about something important." Frank sat down and folded his hands on his desk.

"Wow. Something must be going on at his home," she murmured. And it probably has everything to do with Linda and their unborn child; she finished the thought in her head. She knew Evelyn Richards wanted her son to keep the baby and she'd even offered to take care of her grandchild for as long as it took them to get started in life after college. Daddy, of course, was adamantly against it, citing statistics galore as reasons to end the pregnancy. At least Frank had his mother on his side, even though his father ruled the family with his iron will.

Frank had turned his head and was looking at her with no particular expression on his face. She dropped her gaze to the floor somewhere under Jeff's desk, as if some mysterious clue lay waiting for her there, something to fix her whacked-out head.

"Ms. Letrell, can I ask a question?" Her teacher continued to write on the board.

"Yes, Claire. What is it?"

"In your experience, do you recall reading about keeping secrets in literature? I mean, is it a good idea or has anyone written about it?" She was babbling. Why? Ms. Letrell turned to face her with an inquisitive look.

"Yes, I have in, Harper Lee's, To Kill a Mockingbird. Why do you ask?"

Ms. Letrell waited a moment for her to answer and then turned back towards the board to continue writing. Claire wanted nothing more than to disappear from the room. Every set of eyes was on her, corralling her, and driving her inside of herself. "What am I going to do next?" She wondered. "Jump up on my desk and beat my wings?"

"Ah, just curious I guess. Thank you." Claire laid her overwrought head on her folded arms, staring at the surface scratches on her desk, which spelled names and depicted all manner of objects. She pretty much went blank for the remainder of class, doing her best to not air out her laundry list of best-kept secrets. But, she would get the book from the library today and take it home and read it tonight, in order to understand what was she'd asked her teacher about – keeping secrets and all.

She raced towards the door when the bell sounded, bumping into Frank in her hurry to escape, propelling her into another person, not missing a beat on her way out. Was today to be a repeat of Monday, where everything that could go wrong, did? "Mindful purpose," she mumbled on the way to her Western Civilization class. She made a detour to the library at the last minute, not caring if she was late to class. She needed a distraction, and the book would serve just fine, giving her something to focus on for the rest of the day. By lunch, she'd read a third of the book and was hooked. She found Rachel in the Atrium, sitting next to Frank, of all things. She hesitated, wanting to flee back through the arches into the crowded seating of the cafeteria, but her feet kept heading for her sister's table.

"Hi. Mind if I join you?" She said nearly inaudibly, squeezing in next to her sister. Frank eyed her but kept eating.

"Claire, these are four of Frank's friends from the football team."

Claire nodded, barely looking at them. "Hey, I'm reading this really great book." She said diving into her salad and shoving a breadstick in with it all. She kept her head down and ate like a madwoman, to which some might agree.

"Are you alright? You're behaving very strangely like I don't know what."

"Muffinyak," heralded the forthcoming flying bits of breadstick and lettuce. Claire started to laugh, and choke at the same time, holding her hand over her mouth to keep from expelling anything more. Her eyes were all crinkled up with laughter wanting to spill out. She endured a little longer, swallowing in small clumps. When she was sure she was in control, she took a drink of milk from the carton to clear her mouth and wash the clod of salad and bread down, which was stuck halfway down the plumbing. "Must you ask? That's what I said." By now, the boys at the table were watching intently, amused by her antics, and doing what boys did best around girls – checking out her equipment. She paid them no mind, hoping her sister would pick up the conversation.

"I ask because Frank said you were behaving oddly in English this morning. He seemed concerned Claire, so what's up?" Rachel said.

She stole a glance Frank's way, a little perplexed at his sympathetic attitude. "Yes, I'm alright. And yes, I was feeling strange in English class and said some rather odd things. But, I did get this great book." She pulled it out of her backpack to show her sister. "This book was written for me. I mean, one of its characters, a little girl, makes me feel like I've known her forever. So, it was worth my being weird in English."

"What secrets Claire?" Frank asked.

She caught herself before she backward off the curved bench seat around the circular lunch table. She scowled at Frank, angry with him for his probing question. Her face was hot and nostrils flared like she was some animal ready to charge.

"I think Claire would probably like to keep those to herself. Otherwise, they wouldn't be secrets, now would they?" Rachel spoke for her sister.

The four other boys laughed at Rachel's comment, but Frank didn't. He had a questioning look on his face like he might know what she was talking about. Not possible, she said to herself. No way.

"Frank," she said picking up the other breadstick and waving it at nothing in particular. "Do you have secrets? Yes? Well so do I, and they're going to stay a secret, if you don't mind." Claire punctuated the last six words with a quiet determination. "No disrespect, but we all have little secrets that quite frankly," she stifled a giggle, "are no one else's business. Am I right?" She knew her last words were a challenge and would tell her something about his intent in asking.

"If you say so Claire," Frank barely lifted his head from taking a bite of his hamburger. "But, if you ask me," he said through a mouth full, "there's something you're hiding. Things were not normal at rehearsal yesterday, now were they?" He raised an eyebrow her way.

"No, but sometimes, there can be no explanation for why events happen, now can there." She mocked his expression. "There is a multitude of unexplained happenings throughout the world every day." His crew of four nodded in agreement, much to the detriment of his point. He seemed to take it in stride though, picking up his burger for another bite.

"Linda told me what happened to her while she was by your side. And, you know what I mean Claire."

Frank shoveled in the last of his burger, his cheeks bulging. He was looking her straight in the eyes now, trying to make her feel uncomfortable, and perhaps trying to force an answer from her. But he wouldn't succeed, not today. She was determined to put this whole incident to rest, once and for all. So, she lied to him about what had happened. It seemed the logical thing to do to cover her bases. In front of her sister and four jocks, she told Frank her version of the truth. "I said a prayer for Linda while we were next to each other. I prayed she could find peace and solace in her and your decision to defy the will of three of your parents and follow your own path in life. That's what happened. The light show was coincidental, but it made the prayer seem more real to her. Now I'm sure all your buddies here have said a prayer for a fellow player who got hurt during a game. Heightened emotions Frank. They mean a lot when it comes to our believing something." She watched the faces of the four oversized males examining memories, some agreeing, some not. By Frank's silence, she took it to mean he agreed to some extent. He had on a poker face and was not revealing his thoughts or feelings, meaning, the discussion was over for now. She forked some salad into her mouth, never taking her eyes off him, not wanting to miss a clue of what was going on inside of him. After a long pause, he and his friends left not saying a word, nor giving her a look of any sort. Surely, one of them had something to say about the oddness of their conversation. She didn't understand their behavior.

"I'm sorry if I spoiled your lunch, but this has been brewing since yesterday. And no, I didn't just tell a complete lie. I did pray but prayed for the strength to help Linda. At least I think I did. Things got a little out of hand." Claire looked at her sister for agreement but found her poised to pounce.

"A little out of hand? Really, Claire, you have a flair for understatement. You revealed yourself to Linda plain and simple. You're just lucky Arthur was listening to the rumblings you call organized thought. He saved our butts and you know it. Tell me something. What is the difference between a bald face lie and a little white lie? Hmm?.......... Exactly!.............. Nothing! ....If you're so smart, then why do you have to lie to cover your tracks?"

Claire was feeling bad about what she'd done, but not so much as to not know when her sister was just giving her a hard time because she'd left herself wide open. "You're right of course, about the lie. I shouldn't be doing that, should I? I don't seem to have much willpower when it comes to Linda's problems. I just fall into the pity pit and then have to resort to angel tactics to save my heinie. You're right of course; by all means, throw me to the dogs." She could hear the ruminations inside her sister's head, building to a climax. Claire was ready for what came next; at least she thought she was. Rachel's giggle betrayed her real feelings and triggered the same feelings in her. It was like a countdown to one before they were laughing uncontrollably. Claire laughed so hard, she had to gasp for air, surprised at her body's reaction to something as harmless as laughter. Rachel put the crowning touch on the whole incident with a high-pitched squeal of delight, which got the attention of everybody in the atrium. She shrugged her shoulders at those sitting close-by, extracting herself from the circular bench seat, staggering with laughter to the trashcan to dump her half-eaten lunch. But it was worth it. She didn't know how she'd lived all those centuries without her sister.

They parted ways in still tied in fits of giggles, getting stares from everyone they passed. She wondered what Lu would have for her today; quite sure yesterday's rehearsal was being talked about around school. As it turned out, Lu was absent, allowing her some breathing room before another rehearsal – hopefully a more normal one.

She spent most of the afternoon, thinking about the discussion at lunch and why she'd felt it necessary to lie to Frank, even though it wasn't all a lie. Some of it was true. But the reality was, she'd lost control of herself and merged with Linda's misery, actually, horror was a better term for what she'd found inside of that poor girl. It hadn't felt much different than what lay within the dark cavern – utter, unmitigated despair. She'd been horrified at the thought of one more second inside of Linda's head, taking the easy way out and using her Angelic Powers to dismantle at least a part of what resided in Linda. She did say a prayer – she was sure she had. Prayer is kinda built into Angels, it's the way they think normally. So no, she didn't really lie, she told herself.

"I see you're still talking yourself into it, Claire." Her sister said as she sat next to her in Theater class.

"Yeah. I'm still going over what happened, but I didn't lie Rachel. Stretched reality a little maybe, but not an outright lie."

"I know. I was just giving you a hard time of it. Gotta take advantage when I can, you know."

Frank and Linda snuck in just before the bell, sauntering by them like they owned the world. "Well, there's a change worth noting," Claire whispered across the aisle to Rachel. Something must have happened since the lunch discussion because Linda looked better than she had in quite a while. Mr. Clark came in a little late and said they'd be moving to the auditorium to begin rehearsal early, and those who were not a part of the production could stay and help if they wanted, or leave early for the day.

Frank was waiting for them backstage, leaning up against the controller's worktable, and looking ready to do battle. His eyes followed their approach, two tiny crows' feet accenting his smug face. "Why Frank, I guess you have some sort of apology for Rachel and me." She was trying to throw him off balance when really she was a little scared.

"In your dreams. You two are lying about who you really are. I had my dad's secretary look into who you say you are and the alleged accident that killed your mothers. Sorry. Busted. There is no record of the accident. So Claire Tate. Who are you?"

She did her best to stay calm, yelling for Arthur to pay attention to what was going down here. She was sure Sandy would have covered all the bases because Arthur's guardianship required multiple government agencies and loads of paperwork, all of which would be in the California data banks. She took a deep breath, examining his eyes and body language, looking for anything to use at the moment. He did have handsome blue-gray eyes if nothing else. Rachel was ready to attack, the way her feet were shuffling and the taught stature of everything above them. "Well, Frank. I guess she made some mistakes in identifying us for the computer. Oh, and don't you need a court order to learn about the guardianship? I believe you would need to vacate the protection order assigned our cases." She was saying things she knew nothing about but didn't really care if they were right or wrong. Sandy would fix what needed fixing – if anything was needed. Frank grunted, pushing off the table, and walked away. "Nice try Frank," she said in a sarcastic tone and realized right away that it was a mistake. "Ops." Frank stopped dead in his tracks and turned around, his face distorted in anger as he walked towards them.

"Great. Just great Claire. Now there is going to be a confrontation." Rachel shouted in her thoughts.

Rachel pulled on her arm, wanting to flee. Claire stood her ground and waited for the big lug to get in her face – which he did.

"Liar. Both of you are hiding something. I know it."

Frank pushed her with his body, causing her to stumble backwards. She grabbed his shirt with both hands to keep from falling and pulled him right back into her face.

"Frank!" Mr. Clark bellowed from across the stage. "Let go of her and back away."

Claire released Frank, as he pulled away, thankful he'd obeyed Mr. Clark.

"Now, what's going on here? One of you speak-up."

"Frank doesn't think we are who we say we are. We're lying according to him. Oh, and by the way Frank, thanks for the sympathy about our deceased mothers. I'll be sure to reciprocate it."

"Stop it, Claire. You and Rachel join the rehearsal with Ms. Newman." His finger pointed the way.

She and Rachel were a few steps away when she turned her head and heard Mr. Clark.

"Frank, a word to the wise. Just because your father is a Councilman, doesn't give you license to do as you please."

"Arthur, were you listening? I hope you were. Arthur?" Claire's face squiggled up with irritation, mostly directed at Frank and his utter lack of brains when it came to other peoples' feelings.

"Yes, Claire. I heard. Sandy said your presence here is sewn up tight with all documents accounted for. I wouldn't worry; Frank was just blowing off steam, probably about his situation, not yours. Please don't confront him again though. He does have a temper, and it's usually affixed to physical violence. He could easily hurt you and Rachel and complicate the assignment. Enjoy rehearsal."

"Did you hear all that?" Rachel nodded. Meanwhile, Ms. Newman was explaining some of the emotions parents have with their children, to Evan and Liz, the parents of Frank and Linda. She said that when they bring the two homeless girls home, there will be consequences to deal with: the laws governing minors, the police and local Welfare Dept., the newspaper and TV reporters, and the needs of the two homeless girls, like medical, dental, clothing, and where they'd sleep. Ms. Newman watched as Frank joined them, late again, giving him an irritated look. Frank scowled back at her and folded his arms tightly across his chest, looking defiant standing next to Linda.

"I'm not going to repeat myself, Frank Richards, so you can ask Linda about what I said."

It was a standoff as far as Claire could tell, neither giving up any ground. Ms. Newman said she wanted to see a walk-through of the scene, so she and Rachel took up their station at the fence to wait for the dog-walking rescuers to arrive. It was interesting to watch Linda and Frank interact when one of them was in a mood because it always seemed to set the other off in the same way – like trading emotions and sides. They flip-flopped twice before Linda hit Frank on the arm with a closed fist, stopping the action and sending Linda to the left wing to sulk. Claire was confused as to why Frank was so pig-headed about things, especially when it involved Linda, the mother of his child.

Things escalated quickly when Mr. Clark stepped in, took Frank by the arm, and tried to walk him off the stage. Frank pushed him away and was ready to strike, his clenched fists slowly rising from his sides. Mr. Clark hesitated, but stood his ground against Frank, perhaps knowing he would lose badly if it came to blows. Claire's heart was in her throat and pounding in fear. She was glad her teacher had decided to stare him down in a battle of wills. Claire's insides boiled with her sister's rage for Frank. Her sister was ready to do battle with the one who'd pinned her to the lockers in a choke hold; but Ms. Newman beat her to the punch, arriving in front of Frank, and stood on her toes to stick her face up into his as far as she could.

"My office. Now!" She said through gritted teeth.

And that was how rehearsal ended. Frank followed Ms. Newman to her office, leaving the cast and crew gapping at them, wondering if the musical was really going to happen.

GRIDLOCK

Dinner was a quiet affair, and afterward, Arthur sat them all down in the living room, saying he had some things to explain about their encounters thus far. They got comfortable, snuggling together on the sofa, and covered themselves with one of his tattered quilts.

"Today, you both witnessed a scene that has played out many times in Ms. Newman's life. Confrontations with men have not all ended so well for Gail. You see, she grew up with an abusive father, one who cost her most of her childhood. Gail had to be strong for her mother, who though never beaten, suffered at her husband's ire, with an endless stream of demeaning words throughout their marriage, which ended when Gail was sixteen. Although Gail's father never touched her, she was abused in the same way as her mother. She had no siblings to seek solace from, and her mother's constant depression allowed for a little comfort. Gail never got to date at all, but she did have a Jr. High and High School sweetheart, someone who cherished her beyond words, doing everything in his power to help her endure. His name was Roy Clark, your Theater teacher. They're both in their thirties now and have never married, not that Roy hasn't asked. Gail, like Frank and Linda, used music and theater as an outlet for her emotions, graduating from the same university as Roy, and even acted with him in productions. But, she has always refused to marry, perhaps because she was afraid of what her abusive childhood could do if they had children. The confrontation with Frank today ended well for all, but it took a toll on Gail, something only Roy could know about, because of their past together. Both Gail and Roy are a part of my assignment, along with you two young gals. So, now you know a little of their history. This musical, which I helped them to finish, is a way to help Roy, Gail, Frank, and Linda, move through some of their barriers and find a fulfilling life. And, we're the team to get it done. You know, when Sandy was dreaming up this assignment and trying to choose who would be in your shoes, she came to me for advice. I told her she needed experienced Angels for such a difficult assignment, but she said sometimes inexperienced Angels do the very best of work there is. We all knew each other from long ago, and we too have a storied history to work out, which is why she and the Higher Ups chose you both, knowing that together, we would be stronger because of our past. So here we are, just out of a cat fight, and getting ready to jump headlong into . . ." He paused. "What should we call it?"

Bosco appeared out of nowhere jumped into Claire's lap, his motor running full tilt, with the meows coming nonstop. "Let's ask Bosco what he thinks. He seems tuned into what's going on. Mr. Bosco stuck his nose on hers, purring softly now. "A very wise cat you have Arthur. He says to keep up the good work and remember to feed me." She set him down on the floor and brushed the cat hair off her. "I'm going to bed early if there's nothing else urgent to discuss." She gave Rachel a hug and Arthur a kiss, and went to her room; stopping at the top of the stairs to yell: "How about calling it Arthur Organ's Fix a Life Class?"

The next morning, she made a point of avoiding Frank in English class. She was not ready to take him on again. She kept to herself all morning and never did meet up with her sister for lunch; sitting instead in a corner of the cafeteria with a few other girls who seemed to be hiding out like her.

She barely listened to Lu in Science class, just nodding at what seemed an appropriate time. Her mind was a long way off and walking on her mountain path filled with wildflowers. She was so far away, in fact, Mr. Boswell had to shake her shoulder to get her back into the classroom to answer his question.

"What? Oh, I'm sorry. I was thinking of . . ." She stopped herself before she blurted out an explanation that would make no sense to anyone. "What's the question?" She smiled up at him.

The laughter in the room succeeded in waking her and brought her back into reality. She smiled politely. "Sorry."

"Like I was saying," he continued . . .

She tried to pay attention for the remainder of the class but was still having trouble focusing on anything except the fiasco in rehearsal the day before. She worried the same thing would happen again. Frank was out of control yesterday and had nearly come to blows with Mr. Clark. Her sister wasn't far behind either. "I need a plan." By the time Theater class arrived, she thought she had one to deal with Frank and was mulling it over when she sat across the aisle from her sister.

"What plan?" Rachel asked.

"Still working on it," she shrugged.

Mr. Clark ended class early again, saying they needed the extra time for rehearsal, and walked them backstage, where Ms. Newman was talking with three scene painters. Ms. Newman didn't look any the worse for wear from yesterday, so Claire was hopeful today would go much better for her.

"I'll be right with you. Please get ready to pick up where we left off yesterday." Ms. Newman said.

Mr. Clark positioned himself center stage, perhaps to keep order after what had happened yesterday. She came up behind him and tapped him on his shoulder. "Mr. Clark, I'm very sorry about what happened yesterday. I know it must have been hard for you and Ms. Newman. It's just that Frank and Linda have had it out for me and Rachel ever since we replaced the other two sisters. Frank and I had a bad day yesterday, so it's partly my fault for what happened." His eyes never left Frank and Linda when he answered.

"Whatever it is between you, I suggest you lay it to rest because we have a lot of work to get done before performance night."

"Yes. We will. Thank you for being patient with us." She studied his face for a moment, in all of its intensity, feeling partly responsible for what had taken place yesterday. His normal, kind, and placid features locked into rigid lines and a taut jaw. She was sorry it had to come to this. Rachel tugged on her arm and led her to one side of the stage; her eyes motioned to the opposite side and the approach of Frank and Linda.

"Here comes trouble." Rachel said.

Claire nodded, watching Frank and Linda. They were arm in arm, almost looking normal today, just two high school lovers in a musical together. They skirted around Mr. Clark and headed directly at Claire and her sister. Rachel pulled her back as she stepped towards them, leaving her to wonder what she had up her sleeve.

"Hello Linda, Frank." Rachel reached out to take Linda's hand. "My sister and I are concerned we upset you yesterday and we wanted to apologize. We're really very sorry your friends lost their parts. But we have a musical that we're in together, so we might as well make peace and try to get along. The show is more important than any of our differences of opinion. Besides, I hear the head of the Theater Department at American University will be attending, and looking for prospective scholarship candidates. So, it's important for everyone in the cast."

Rachel stepped back beside Claire, to await their response, and as she did, Claire could see the pain in Linda's eyes.

"Really? Dr. Rideout will be there?" Linda responded.

"Yup. that's what I heard." Rachel confirmed.

"And how is it you know this?" Frank said still holding Linda's arm.

"Why Claire overheard Ms. Newman on her cell phone, calling the man by his name, and thanking him for his interest. She said it was going to be the best musical he'd ever seen." Rachel reached out to pat Frank on the shoulder.

"Frank, I think the lighting crew could use your expertise with lighting the scrim for the small stage where Rachel and I have to enter and return to several times." Claire knew she was stretching his abilities a bit, but the crew was having a hard time getting it right, and Frank had an eye for details on the set, according to what she'd heard.

"Yeah, sure. I've worked the gridiron before."

Frank's gaze drifted up towards the framework that the scenery hung from, as well as much of the stage lighting. It seemed to take his mind off their problems by giving him something constructive to do with his hands. While Frank was studying the lighting high above, she leaned closer to Linda.

"Are you alright?"

"Yes."

Linda's sharp tone said she wasn't alright in Claire's mind. But what could she do about it? Nothing.

Ms. Newman cleared her throat loudly and looked directly at her and Rachel. She waited for them to return to their marks on the stage.

"Claire, Rachel, we don't have a lot of time for rehearsals."

"We're sorry Ms. Newman, we were making peace with Frank and Linda so a repeat of yesterday wouldn't happen. I think all is well." Claire sat down on her mark and leaned against the fence, her sister following suit.

"Yesterday wasn't any of your doing," Ms. Newman smiled. "Frank and Linda have other issues they let get in the way of the rehearsal. They know better and will buckle down to do whatever it takes for the performance. We'll get started in a moment. Where did they go anyway?"

Claire pointed to the backstage area. "She didn't seem at all rattled by yesterday, did she?" Claire said after Ms. Newman had left to check on the two. I wonder if Arthur was mistaken."

"We're about to find out," Rachel pointed at the approaching threesome and the dog.

It was not the same dog as before, this little guy was a little shy and unsure of himself, stopping and starting, and looking every which direction. Claire giggled when the dog went promptly over to the fence and lifted a leg. "He doesn't look too shy to me. If he does that the night of the show . . ."

"Yeah, a real show stopper." Rachel elbowed her sister.

"Stop it." Claire grabbed her sister's arm and studied Linda's face. "She's in pain." She stood up to get a clear view.

"It's dark. Maybe it's just the way the light's making shadows on her face." Rachel said.

Linda twisted to one side with her arms holding her midsection. She folded over letting out a painful cry as Frank caught her before she collapsed onto the stage floor. Linda's cry of pain turned everyone's heads towards her. Claire flew to Linda's side and saw blood trickling down her leg, making a small pool on the black stage floor. Ms. Newman was alongside them now.

"Frank! You got your phone?" Ms. Newman's strong voice got Frank's attention. "Call for help. Now!" Ms. Newman helped Linda to lie down.

"What's wrong?" Claire's voice cracked with fear – not her fear – the fear in Linda's eyes.

"Miscarriage. We need to get her to the hospital. Frank. Did you get through?"

Frank nodded, his face filled with fear, his voice vanquished. "Frank. Take my spot by Linda." Claire waved him to kneel beside her. She moved to above Linda's head, placing her hands on her and praying – praying like she'd never prayed before. She was afraid for Linda, but she was almost more afraid for Frank. His face was contorted in pain and anguish, knowing he could do nothing about what was happening. A few minutes later, Linda let out a blood-curdling scream, the same time the paramedics were running down the center aisle in the auditorium. Linda was loaded and gone within two minutes, leaving them all shaken to the bone. In the few minutes of terror on stage, Ms. Newman had transformed from being strong and in charge to visibly shaken; so much so that Mr. Clark's face was filled with the same pain as his childhood sweetheart.

"Arthur," she whispered. "We need you. Rachel and I are going to the hospital with Ms. Newman and Mr. Clark. Please come as soon as you can."

LINDA'S TORMENT

Mr. Clark called Linda's parents, knowing that Gail was quickly losing the battle with her past, and unable to help others. Claire watched in pain as Ms. Newman slowly began shutting down and collapsed center stage, consumed in grief. Gail Newman's past came rushing to the forefront, crashing down on her, and laying waste to what semblance of a life she'd made for herself. Claire knew this, because Gail's past was playing out in her mind, and filling her with despair. She was on a carousel of anguish with: Frank and Linda; Gail and Roy; Adam and Evelyn Richards; George and Sharon Connor; and Rachel and herself. She was dizzy and at a loss to help anyone, including herself. Roy relieved her of some of her fears when he sat beside his sweetheart and held her in his arms, giving her the only support she'd ever known. Claire looked around at the cast and crew, all of them not knowing how to deal with any of this. She counted herself as one of them. What more could befall Linda and Frank? And what would become of them now?

"Could we go with you to the hospital?" She whispered to Mr. Clark, after composing herself.

"Yes. But first I have to attend to Gail." Roy's eyes never left the woman he had loved since seventh grade.

Gail's red, tear-swollen eyes gazed into his, holding on to the love they'd always felt for each other. Claire knew this look. It was the same look that Rachel had when she and Arthur came for her. The hope of a thousand years come-to-pass. Ms. Newman looked at Claire with tears welling up. Claire touched her on her shoulder, doing her best to impart some of her birthrights, without it being obvious. Gail's eyes brightened, no longer in such dire distress.

"We can go now. I'll be alright. Help me up, Roy."

"The EMT said they were going to Sibley Memorial, for those of you who want to come. Make sure you call your parents and tell them where you'll be." Mr. Clark said.

Claire helped with getting Ms. Newman to the staff parking lot. It took them fifteen minutes to get to the hospital, an eternity in her mind. She settled down some as they walked into the Emergency waiting room and stopped at the admittance desk to ask about Linda. They had a seat and began the waiting process. Since they were not family, they would be told very little about Linda's condition. Claire was not doing well with it at all. Rachel seemed content to sit and wait by herself. Claire began to pace among the chairs, more nervous now than when it had all begun.

It was not terribly busy in the ER when they entered, but several ambulances came thirty minutes later. Shortly thereafter, Linda was brought out in a wheelchair, and parked by the admissions desk. Claire raced over to be with her, as did Ms. Newman and Frank. There were still no parents present. A nurse brought Linda's paperwork out a minute later and told her she would be sent for an ultrasound before they could decide what was next if anything. She may go home and come back tomorrow. The nurse also said that the ER had a multiple injure automobile accident inbound, so it may be a wait of several hours if she did need treatment. In any case, the hospital preferred having the consent of her parents beforehand, if there was a procedure involved.

All of this was not sitting well with Frank, who was more agitated than Linda. He was nervous and flighty, and checking his phone constantly for a message or missed call like he couldn't hear it if he was called. Claire wanted something to happen; anything would do about now.

"Linda Connor," a hospital aide called out from the other side of the admissions desk.

"Here!" Frank raised his hand from its place on Linda's shoulder.

"I'll be taking you to the Radiology Department for an ultrasound. Is there a family member here to sign the consent form?"

"Not yet," Linda answered. "But I'm sure they'll be here soon. Do I have to wait?"

"No. You can sign and we'll get it done now." The aide said handing her the clipboard and pen.

Claire watched as Linda was wheeled away with Frank by her side, insisting he be allowed to accompany her. As they disappeared down the hallway, Claire watched as Frank answered his phone, just as the double doors closed behind him. Now there really was nothing to do but wait, and her feet were feeling like they needed to pace some more, anything to do was better than just sitting.

"Ms. Newman, what do you think will happen? Will they keep her overnight?"

"I don't know Claire, but I'm sure Linda will be fine. Did you get a hold of Arthur to tell him where you are?"

"Yes, he said he'd be over shortly. Do you think we'll be able to continue with the musical?"

"We'll do our best, as I know Linda will too."

Roy Clark put his arm around his sweetheart's shoulders, pulling her close, and returned to their chairs. Claire was moved by his empathy for the woman who couldn't find the strength or resolve to marry the one person in the world who loved her and knew her heart better than anyone. Maybe that would all change if she and Rachel could succeed with Frank and Linda, and Arthur could somehow help Gail to open up to Roy. "We need to talk," she whispered in Rachel's mind, patting the seat next to her.

"You mean about this mess we are calling our assignment?"

Rachel sat next to her sister, pretending to look at a women's magazine. Claire folded her hands in her lap and stared off into space, focusing on how short the time was for the musical to come together. "We need to take charge of Linda when she goes home. I know she wants to play her part, but she may not be physically able to right away. I want to be there for her, help her rehearse her part, and lend a little emotional support, whatever I can do. Otherwise, I'm feeling as if the show might be canceled if she can't keep up. I think I'm going to have to enlist Ms. Newman and Mr. Clark's help convincing the Connors that I'm needed. I just hope Linda accepts my gesture of help. I think she will. Rachel, Frank's a mess, and it may only get worse if there's a conflict between him and the Connors. Would you stay by his side for whatever it takes to keep him calm and level-headed through all of this?" Rachel made a face at her but nodded she would. "Why aren't her parents here yet? Mrs. Connor is less than two miles away at American University."

"If she's teaching she may have her phone off. There's no way we can know, and neither do we need to know. What Linda's parents do is not a part of our assignment, at least not directly."

"I disagree," Claire responded in a sharp tone. "They're very much a part of our assignment if they stand in the way. We can't go against their rights as parents, but you know . . . Look, there's Linda's father. I recognize him from the police station when he picked up Linda. He's still in scrubs." They both watched as he questioned the admitting person behind the desk. He disappeared through the entrance doors to the ER Ward. "I wonder who he's going to talk to." She got Roy and Gail's attention, telling them Dr. Connor had just walked into the ER.

Things happened more quickly after that. Linda came back from Radiology pretty much the same time as her father emerged from the ER, meeting face to face next to the admissions desk. He gave her a quick hug and handed some forms to the staff person. He bent low and kissed his daughter and pointed to the staff person, then used the desk phone. The staff person wheeled Linda off the way she'd come with a lap full of paperwork, hopefully, to be treated. Mr. Clark was walking towards Dr. Connor as Linda was leaving. They talked for a minute or two, shook hands, and Dr. Connor left.

"He said everything was taken care of and Linda would be fine," Roy said. "She would be able to leave in a few hours if everything went as planned. He said not to worry, this sort of thing happens more often than you think. He said his wife would be here soon. He has another surgery, so he couldn't stay. As soon as Arthur gets here, we're going to leave. Gail needs to go home and rest."

"Rachel and I are going to help Linda and Frank in every way we can Ms. Newman," Claire said as they sat down to wait for Arthur. "I'll help Linda with her part as soon as she feels up to it. I know they both want to see this musical happen. It's important to them." Claire laid her hand atop of her teacher's.

"Thank you, both. Things will work out for us."

Ms. Newman voice was barely audible, but she smiled a little, patting Claire's hand. Claire was confident too, that all would work for the best. They had to accomplish their task because their assignment was really a test for whether they could successfully find their way back into the Angelic Ranks. "Well stated Claire," Arthur said in her thoughts as he came into the waiting room.

"Sorry, I'm late. I trust Linda is being well cared for."

"Yes. Dr. Connor was just here and took care of everything. His wife is on her way." Roy said. "We hate to duck out too quickly, but I want to get Gail home."

"Of course," Arthur hugged Gail and shook Roy's hand. "We'll wait for Ms. Connor and tell her what you did for her daughter. I'm sure her husband has already filled in the details for her in a voice mail. Good night then."

Claire hugged Ms. Newman, as did her sister. "Thank you for all that you did for my friend," Claire said. "I'll try to not worry like you said not to Ms. Newman." Claire looped an arm around Arthur's back, leaning her head against him, feeling herself relax, and the carousel stop for the first time in an hour and a half. They sat down to wait for Ms. Connor, and all she could think about was how hungry she was, and how much she wanted to leave this place.

"We'll fix that right now," Arthur gave her arm a squeeze. "Sharon has arrived."

The three of them approached Ms. Connor, who was actually a Dr. as well; only hers was a Ph.D. in Political Science. She was a striking woman, her cheekbones lifted and prominent, setting off her soft blue almond shaped eyes. She was as tall as Arthur, and equally as fit and trim. Linda had her eyes, but her father's thick bones and muscular physique.

"Ms. Connor. I am Arthur Organ, and this is Claire and Rachel. We're very sorry about what's happened to Linda. I wasn't there, but Mr. Clark and Ms. Newman were. They came over with your daughter, but had to leave, because Ms. Newman was so upset over what had happened. They send their prayers, as do we."

"Thank you, Arthur. My husband called and explained everything to me. Where is she now?"

"I think she was taken to a treatment room ten minutes ago. Perhaps the admitting person has more information."

Ms. Connor waited for the admitting person to finish on the phone, and then they spoke for a few minutes. The woman jotting down some notes for her and pointed down the hall. Ms. Connor turned to them, dabbing at a tear. Claire started to reach out to her, but Arthur told her to wait a moment in her thoughts. He was right of course. Sharon Connor, who had been against Linda marrying Frank and having the baby, was struggling with her emotions as a mother. She had lost a seven-month-old child when Linda was six. Now her daughter was in a similar scenario and needed her support. Claire was beginning to understand what it meant to be human and experience all the emotional turmoil, which was part of everyday life, but especially at times like this, with the loss of an unborn child. "Arthur, is this even the right time for me to ask?" She whispered in her thoughts. "Be patient a bit longer," he responded.

"I'm sorry. It was very confusing having to leave a class halfway through. Claire, is it? You looked like you were about to say something."

"Yes I would, and you're very perceptive. Ms. Connor, I would like to help Linda when she gets home. With the musical, I mean. I know how important it is to her and I don't want her to feel like she is falling behind by having to miss rehearsals. Linda and I have sort of connected in the short time we've known each other, so I think I could help if you think it's a good idea."

"Let me think about it. Now I go down this corridor, right?" Sharon said.

"Yes," Arthur said.

As Ms. Connor walked away, Claire had a good feeling about her, that she would find it within herself to support her daughter better than before.

"Yes, it would be a good thing," Arthur said. "Come on. Let's go home. You can call her tomorrow."

"Sort of connected?" Rachel's sarcastic tone reverberated in Claire's head, as they left the ER. "You have a gift for understatement."

ANGEL OF MERCY

With all her heart, Claire wanted to help Linda, no matter what had happened between them. Her life depended on fulfilling her Angelic Duties, and her assignment was Linda. It was, after all, the reason she existed; to serve humanity, and for today, that was Linda. She bolted out of bed and showered, dressed and fixed her hair with lightning speed. Racing downstairs, she found Arthur already in the kitchen, having had his coffee, and awaiting her entrance.

"Breakfast," he pointed to a bagged sandwich. "Phone," he handed her the phone to call Linda's house. "Books," his eyes fell on her backpack on the kitchen stool. "Smooch," his finger tapped his cheek.

Claire kissed her mentor on the cheek and smacked him in the behind for good measure. "Thank you." She dialed Linda's house number to talk to Ms. Connor. It rang three times and transferred to a message service. She left a short message and her number. She dialed Linda's cell and got her service too, leaving a message. She placed the house phone in its cradle and got her cell phone to send a text to Linda.

"Want some company?"

Discouraged, she plopped on one of the stools and hung her head.

"Be patient, young lady. Don't feel like you have to rush into the day. Let it come to you, one moment at a time. You'd be surprised how well it works." Arthur smiled and rubbed her shoulders.

She sighed, setting the cell on the counter, nudging it away with her finger. She folded her arms on the counter and rested her chin on them, trying to smile for Arthur. "Maybe this isn't going to work the way I thought it would. What if they don't want me over there? I could understand why. We barely know each other."

"Ah, but that's not entirely true. You see, Angels know every person in this world because we're connected to them – some more than others – but, they have to initiate our services. You know free-will and all. You just sit there and focus your thoughts on Linda and how you can help her. I guarantee you'll get results. Now close your eyes and concentrate."

Claire followed his instructions, sitting up straight and closing her eyes; visualizing Linda and herself sitting together, talking, and just being teenagers. She set aside her wishes for any big monstrous flashes of inspiration and the like. She breathed long and slow, listening to her heartbeat, and falling in cadence with it. Claire literally fell into Linda's bedroom with them and found herself overwhelmed with grief and sorrow. Linda was in bed with the covers pulled over her head, and her mother was sitting in a chair crying softly. "Now tell them they are loved and will be cared for," Arthur's gentle voice filled her with compassion. She said those words as quietly as she could, not wanting to disturb them. She said them over and over until she felt as if she was the one being cared for, she was being lifted out of her grief and sorrow. So strong was the feeling, that she began to cry with them, completely unaware she was sitting in the kitchen at home. She wasn't there; she was in Linda's bedroom. She'd startled herself right back into the kitchen nearly falling off the stool, her eyes opening to find

Arthur sitting next to her with his chin on top of his laced fingers and elbow resting on the counter.

"Good job. You've got the hang of it I think."

The cell phone rang, finishing the job of her return to the kitchen.

"Hello, this is Claire."

Her face flushed with energy, feeling tingly and expanded.

"Yes, I can do that. I'd be happy to. I'll be a few minutes. Bye."

She laid the phone on the counter and looked into his delighted eyes. "Can you give me a ride to the store and drop me over there?"

"Anything for you." He said. "Shall we then?"

Arthur drove her to the bakery to pick up the cinnamon rolls Linda had asked for and then dropped her off, reminding her to call him before dinner, in case she couldn't make it. The Connor's had a big colonial two-story, set among large oaks and other trees, which she didn't know the names. Compared to Arthur's place, this was a mansion, complete with a three-car garage and living space above. She walked up the red brick walkway that curved around a large oak, and rang the doorbell. Ms. Connor answered, and without saying a word, led Claire directly upstairs to Linda's room. It wasn't a lot different from her bedroom, except larger, and with a dormer cut into the roof, which held a desk and view of the trees in the front yard. Linda was in bed with the covers pulled over her head, just as Claire had seen.

"Do you drink tea?" Ms. Connor asked quietly.

"Yes, thank you." Claire smiled pleasantly. She sat at the end of the bed. There were stuffed animals everywhere, big and small, old and new. One old teddy bear sitting in a child's rocker next to Linda's bed caught her eye. It was missing a lot of fur and there was a rip in its side. "Hi Linda," she whispered almost

225

inaudibly. Linda's feet moved a little and a hand moved under the covers close to what she thought was Linda's head. It was hard to tell because there were stuffed animals both under and on top of the covers.

"Hi," the muffled voice said from under the covers.

"I brought you those cinnamon rolls you asked for. I think your mom is warming them up."

"That's nice of you."

A hand extended and curled over the top of the covers, pulling them down to expose Linda's head and very bloodshot eyes. "There you are. Thank you for letting me come over." Claire's eyes welled with tears and her heart swelled creating a lump in her throat. "I'm sorry." She croaked. Linda extended her hand out to Claire's, fishing around to grasp it. She scooted closer and took Linda's hand, using her other to wipe her own eyes. She didn't know why she was weeping but thought it may have something to do with Arthur's little visualization and focus session, which got her connected with Linda on a deeper level. Claire was momentarily paralyzed and transfixed by Linda's eyes, like a deer frozen in a car's headlights. There was so much pain being conveyed, it took Claire's breath away.

"Tell me how I can help," she said clasping Linda's hand between hers. Linda's eyes welled up with tears, her expression one of desperation. "I can't begin to know how you feel. Can you help me?" Linda nodded wiping her eyes and nose on her PJ sleeve leaving a wet streak. For some reason, it made Claire giggle a little bit because it was so graphic. It sparked a giggle in Linda as well. Her mother came in as they giggled together, stopping her in her tracks, melting the gloomy expression on her face. She set the tray down on the nightstand, sat beside her daughter, and hugged her for a long time.

"I'm so sorry for what I said to you and the way I treated you. You didn't deserve any of it." Ms. Connor said in deepest sympathy.

"Mom, that hurts."

"I'm sorry," Sharon said sitting up and wiping the tears from her face. "It's good to see you happy for any reason." Sharon looked back at Claire after a moment. "What was so funny?"

"Nothing much," Linda said. "I wiped my nose on my sleeve and we laughed at how gross it looked. Ouch." Linda winced. "It hurts to laugh," she giggled again. "But it feels good too."

"Your mom fixed us tea," Claire said, seeing three cups on the tray. "And hot cinnamon rolls. May I pour?" Linda nodded. "Milk and sugar of course." She waited for the nods. Linda's mother placed two more pillows behind her daughter's back and head. "Did they give you something for the pain?" Linda pointed to the prescription bottle on the nightstand. Claire handed each a cup and saucer, setting the plate with the precisely cut rolls on it, next to Linda. Ms. Connor got up and opened a hall closet just outside of the bedroom, retrieving a bed-tray with short legs, and brought it in for Linda to use.

"It was very nice of you to come over Claire. It means a lot to Linda and to me that you care so much. So, are you just visiting with Arthur for a part of the school year?"

Linda had a pained expression at her mother's questioning her friend. "Yes. For quite a while actually. Both of our mothers died in a car accident together several months ago, and the courts awarded Arthur guardianship. We'll be here next year too." Claire sipped her tea, guarding against saying the wrong thing – she was telling lies, but necessary ones.

"Oh. I'm so very sorry. It must be hard for you both." Ms. Connor looked directly into Claire's eyes.

"Yes, it is. We have our good days and bad days, but Arthur has helped us both a great deal. He's very understanding, and we both like him a lot."

"So you're cousins then?"

"Yes, but we act like we're sisters. We grew up knowing each other pretty well."

"Well, I've got a class to teach. I should be home by 3:30 p. m. Dr. Connor won't be home until early evening. There are lunch fixings in the refrigerator. Be sure to rest dear and take your pills."

"Yes, Mom. I will."

"Thanks again for letting me come over Ms. Connor. Bye." Claire smiled at her as she left. "Your mother seems really nice Linda," Claire said fishing for whatever Linda would tell her about their relationship.

"She can be sometimes. Was your mom nice to you?"

The question required her to lie again for the umpteenth time. "Yes, she was a lot like your mom, smart, pretty and always pestering me with twenty questions."

"Do you miss her? Oh. I'm sorry. Of course, you miss her. How thoughtless of me. Tell me about Arthur. He seems very clever and quick to pick up on things in his classes. Frank and I are taking his Web Design class this year. He never lets us get away with anything, especially Frank."

"Arthur has helped us a lot. Besides being a good cook, he knows how to help Rachel and me with most anything, except for girl stuff. We stump him on that." She giggled with Linda. "How about your father. What's he like?"

"He's an orthopedic surgeon, so he's really smart, but like Arthur, he's not too good with girl stuff. He works a lot, so he's not home much at all. We have our differences, but we get along okay, I guess."

Linda's eyes glazed over, telling Claire she was off somewhere thinking about her parents. She waited for her to come back, quietly staring at her, trying to get a feel for who she was.

"So tell me, Claire. Why are you really here?" Linda said

228

coolly.

"Well, let me see. Because you just lost your baby and you're parents don't really approve of your relationship with Frank, but mostly because I'm an angel sent to help you, and I'm doing my best not to screw it up." Claire said, as a matter of fact, folding her hands in her lap, and twiddling her fingers, glancing up several times to see the look on Linda's face. Linda giggled after she couldn't hold it any longer.

"Still sticking to that same angel story, eh? You know, I don't know exactly why, but I trust you more than I have ever trusted anyone. I can't seem to figure it out. I hardly know you, but I know you. Seems rather odd, doesn't it? But, I'm really glad you're here. I was a mess last night after I woke up from the anesthetics. I couldn't sleep at all last night, and it wasn't just from the pain either. I felt like somebody ripped me apart and stole my soul, but at the same time, I am relieved not to be a mother so soon. I'm not ready. It all happened in the heat of the moment, and felt like it was forced on me, not that I didn't want to, mind you."

"Is everything alright between the two of you? I mean, you've been through a lot this past month. She wanted to say more but thought it best to wait and let Linda bring it up.

"It's Frank's father. There's something weird about him, like it's from his past, maybe his father. I don't know. All I know is, it has scarred Frank deeply, and he can't seem to break free from it, at least not for any length of time. We both have a lot of issues, but that's what drives us together. Frank is very smart and a good actor. I know he wants to take it as far as he can if his father would ever leave him alone long enough. You're an outsider. What do you think?"

"Frank hasn't told you anything about his grandfather Merrick?"

"Merrick's his name?"

Without the slightest thought to what she was doing, Claire launched into an explanation, giving Linda what she wanted; a new insight into Frank's family. Linda's need was her command. "You have to swear you'll never reveal what I'm about to tell you. Swear it, Linda, it's important if you two are to have a chance at a life together." Linda gave her an odd look.

"How do you know about his grandfather? Who told you?" Linda said defensively.

"I can't tell you. Just let it be enough that I do know and I think you deserve to understand the man you love. His family has a history." Linda sat herself up straight, adjusting the pillows, wincing several times.

"Alright. I swear I won't say a word, not ever."

"Merrick committed suicide at age forty-three, because the woman he was having an affair with got pregnant, and threatened to tell his wife if he didn't agree to compensate her and provide for the child's future. At the time, Merrick's law firm was in financial troubles, because of two high profile consignment cases they'd lost, and his new house ate up most of the firm's capital reserves. He overdosed on his wife's prescription sedatives in his office after everyone had gone home. A clerk found him the next morning. Frank's father was a sophomore at Georgetown University at the time, and it drove him into a deep depression for months, until he learned of his father's affair. He flip-flopped and sent his depression straight into a rampage of prolonged anger, which landed him in the hospital with heart palpitations. Frank inherited all of his father's emotional baggage and didn't even know why. He still to this day, does not know the why, which is the reason you must keep this information close and never say a word about it. Frank's father developed a deep distrust of women, which he passed on to his son. Frank used athletics as an outlet for his anger, as you well know, and now he doesn't have that, because of his injury. You remember the day at Frank's house when his father came in. You got a good look at the way Frank grew-up with the intimidating size and voice of a very disturbed, yet intelligent man. That's everything I know about his grandfather and father. Rather than holding it against Frank, use it to understand him and help him move beyond its influence. You can help him, because of the love you both have for each other." Linda was silent a long time, thinking about what she'd heard. Claire knew it was a lot to load on her right after losing her baby, but the more Linda knew about Frank's family, the better she could help him.

"I wish you could tell me how you came by this information. Why didn't his father explain it to him? He's old enough to understand. It must have really hurt his father deeply for him to hide it all these years. Maybe that's why he likes to act and is so good at it."

Claire nodded. "Do you want some time alone to think? I'll put some more water on for tea and make us a sandwich for lunch."

"I may rest for a while. Thank you, Claire. No one has ever talked to me like you just did. It was difficult to hear, but refreshing at the same time to have an understanding of someone I care about. Thank you."

Claire pulled the extra pillows from behind Linda and took the tray downstairs, glad to be alone for a few minutes. Ms. Connor kept an ultra-neat home, everything spotless, and everything in its place. It was no wonder Linda upset her so with her unpredictability. Claire sat quietly getting the feel of the Connor home before she opened their huge fridge, finding leftover chicken and roast beef she could use for the sandwiches. Linda's mother liked fresh whole wheat bread from the bakery it seemed because there were two new loaves in the bread-barn. She was in the middle of slicing bread when

Dr. Connor came in from the garage through the door beside her. She jumped out of his way, with both equally surprised.

"I'm sorry. Did I hit you with the door?"

"No. I leaped over here first." She laughed catching her breath from being startled.

"Sharon said you were here helping with Linda. Thank you, Claire. I came home before rounds to check in on her. I'll just go up."

"I was making sandwiches. Would you like one?" She smiled.

"I'm partial to the roast beef."

Claire watched as he moved quickly out of the kitchen, to see his daughter. The look on his face spoke of a kindness she'd only seen in one other person – Arthur. "He must have many happy patients." She murmured and continued making two roast beef and one chicken sandwich. She'd forgotten to ask what they like for condiments on them, so she raced upstairs finding Linda's father embracing her and stroking her hand. She stopped short, but Linda had seen her. "I'm sorry to interrupt, but I forgot to ask what you like on your sandwich."

"Mayo and mustard if it's chicken, otherwise ketchup and horsey sauce." Dr. Connor said.

Linda nodded in agreement. She left them alone and returned to finish the sandwiches. She sat and waited for Dr. Connor to come down, taking the time to query Arthur, to see if he'd been listening to her, which he hadn't. He said it was her private business with Linda, which she was more than capable of handling herself. Dr. Connor interrupted her silent conversation with Arthur on his way out, pointing to the sandwich on the counter by the door. She nodded and he was gone. She took the kettle from the stove and filled the teapot, put everything on the tray and headed back upstairs for round two.

"I'm glad you got to meet my dad. He never comes home at lunch, so today was special."

"He came home to see you because you're special to him." Claire set the tray on the nightstand. "We got chicken or beef, your choice." Linda's eyes widened looking at the sandwiches. "What? Did I do it wrong?"

"They're huge." Linda laughed and winced at the same time.

Claire picked up the prescription bottle and read the label. "Is it time?" Linda nodded. Claire took out one tablet and handed it to her with a glass of water. She picked up the knife and cut the sandwiches in half, setting the tray next to Linda, so she could reach.

"I can't even get my mouth around this," she giggled. "But it's really good," came the muffled voice.

Claire was glad Linda was feeling better. "Your mother's kitchen is so clean, I didn't want to mess it up by making lunch." She said with her mouth full, making some funny sounds for words. They both laughed. When the sandwiches were half gone, it was naptime for both of them. They had expended a lot of emotional energy in their conversation and needed to rest. She took the leftover sandwiches to the fridge and returned, sitting in the chair with the ottoman where Linda obviously read books, because there were stacks of books on the table beside it, with a floor lamp, which overhung the chair. There was a comforter beside the chair she covered herself with, and promptly fell into a half awake and half dream state, bouncing back and forth between Merrick's land of desolation and Linda's bedroom. She shifted in the chair and focused on the oak trees outside the dormer window. She fell asleep several more times, finally waking to Linda's snoring. She got out of the chair and stood behind the desk, looking out at the bare branches and semi-green grass of late Fall. Several sparrows landed in the tree, poking about for something to eat.

"What are you looking at?" Linda murmured.

"Sparrows foraging for food. They must have to eat a lot to keep warm all winter. I wonder what they're finding in your oak tree." Claire's eyes widened as Frank's car pulled into the driveway with Rachel in the front seat. "Frank's here." Linda's sleepy eyes brightened.

Claire went downstairs and opened the front door for them, seeing the surprise on his face at her presence. "Hi, Frank. Rachel. I bet you're wondering why I'm here."

"Are you alone with her?" Frank asked.

"Yes. You just missed Dr. Connor and Ms. Connor won't be back until 3:30 p.m." Frank walked right past her and headed up the stairs. "How's it going," she asked Rachel.

"Dandy. Just dandy." Frank's been a pain in everyone's neck at school. The counselor told him to take the afternoon off and be with Linda if he needed to. I saw him in the cafeteria and hooked a ride here."

"Did you get something to eat yet? I made sandwiches if you want something. We should let them have a few minutes alone." She got Rachel the other half of her sandwich and they sat down at the kitchen table. "Was Frank nice to you?"

"Just okay. I think he's pretty upset, and not only because Linda lost their baby either. I think his dad is still giving him grief about everything to do with Linda, but I can't say for sure because Frank won't say anything."

"No, I don't suppose he would. I told Linda about the family secret, Merrick, and swore her to silence. I know it helped her understand Frank better, and it let her know what she's up against since Frank doesn't know the family secret. He's going to be furious when his parents finally tell him if they ever do. Linda and I are getting along quite well, all things considered. Maybe some of it will rub off on Frank. It would certainly help our cause." Claire snuck in a bite of the sandwich.

"Not a good idea, sister." Rachel shook her head and took back the sandwich.

They both heard Frank's hollering and then his heavy footfalls bounding down the stairs. He stormed out the front door, slamming it hard behind him. He was in his car and spinning the tires as he left, leaving burn marks for fifty feet on the brick driveway. They looked at each other, both thinking the same thought, and raced upstairs to Linda's bedroom. She was holding her knees tight to her and sobbing uncontrollably. They both knew what had happened as they sat on either side of the bed. Linda had told Frank about the family secret, either by mistake or on purpose.

"Arthur," Claire yelled in her thoughts. "Arthur, you have to come get Rachel. Linda told Frank about Merrick. I made her promise not to, but she did anyway. Arthur, can you hear me?" The only sound she heard was Linda crying. Claire moved up the bed to her side, cradling her in her arms, rocking with her as she wailed her mournful cry. "Arthur, we need your help please."

"Not a very wise choice Claire. You've placed Frank in a very precarious position with his parents. And yes, I'll pick Rachel up, but it'll be thirty minutes until I can. You have a lot to learn about human emotions and their dynamics and impact on lives. Stay with Linda, she'll need your help more than ever now."

"Thank you," she whispered.

"Thaaank yoou?" Linda's heaving voice questioned.

"I wasn't talking to you, Linda. Can you lay back now and try to breathe a little deeper, and relax your stomach and pelvic muscles." Claire could see that she was causing herself pain. She helped her lay back against three pillows, still stuttering in little gasps of breath. Claire moved the tissue box next to Linda, pulling out four or five tissues for her. "Try to breathe a little slower. What's done is done, and can't be changed now. Deep breaths please." Rachel looked at her and shook her head. "Not good. Not a good idea at all." Rachel said in her thoughts. Claire just shrugged her shoulders. "Arthur said he'd be here in thirty minutes, so we'll have to sit tight for now. I'm staying and you're going to rehearsal with or without Frank. We'll deal with him when we can. Besides, he's probably on the phone with his father, cussing up a blue streak, and rightfully so. We need to have a story as to how we knew about his family secret before our inevitable confrontation. And it's gonna be a big one.

TRUTH HURTS

A rthur's knock on the front door was a welcome sound after the wailing session had come to a close, and Linda had grasped the reality of her actions. Rachel answered it for them and returned to the bedroom with Arthur. He gave his condolences to Linda for her loss and after surveying the emotional heaviness in the room, said he'd be on his way with Rachel. He wanted to locate Frank and help him cope with the tragedy of his grandfather's life. Before he left, Arthur reminded Claire that human affairs needed to play out in their own time between individuals, families, as well as the affairs of countries. Their job was not to interfere like she'd done by telling Linda information best left unsaid; better to be exchanged in conversation with someone in the family. She had changed the dynamics of the Richard's family forever. He said these words quietly in his charges' minds, in hopes they'd heed the rules with humans in the future. He expressed his condolences a second time to Linda and left.

"Arthur seems like a very nice man," Linda said.

"Yes, he most certainly is, and very wise too." Claire got up to open a window and watched Arthur and Rachel as they were driving away. Her mentor waved goodbye, telling her that even in the smallest of detail, he was thoughtful and kind, almost to a fault – at least in her case. She'd screwed up again and her mentor didn't seem to mind.

Linda slept a lot, which was the best thing she could have done, leaving Claire the time to chat with her sister on the problem of Frank. He was hiding out somewhere, was all Rachel passed along.

Around 4 p.m., Ms. Connor returned and started dinner after she'd checked in on Linda. Claire had asked if she would be needed for the evening and got conflicting answers, with Linda wanting the company of someone her own age, and Ms. Connor saying it wasn't necessary unless she wanted to stay for dinner. Dr. Connor wouldn't be home until later, which was the norm for him, making late rounds on his patients who'd had surgery in the morning, and the ones staying hospitalized longer after more complex surgeries. Since he did joint replacements for some patients, they always needed a couple of days to recover before being discharged. It had been this way, Linda said, for more than seven years. It was exciting for Linda in the beginning, because her father would take time and talk about his work with her, while he ate a late dinner. Now, she lived alone in her room, never talking much with either of her parents, except when she had to.

Claire called Arthur on her cell phone a little while after Ms. Connor came home, thinking she wasn't needed, and would probably feel out of place when Dr. Connor came home. She was tired and glad to be leaving, having had a day filled with emotionally charges moments. Linda and her sixteen years of baggage was an eye-opening experience for Claire and she gained a great deal of insight into herself through Linda's life. Nothing was said about returning tomorrow, so she took it to mean she would not be coming back anytime soon.

Arthur's house was just as still as still could be, with no latent family history or the like, except for hers and Rachel's. She went straight to the kitchen to make herself a cup of tea and sit for a while. Rachel was upstairs showering, and Arthur was grading papers. Just as she was settling in on the living room sofa, the phone rang, fracturing the silence. Arthur got it in his study and several minutes later, he walked into the living room to announce that Frank was kicked out of his friend's house and was going to spend the night on Arthur's sofa. She had a dreadful sinking feeling in the pit of her stomach as if it were some kind of premonition.

"Not to worry," he smiled. "You'll see what comes of this in the morning. Please try not to interfere tonight and you'll find a big problem you've been wondering about will be mostly gone. You look like you had a tough day, but I know it was a good day too. You and Linda formed an important link with each other, which will serve both of you well. Everything is fine Claire, believe that."

"Okay. I'll try. I guess I'll go to bed early. I'm not hungry, just glad to be home." She lingered a while longer after he returned to his work, sipping her tea and doing her best to undo the knots inside of her. Even her head was tired.

Her first dream caught her off guard when she woke from it, feeling her insides crawling with some strange presence. She glanced at the bedside clock, 9:23 p.m. it said. There were hushed voices coming from downstairs, so she got up to investigate. Donning her robe, she went to the head of the stairs to listen. It was Arthur and Frank talking so quietly she couldn't make out much of their conversation, other than Frank was very angry with his father. She went back to bed and lay worrying for some time before she fell asleep.

In her second dream, she was standing with her sister at the entrance to her dark cavern. It didn't feel bad, but it had all the appearances of being a point of no return to her. Why are we here? What's to learn from this black hole? She turned to her sister and was horrified to find a sinister face glaring back at her, the face of something so evil she shuddered and fainted on the spot. Claire woke up on her bedroom floor, shivering and drenched in a cold sweat, and covered in goosebumps. She untangled herself from the covers she'd pulled from the bed and hurried to Rachel's room, only to find her asleep. She got a glass of water to take back to her room and fell asleep just before midnight.

What came next stunned even Claire. She and Frank were running along the shore of a wide river chasing a man in a rowboat, who disappeared around a bend when Frank got stuck in a swampy area by the shore. Trying to pull his feet free only got him deeper into the mud, which was now up to his knees. Then he began to sink quickly into the mire, passing his waist almost immediately. By the time she'd gathered her wits, he was up to his chest and frightened beyond belief. She reached out for his hand and pulled with all her might, but he still continued to sink, and was now in deadly straits with the mud closing around his mouth, his other hand flailing about, finding hers and latching on with a death grip. She screamed as he pulled her into the mire face first, filling her mouth with the slimy mud. She choked but once, the blackness enveloping her as she followed him down, ever more swiftly. She blacked out, remembering nothing until . . . until she didn't know who she was anymore.

She was lying next to Frank in a pool of mire, her face half under, with only one eye showing. She jerked herself free from Frank and stood, coughing and throwing up globs of muddy water. It was a horrifying feeling, but not half as terrifying as what she saw in the distance. Frank grabbed her ankle as she let out a blood-curdling scream, which seemed to hasten the approach of the thing in the distance. Running alongside the towering beast, was something that sickened her heart and turned her insides into twisted knots of revulsion, frightening her more than she could bear.

She collapsed back into the mire, convulsing, yet acutely aware of what was happening. Rachel's beast stood over her with its hairy-clawed foot crushing her into the soft mud, leaving but one of her eyes above the mire. It reached over her and extracted a screaming and horrified Frank Richards from the muck, raising him up to look at him, twisting him in every direction, while breathing on him in deep snorts.

A hand grabbed her arm and pulled her from under the beast's clawed foot. She came face to face with her sister. Her face was distorted into a crooked smile and her long black hair was a tangle of mud and knots. She was barefoot and had but shreds of a dress hanging on her shoulders. Claire couldn't believe she was seeing her sister in this place, with this thing, and looking this way. It wasn't possible, but she'd know her own sister in any shape or condition.

"Why Rachel? Why are you doing this? Is this some sick joke you're acting out?" Claire doubled over and threw up what little there was in her stomach. A pain like no other washed over her in waves. "This can't be true; it's not possible," the words screamed in her head. Rachel said nothing, fixated on the beast holding Frank. Her sister's face horrified her, the sinister eyes, deformed and shrunken deep into their sockets.

Claire was shown a picture of her sister in Arthur's living room, sitting beside Frank on the sofa. They were talking angrily about how he'd forced Linda to have sex with him. His hand had grabbed Rachel by the throat, his fingers reaching halfway around her neck, squeezing her windpipe shut.

She gasped once and hit him in the face with a stone coaster from the coffee table, and broke free, coughing, and breathing with a raspy wheezing sound. Rachel showed her the marks on her neck to prove it.

"This is what he did to me when he asked me to sit and talk with him. It was 2 a.m. He apologized but didn't really mean it.

It made me so angry that Arthur would let this rapist in our home. This was the second time his hands were around my throat and it will be the last time if I have anything to say about it. I went to wake Arthur in the study, but changed my mind on the way, thinking of my own punishment for Frank, something far worse than anything of this world. Why you were with him, I don't know. Look at him, Claire. Now it's his turn to be scared out of his mind. He's powerless against the beast in him. I had to teach him a lesson he'd never forget."

Claire woke gasping for air, still choking on the mud from the dream, and still horrified by her sister's sinister face and devilish acts. She staggered out of bed and made it to the bathroom, splashing water on her face for several minutes, and rinsing the sickly taste from her mouth. She leaned on the sink for a long time, trying to forget the dream that quite possibly wasn't a dream at all. She checked on her sister, who was sprawled across her bed, still wearing her robe.

"Rachel," she shook her gently. "Rachel." She was dead to the world.

On the way back to her room, she heard uneven breathing coming from the living room, like someone was scared, holding their breath and then gasping for breath, then repeating it all over again. So it wasn't a dream. Frank had grabbed her by the throat. She had retaliated the best way she knew how, by dragging him into darkness and offering him up to her old captor. "Arthur, how can you sleep through all this?" She said in her thoughts. She went back to bed to think and try to clear her head. She knew she didn't want to go downstairs unless it was to wake Arthur. Frank couldn't be trusted, not for one minute. She pulled the covers over her and fell asleep, exhausted.

She was dreaming again, this time she was standing with Frank at a grassy spot by the same wide river. They were looking out over the water at a figure in a rowboat headed straight for them. A large man with a fishing hat was at the oars, taking long powerful pulls, lifting the bow of the boat considerably with each thrust from the oars. It was twilight, so she couldn't make out who this mystery person was until he was almost to the narrow sandy beach at river's edge. "It's Merrick," she said covering her mouth. Frank turned towards her with a look of wonder on his face. Merrick beached his boat and climbed out, pulling it a few feet ashore. He looked different to her from when she'd met him in his desert of no return. He looked younger, happier, and it was obvious Frank recognized him from photos he'd seen.

"Grandpa?" Frank's most inquisitive voice sailed across the grass to Merrick, who smiled broadly.

"Yes, if you're Adam's son." He smiled.

They walked right up to each other and Merrick stuck his hand out to shake. Frank grabbed the hand and pulled him into a bear hug. Merrick was three inches taller and a lot bigger than Frank, but it was pure gentleness that greeted Frank. They separated and looked at each other for a long time, their eyes seeking out every detail, as if they'd never seen each other before, and never would again.

"It is good to meet you, Frank Richards. I'm afraid I have to go now, but I hope we meet again soon. Goodbye for now."

Frank was stunned, as his grandfather, who he'd never met in life, turned quickly and pushed his boat back into the river and turned it to face downstream, and rowed away, lifting his hat to them. "Thank you," he called out across the river and disappeared around a bend in the river.

"I should be the one thanking him," Frank scratched his head.

She woke up with a start, feeling energized and clear-headed. She sat up in bed, looking around the room, making sure she was awake and at home in her room, and not still dreaming. It had been a night filled with strange dreams, unlike any before, leaving her with the feeling that Arthur was involved with all of it. It had him written all over it. She got up to get a drink of water and pee and heard Frank snoring on the sofa downstairs. She wondered if he really had grabbed Rachel by the throat, sending her into a vengeful state in the wee hours of the morning. She poked her head into her sister's room, finding her still sprawled across her bed and sleeping soundly like nothing had happened. Maybe it was all in her head – she didn't know. She returned to her room and pulled the covers over her head, and left a small opening to breathe through, thinking she'd ask Arthur about her dreams in the morning. It was 4:43 a.m. when she closed her eyes and fell asleep, hoping to be undisturbed the rest of the night.

She went downstairs early to find Arthur in the kitchen. She wanted to talk with him before Frank or Rachel was awake. She'd only slept for another hour, waking to Bosco's meowing in the garage, where Arthur had put him for the night – he would have pestered Frank all night otherwise. Arthur was sitting at the counter with a smile on his face.

"Water's hot for tea," he said.

She made a pot of tea and sat at the counter with him. He looked like he was expecting her to rise early to talk with him. "Busy night," she started. "I don't suppose they were just dreams, were they?" He sipped his coffee and continued to grin. She hated it when he got this look like she was going to have to answer her own questions. She poured a cup of tea from the pot, adding milk and sugar, and sipped it, waiting for him to say something, anything. After last night's wild and woolly barrage of dreams, she wasn't especially in the mood for his practice of the Greek Stoicism philosophy. He actually laughed at her in her thoughts – well chuckled anyway. "Thanks.

Thanks a lot." She folded her arms tight around her midsection, thoroughly put out with him. "Nice try," echoed in her thoughts. He lifted his cup to his lips, his eyebrows raised in anticipation of something. She waited for him, mimicking his coffee sipping expression.

"What do you think went on last night?"

"I think I'm going crazy because of this assignment. It's so convoluted and complex, I don't know if there will ever be a resolution for anyone, especially Rachel and me. I don't think we were ready for something like this. You and Sandy may have underestimated the complexity of the whole Frank and Linda thing. That's what I think. Last night, well, last night was flat out weird. So weird in fact, I don't . . ." "What did I tell you before you went to bed?" Arthur's voice again echoed in her in head. "You said not to worry. Well, I am worried and not about Frank and Linda either. I'm worried about Rachel and my future as . . . well, as Angels. We're not doing so good right now. I think I can speak for my sister. If what happened last night was real, then Rachel has headed the wrong direction. She scared the crap out of me last night. I can't imagine how afraid Frank was." Arthur held up his hand for her to stop her ranting.

"I did say not to worry, and I also said that a big problem would be gone in the morning, or at least on its way out. Try a little harder not to doubt yourself and your capabilities, Claire. I have the utmost faith in you and so does Sandy. We were watching it all play-out and neither Frank nor Rachel were ever in any danger. I think he needed what Rachel did for him, a shock to dispel his anger – his choice, you know. Meeting his grandfather was his idea, his desire. Sandy just made it easier for them. It would have happened eventually because it's what they both wanted to have happen. Merrick got his healing because his son, Adam, prayed for him on and off through the years, even though he never lost his anger towards him."

Arthur gathered up her hand and patted it softly, his eyes dancing with delight at his charges' accomplishments. She was resisting giving in to his Angelic smile, still a little mad at his and Sandy's tactics, and lack of compassion for her and her sister. But who was she to doubt the pros? Sandy and Arthur had been at this for a long time, so they must know what they're doing. "Do you? Do you know how everything is to be?" Her defiant eyes conveying her fiery disposition and her need for certainty.

"Of course not. You know that's not the case. Perhaps we should finish this later. There are others involved who have questions too." Arthur nodded towards Rachel standing in the kitchen archway. "Good morning Rachel."

Her sister's wet and red eyes spoke worlds to Claire about last night's drama. It was all true because here was her sister, clearly shaken, by seeking retribution through her actions last night. Claire went straight into her arms, drawing her into a tight embrace, and took on all the wild feelings inside of her sister; drinking them in like there was no other way to deal with them. She collided with the horror of Rachel's revenge on Frank and was once again, choking on the memory of the fall and the evil sedition she witnessed in her sister's face. She squeezed her so tight that Rachel beat on her back with her fists, gasping for breath when Claire finally let her go. There was nothing in the Angel training manual about this, she bet. Rachel's terror lingered on from the place she'd dragged Frank, and it wasn't getting any better. She stood face to face with her sister, with all the despair within the dream, smothering her all over again. Was this to be their reality for the rest of their lives? Forever crossing back and forth between the need to do good and the incessant draw of evil? Claire grabbed her sister with such force, the breath went out from them both. She didn't know what else to do. Claire was hopelessly lost in her sister's need for closeness; the haunting memory of their centuries of separation filling them both with the desperate need to make this work, to do what was required of them.

"I'm sorry," Rachel, sobbed.

"So am I," Claire whispered. "So am I."

"Ahem," Arthur cleared his throat. "We have a guest."

Frank was shuffling towards the stairs. She drew back from Rachel and wiped her face with her sleeve. Arthur handed them both a couple of napkins to do the job right. She giggled as she blew her nose, making a loud funny sound that could only be made this way. Her sister's eyes were squinting above the napkin she held to her face. Arthur laughed and handed them a wad of napkins, taking the wet ones and throwing them away.

"Breakfast anyone?" He said opening the fridge. "How about pancakes. I'm sure Frank would like some pancakes. Bring yourselves in here and we'll make them together."

Frank had gone upstairs to shower, so by the time he came down, they had a plate full of pancakes, and had set an extra place at the kitchen counter, grabbing a spare stool from the garage storage closet.

"Good morning Frank," Arthur said. "Hungry?"

Frank was halfway in kitchen, when he stopped, and seemed to be surveying the situation. He looked unsure of himself, not something he was accustomed to feeling. Claire slid off her stool and walked over to him. She took his hand and led him to the counter, pulling his stool away from it for him to sit. "Good morning Frank. It's okay, we don't bite – very hard." She stifled a giggle, not wanting to intimidate him any more than he already was. He sat down, his eyes darting from counter top to each of them and back down again. If she didn't know better, she'd have to say that he remembered some of what had happened in his dreams. It was obviously way out of the ordinary for him. "Syrup and butter?" She said sliding them over to him. He fixed his cakes and paused with his fork ready to cut a bite.

"I apologize for any inconvenience I caused you. Thank you for letting me stay the night."

"No need to apologize," Arthur said. "You're welcome to stay as long as you need."

Frank nodded, his eyes darting away, perhaps afraid to think his father would still be angry with him. His fork eventually found its way into his mouth and then continued cutting bites in quick succession. Maybe he didn't remember, she thought. Arthur shrugged his shoulders when she looked his way. Maybe something had stuck with him, because he seemed a changed man this morning, and he had every appearance of a scared animal, ready to bolt. Either way, Claire thought they'd succeeded.

RECONCILIATION

Reconciliation was an unfamiliar word to Frank Richards unless of course, it was to reconcile someone else to Frank's way of being, doing, and thinking. When he left their home, his belly was full, his mind was numb, and his heart was confused by the few hours he'd been with Them – the motley crew of crazy-young Angels and their mentor. Yes, Frank Richards was a man profoundly changed in ways he'd yet to fathom. Her sister had done a number on him and they were going to find out if it took, when they all met at rehearsal. Claire hoped that Linda would be able to get out of her house and attend, even if she didn't participate. Arthur had not really addressed Rachel's treatment of Frank, but he often delayed his assessments of their misguided doings, giving them time to think it through and feel their own brand of – what goes around comes around. It had worked in the past, so it was probably indicative of his intended silence this morning with Rachel. They were halfway to school before her sister said a word to her.

"You probably think I'm the evil stepsister, and maybe I am. If you're wondering what happened last night, I taunted Frank when I went to talk to him. I did everything I could to make him angry and lose his temper so I could justify what I did in return. I don't mind telling you I was scared for my life when he grabbed me by the neck, and with only one hand, he proceeded to crush my throat. For a moment, I thought I would die, but only a moment. I didn't care about anything, except my revenge for what he did to me in the hallway at school, and what he did to Linda. Last night was all about revenge, and I suppose that makes me an evil person. It's like a disease that overpowers me, consuming my every thought with its pervasive evil, and renders me helpless. I don't even know why you would still want to be my sister; we're such polar opposites, you wanting to do good, and me the anger addict. Tell me I'm wrong and I'll believe you. Tell me there's hope for me, something I so want to believe. Oh Claire, I never left the dark cavern, not really. You came for me and took me away, but it still exists in me, and controls me, never letting me stray very far from its grasp. It's like Frank's choking grasp last night, the brutality of mindless anger, raging and spewing its venom indiscriminately, blinding all those it touches. Even you were horrified in that place, I could see it in your eyes, the fear of what I'd become and could do. Claire, I'm afraid I am going to fall again. Only this time there will be no second chances, no light of day, only the stark icy chill of the beast sucking the life out of me for all eternity."

Claire was overwhelmed with her sister's anguish and her cry for help. It was as if thousand pound weights were shackled around her neck, dragging her down into the same pit that had befallen her sister in the dream, which wasn't a dream. It was the reality of her sister's past, come to life in her, and she was afraid. She backed away, slipping off the curb in front of a car that swerved and screeched to a halt, the young teenage girl's face horrified at the thought of hitting a person with her car. Claire staggered back onto the sidewalk, kneeling in the browning grass, feeling sick inside. "Arthur," she whimpered lying face down in the grass. "Please tell me I can handle this. I don't think I can, it hurts so much." She emptied her stomach in the grass, wishing she would just die here and now, and get it over with. She couldn't go on like this, being too weak to face even her own sister, let alone the likes of Frank Richards or Linda Connor.

"Are you okay?" The girl asked.

There was a great deal of fear in her voice that reached inside of Claire and began to turn her away from the path she was headed. She nodded her head weakly, spitting, and starting to cry softly.

"Claire, this is not who you are," Rachel said, kneeling beside her. "You're not me, you never were. Don't take my failings upon yourself. They're not yours, they're mine."

"Wrong on both counts," Arthur's voice said from behind them.

He helped Claire to stand and wiped her mouth, holding her by the shoulders. "You can do this," he whispered in her mind, his confident eyes softening the blow. "Believe in yourself Claire, it will be enough."

"I think she's okay," Arthur said to the young girl. "Thank you for stopping." He smiled the faintest of smiles.

The girl got back in her car and slowly drove off. Claire was very sorry she'd scared the poor girl, who'd done nothing wrong, other than being in the wrong place at the wrong time to be the recipient of someone else's grief. She looked into her mentor's eyes, thankful he'd followed them to school, probably knowing she was still vulnerable to everything that happened the night before. He was being Arthur, the ever-present, all-knowing mentor – her mentor.

"You know, my pancakes don't look so good like this." He pointed to the chunky pile of puke, laughing.

His laughter had always been contagious, and this time was no exception. She stared down at the puddle weighing heavily on the longer blades, still dripping from some. This was where she'd been ready to throw the towel in, and declare her life finished and unrewarding. She began to laugh hysterically, doubling over and unable to stop. Her sister wasn't fairing much better, her arm across Claire's back, laughing just as hard beside her.

"You know, some dog's going to thank their lucky stars they happened upon this treat." Arthur howled like a dog and then laughed equally as hard. "You should get going or you'll be late to class."

Claire wiped the tears from her eyes and nodded, not yet able to speak. She and her sister were walking away, doing their best to end the calliope of sounds their laughter produced. She resisted looking back at Arthur and the whole scene she'd created, knowing she'd begin laughing hysterically again. With their arms around each other, they finished the walk to school, arriving just as the bell for first period sounded. Arthur's cure had worked its magic, as always. She completely ignored Frank in English class, surprised to see him there after what he'd been through last night. She'd deal with his presence later in the day.

Meeting Rachel for lunch turned out to be interesting enough, as she was sitting with Liz and Evan, who played William and Catherine Coleman. Sitting down, she eyed her sister, wondering who sat with whom. She wasn't up for any more drama, at least not until rehearsal, when it might become necessary. "Hi Liz, Evan," she said. "What a pleasant surprise. How are you guys doing?"

"We're good," Liz responded. "We were talking about our character's family problems in the musical, saying they posed an interesting dilemma, one which we all probably have faced at home with our parents."

"Part of growing up," Evan said. "I never had troubles like my character though. My parents are mindful of my need to learn from my mistakes, unlike our parents in the musical."

"What do you think Claire?" Liz asked.

"I'm not sure it applies to me and Rachel. You see, our parents divorced when we were quite young, and our mother's both died in a car accident together, six months ago. That's why we're living with our uncle Arthur, who was awarded guardianship of us by the courts in California." Claire dropped the bomb and waited to see what came of it.

"I'm sorry," Liz said. "That's a terrible . . ." She stopped.

"We're very sorry for your loss," Evan said in a hushed tone. "It must be hard on you both."

"Yes, but Arthur's been great, very understanding, and forgiving, allowing us room too. . ." Now it was Claire's turn to stop herself before she said something she couldn't take back. "Thank you."

"Yes, thank you for caring about us," Rachel said swing her leg over the bench seat. "Sorry, I've got to be early to my next class."

Abandoned by her sister, Claire sat eating her lunch in silence, not daring to start up another conversation she'd probably not want to finish. Liz and Evan excused themselves when they'd finished and left her alone, which was fine with her. She had way too much baggage from last night and this morning, all threatening to pop up and make a scene.

Claire looked forward to rehearsal all day, hoping it would be the one place where she could enjoy herself. And even though she didn't feel at all well today, she still felt as though it would help lift her spirits; like Arthur had this morning, saving her from herself and her dark thoughts of failure. Frank was subdued in Theater class, neither engaging in class discussion nor paying her and Rachel the courtesy of a nod or greeting, which was okay with her. She and Rachel stood in the wings waiting for rehearsal to begin, both tired, but willing. Ms. Newman drifted in a few minutes late with Linda, whom she'd given a ride to rehearsal since her mother was teaching.

"Your attention, please. Linda is feeling well enough to follow along from the front row, but won't be speaking any lines today.

She says she is doing better and will be back on Monday ready to rehearse again. We'll keep it simple today, going over orchestra and choir cues, so we don't forget their importance with transitions and the songs. The remainder of the time will be spent on solos, duets, and the closing song with the full cast, and choir."

It was good to see Linda. She was a real trooper, not wanting to fall behind, no matter how she felt physically or emotionally. Claire was proud of her. And Frank, well he was the perfect pawn, moving everywhere he needed to be, paying attention, and keeping his mouth shut throughout rehearsal. She was impressed and thankful she didn't have to engage with him much at all, and even being in close proximity to him seemed safer than it had. It was slow and methodical as they walked their parts and paid attention to every cue, whether it was theirs or someone else's. Ms. Newman said it was important to know everyone's part because it would help each to fit in and know that they all were working together as a unit, and not independently from one another. It was a short rehearsal, but a good one for all, because they were all in a way, recovering from Linda's trauma two days ago.

Arthur had brought home a simple dinner of vegetable soup and fresh bread from the deli a few blocks away, and he'd baked brownies. After dinner, they sat in the living room, where Frank had slept, accosted Rachel, and been retaliated against by her, and ate the brownies.

"I have news about the Richards' family from Sandy, who looked in on them for us, so we can understand what's going on in Frank's life. Sandy said they had pulled Frank from school in the middle of the day, and Adam had cleared his appointments so they could have a family meeting about what had happened. She said it went well, and Adam actually apologized to Evelyn and to Frank for his behavior and the argument concerning his father, whose name he mentioned aloud for the first time in decades. The family secret was discussed in a quiet, non-offensive tone, lending some forgiveness to Merrick's suicide, something that had never been talked about before in the family. Frank's father didn't talk a lot about himself and the trauma that Merrick had caused in his life, but he did forgive his father for his suicide, making note of the financial difficulties his firm was having at the time. Sandy said that Frank had not said a word until the meeting was concluded and only then did he tell them about his dream of Merrick. Sandy said what happened next lit the fire of reconciliation for Frank and his father, because Adam said he had the same dream about his father the night before, waking him, and keeping him awake for half the night because it was so real. Sandy was responsible for Merrick's appearance, noting that he'd come a long way in his healing process, and wanted to somehow contact his son and his family. She accommodated his request with pleasure. That's what happened at the Richards' home today. Sandy said she needed to make this happen in order for Frank to have any chance at a life free from anger. It was her assignment, she'd said. And just so that you know," Arthur's eyes met Claire's, "there was no mention of your telling Linda about the Richard's family history."

His point hit home, warming her face. She knew he wasn't trying to make her feel guilty, only reminding her of the complexity of human affairs, and not to interfere. His words hung in the room for some time, as she and Rachel absorbed what Sandy had done for the Richards. Merrick had been freed, but so too were his descendants. "That's good to know," Claire finally said. "I don't think Rachel and I would have gotten anywhere without help from both of you. Thank you, Arthur, for this morning. I was floundering in my fears and so afraid for what could befall Rachel. Anyway, thank you again." Rachel was crying softly as Claire spoke. Arthur comforted her as best he could, but it was up to her to deal with what she'd set in motion for herself.

Arthur had always been very clear about the duty every Angel assumes. Self Determination was tantamount to an Angel's life of selfless giving to the humans of this world and in their afterlife, wherever it took them.

"Rachel, you know you can always count on me to assist you, but you must choose your path, and then follow it wherever it leads. Your sister Claire is there with you every step along the way. So, never think that you are alone." Arthur jostled her shoulders with the arm he had around her.

Rachel nodded, wiping her tears away. It truly hurt Claire that her sister was in so much pain, but she needed to break free from her past, in order to move on with her life. Claire wiped her own tears away, feeling the heavy burden on her sister. Rachel's moment of weakness in her revenge on Frank had cost her dearly and still threatened to drag her back into her past and Claire along with her because they were bound together in their love as sister's forever.

DRESS REHEARSAL

To clear the air the next day, Claire had taken time for herself to get her head screwed on right. If she was ever to be of any assistance to her sister, she needed to first address her own problems and come to grips with them. There were eight days left of rehearsals, the last three of which were full dress with orchestra and choir. There was not a lot of time left before the performance for her and her sister to practice their duets, and neither one of them was in any kind of shape emotionally to deal with some of the songs' intensity, as well as their providing pivotal changes to their characters and to the theme of the musical. She felt confident they could sing the songs together, but like Ms. Newman had told them at their audition, songs need life to be breathed into them in order for them to touch the audience, and tell their story. Claire worried she'd fail because she was exhausted and had little to give.

"Try breathing. You'll find it works wonders." Arthur's voice drifted upstairs into her room.

"Very funny. I am breathing." Claire yelled towards the open door. She knew what he meant though, with all that meditation stuff. She'd spent eighteen hundred years doing it, and what good had it done her? She knew he was listening to her dribble; he always did when his charges were having a difficult time adjusting. "Adjusting to what?" She murmured. "To myself? Well, there's one for the books, eh Arthur: Angel Can't Adjust to Life as an

Angel, Calls it Quits." She could almost hear him chuckling downstairs, not even bothering to hold it in. "Am I that funny?"

"Sometimes." He said walking in. "You might as well get used to it because it's not going away until you say it is."

"Oh hey, thanks for the help. What, did they send you to the University of Angelic Humor for your degree?" Claire was pouting now, feeling singled out by her mentor.

"You're quick Claire. that's part of what I like about you. Now, if you're quite done, let me show you something." He sat next to her on the bed. "Close your eyes and think about the thing you like best about this place and your assignment. Don't try too hard, just let it come to you. And breathe so I can hear you."

Claire tried to follow his instructions, but was trying way to hard to figure out what she liked best – and nothing was coming to mind. Arthur climbed around behind her and started to massage her shoulder and neck. "Ouch. Not so hard." She winced at the pain and tightness stored in her muscles.

"Breathe deeper when there's pain. It'll pass."

She complied with her mentor's directive, and as she did so, her mind came into focus. "Singing. I like singing with Rachel. That's what I like best about this place. It's a wonderful feeling to sing when you have a physical body; it resonates and responds with a rush of . . . ." She couldn't remember the last time she sang aloud. Was it really eighteen hundred years ago in France? "Good call," Arthur said quietly in her thoughts. He sat beside her and took her hand in his. "Now come with me to a very special place in my memories." As he said the words in her mind, she was drawn into his memory of France, when she was brand new to being an Angel, and living in a physical body. "This is your memory too, Claire, and that was your name at the time as well." She was flooded with memories of her life in the south of France when she sang wherever she went, but she had a special song for her teacher.

Angel Bright on starry night
Shine your light with all your might
For all to see and me to follow
Angel Bright on starry night.

"Arthur!" She opened her eyes to look at her beloved mentor from France. "I remember now. I always loved to sing, and I used to sing with another girl from a neighboring farm. That was Rachel wasn't it." Her eye caught Rachel standing in the doorway.

"I remember the song too. We sang it together a lot, but there's more to it. Do you remember?" Rachel came in and sat on the bed beside her sister.

"I don't remember, but we could figure it out between the two of us, I'm sure." Arthur patted both their knees and got up to leave, his work being done. "Thank you, Arthur. You always were the best teacher."

"As in, your only teacher." He said from the hallway. "This is only our second time together you know."

"Right. I'm still the same old rookie aren't I?"

"I wouldn't say that." His voice carried from the stair landing.

"Rachel. I know how we can fix all of our problems. We have twelve days before the performance and only eight more rehearsals, including the three dress rehearsals. If we sing together every day, I think we can eliminate our difficulties adjusting to this life. What do you think?"

"I think Arthur's been messing with your head. That's what I think. But yeah, it's a good idea. It certainly couldn't hurt anything to give it a try. Besides, we've got a few rough spots in our duets, last time I noticed."

"Atta girl," came rolling up the staircase.

"Thanks, Arthur," they said together.

Rachel returned to her room, leaving Claire alone to continue her train of thought on her problem of giving away the control

259

her own life. It was the same old problem she'd carried around since the incident in the south of France on her first, and only other excursion into the human world. She'd run away after breaking the Angelic Rule on non-interference with the outcome of a human life, something reserved for the individual and definitely not some rookie Angel on her first assignment. Altering a person's life was not in their best interest. "Or something like that," she mumbled to the walls. She waited for Arthur to chime-in with his short one-liner, but he didn't. She lay back on her bed and stared at the ceiling as if there would be some revelatory script scrawled there, which of course there wasn't.

"Arthur," she said aloud. "If I'm so good at thinking I'm always doing something wrong, then how am I ever going to break away from this prison? I mean, I've spent over eighteen hundred years locked in a mindset, and now all of a sudden, you all think I can just break the mold and live happily ever after. Where's the logic in that?"

"Pigs wallow and angels fly. Now if you'd like to give pig wings, then go right ahead." He said loud and clear.

"Oh, now there's a great metaphor," she chuckled to herself. But he was right. She was giving wings to her long-standing belief she was destined to, forever fail. After all, that's just what she'd done in her little world; wallowed in self-pity for all those centuries. A distant thunder came rolling up the staircase and into her room with her answer.

"Oh yeah. Practice makes perfect."

"But, I don't understand why." She blinked as a light went off in her head. The word, guilt, rang in her ears. She'd thrown her life away, simply because she'd felt guilty of breaking the rules on her first assignment, and had banished herself to the hinterlands to wallow in her mistaken beliefs. She'd punished herself, and done a great job of it, all eighteen centuries worth.

"The Richards family did the same thing because of Merrick's suicide. They passed along the stigma of guilt to the next generation, thus burying the family in regrets and anger of something they'd had no part in. Perhaps now, you see the wisdom of yours and Rachel's assignment – kind of a group project – Angels and humans with the same problems. Interesting, eh?"

Arthur's kind voice reverberated in her head. It was so simple, but so hard. "So, does that mean I'm cured?" The long silence that ensued was answer enough for her. He was allowing her the freedom to choose. "Guess I'm in for the long haul; no free lunches." Again, a rolling thunder arrived from downstairs.

"Practice makes perfect."

"Thanks for the sound effects." She hollered in her thoughts. In the meantime, there was a musical to get ready for, songs to work the kinks out of, and lines of dialogue that needed her attention, not to mention her assignment with Frank and Linda. "Thanks, Arthur. I feel better."

****

The next week was an intensive study on her part, and her sister, of the songs they'd be performing and their meaning both to her and to the musical. She and Rachel both struggled with maintaining the intensity of emotion the songs required, but with each day, they found the added strength they needed, and the songs took on a greater depth than previously sung. Rehearsals became the proving ground for them to conquer their faults, and taken aside, Frank and Linda received valuable insights from the two Angels playing angels in the musical.

On Monday of the following week, Ms. Newman had the cast and crew meet in the orchestra rehearsal room that surrounded the backstage area, introducing them to each other, and saying how proud she was of their efforts to make this musical the best they'd ever produced at the school. Ms. Newman stayed to conduct the orchestra, while Mr. Clark would direct the cast. On their way back to the stage, Claire saw Jeff from her English class, seated at the mixing boards for the orchestra and choir microphones. He had a monitor linked to the Director's board and a headset to stay in constant contact with Ms. Newman during the performance.

"Hi, Jeff."

"Claire? I didn't know you were in the musical. This is great. I'll be able to see you on this monitor for the entire show."

Jeff pushed a toggle switch and the stage came up on the monitor. "How do you keep track of all these settings? There's so many."

"Most are presets, but you get used to it after years of practice. The school just purchased the board and a dozen new microphones and eight wireless headset mics for soloists last year, oh, and great software to run everything automatically, even the lighting, but it's controlled on the Director's board." Jeff said.

He fingered another switch and the Director's board showed on the monitor. He toggled two more, and the monitor had a split screen of both.

"If you look up, you'll see two ready-lights, to give the orchestra and choir fifteen seconds advance notice."

"Thanks, Jeff. Sorry I can't stay longer." Claire turned and followed behind the last of the crew headed to the stage.

Until now, she'd never realized how many students were involved in the production. There were only six cast members, not including the dog, but there were forty-seven members of the orchestra, and twenty-three in the choir, not to mention the fifteen in the crew. It added up to ninety-one students Ms. Newman and Mr. Clark had to coordinate, which was a lot. She caught up to Rachel, who was waiting for her on the lift. She was all ready to be lifted into heaven.

"I stopped to talk with Jeff, who's running the mixing board for the sound system." She ducked under the shoulder harness of her wings, buckling her safety belt on and hooking on next to Rachel's clip. Rachel handed her a headset, which she threaded through her hair and around her ear, clipping the battery pack onto the back of her costume. Mr. Clark was at the Director's board fiddling with the laptop computer on the opposite side of the stage from them. She waved they were ready, but not before the lift operator checked their harnesses and lanyards, and gave him the thumbs-up. Every crewmember had a headset on to get directions from Mr. Clark, but they also used hand signals as a backup. Claire was beginning to see just how complex a production was, and once the show started, everything had to go like clockwork, in order for the illusion of the story to remain intact for the audience. As the lift engaged, she recognized that life was like that too, a theater of billions working together for the common cause of the species, which was but one of billions in the vastness of Life. "What a nightmare," she let slip, wondering how anyone could keep track of it all.

"What's a nightmare?" Rachel gave her sister a puzzled look.

"Nothing. Just thinking aloud."

The lift stopped at nine feet above the stage floor, where the musical would begin with the opening theme and choir, and then their duet, What Will I Be. All the practice the week before paid off in the first of several duets. Their voices melded together perfectly to create the mood for the scene in the alleyway. They got their angelic directions from the Higher Ups before they descended, and halfway down, she caught a glimpse of Frank and Linda waiting in the wings, their arms around each other's backs, looking better than she'd ever seen them. She forgot she was attached to the railing and was jerked backwards when she tried to step off the platform. Rachel giggled at her as she unhooked her lanyard and helped her take off the safety belt.

"We got the songs down pat . . ." Leaving a pregnant pause. "But the rest is up for grabs."

Claire made a face at her and followed her to the fence in the alleyway, where they'd huddle together in the snow.

"Remember you've got your headset on please. Everything you say gets amplified." Mr. Clark said from his place at the Director's board, just behind the proscenium.

"Sorry," they both waved. He frowned, tapping the side of his lips to remind them again. Claire shrugged her shoulders, feeling self-conscious about screwing up twice already. Mr. Clark pushed up both sides of his mouth in a smile sign to them. "It's a good thing we have two more of these dress rehearsals to get things right." She said in her thoughts to her sister. "Yeah, I bet we could crack an ill-timed joke and get a rise from the audience with these things." Rachel giggled in her head.

As it went, she only messed up a few more times in the first Act, which she didn't feel as bad about as the first two. She became a little more conscious of everything going on around her, something that hadn't really sunk-in during regular rehearsals, because they hadn't used headsets, or rehearsed with the orchestra and choir. Mr. Clark was patient with them, knowing that this was their first time on stage, patting her back in reassurance, and telling her they'd get the hang of it by the end of the second dress rehearsal.

After rehearsal was over, she asked to hear two of their duets from the recordings Jeff had made. Mr. Clark took them to the orchestra rehearsal room and asked Jeff to stay a little late to accommodate her request. Jeff gave them both a set of noise-canceling headphones and spent some time looking for their songs on the recording.

"If you would have told me you wanted to listen to your songs, I would have made a note of their placement on the recording. I'll do it in tomorrow's rehearsal. We will be recording the performance for anyone who wants to buy it, in case you're interested." Jeff said.

They listened to their duets and made some notes of things needing attention for tomorrow's rehearsal, small things, but important for conveying the right feeling to the lyrics. They stayed for thirty minutes, thanked Jeff, and left feeling good about their performance overall.

The next day's rehearsal went well, with cast and crew more relaxed and attentive to details, like Mr. Clark had said, except for Claire. She was obsessing over details. That night, she tossed and turned much of the night, dreaming about every detail straight through until dawn, waking exhausted, and worried she'd forget something in the performance.

All through the final dress rehearsal, she was so nervous and thought she was continuously messing up when in reality, everything was fine. She never made one mistake, but it didn't feel that way inside of her. The butterflies had turned into Pterodactyls, threatening to carry her away. Rachel said she was being overly active with her negative premonitions, and she should enjoy their time together because the performance was only for one night. Claire agreed, but it didn't change how she felt, not even at the end of rehearsal when Ms. Newman and Mr. Clark congratulated them all and said to get a good night's sleep. "As if that were possible," she mumbled.

BREAKFAST WITH ARTHUR

Claire dreamed she was holding the hands of two angels who carried her away from the human world, turning to look back at the blue planet where she'd lived. "It is beautiful isn't it?" one of them said in her mind. "Do you think you'll miss living among them?"

"Oh yes," she said, her words filled with emotion. "I will miss them more than I care to think."

"Then you should stay, if that's what you really want." The Angels said.

They stopped their ascent, hovering far above the place she'd come to love. "My sister's down there and I don't want to leave her alone, nor do I want to live apart from her." Claire's words sounded final to her. She was refusing to live apart from Rachel. The two female angels turned to face her, enfolding her in their wings.

"Then it shall be as you say." They said in unison.

A rush of panic hit Claire as the two angels let go of her hands, and she began to fall back towards the blue planet below. She was an angel too but had no wings with which to fly. "I am an angel," she yelled watching them get smaller and smaller above her. She fell straight into her body on the bed in Arthur's home, gasping for breath and opening her eyes. It was dark in her room in the early dawn hours and she'd just had a dream, nothing more, so she told herself. But why were they taking me away and where were my wings? "Silly dream," she murmured pulling the pillow over her head.

"Claire, wake up. Claire." Rachel shook her.

"Hmm." She rolled over to face her sister who looked panicked. "What?"

"I just woke from a horrible dream. You left me behind. And I was falling back into the dark cavern." Rachel sat on the edge of the bed.

"It was only a dream Rachel. You're here with me, aren't you? I had a weird dream too. Two angels were taking me away and I didn't have my wings. I said I wouldn't leave you and they let me fall back into bed. Maybe we're nervous about tonight." Claire sat up, seeing there was daylight out the window. "Is it time to get up?" She yawned loudly.

"No. You don't understand. It was real. I could smell the dank putrid decay of the cavern. I could taste the death that lay in wait for me there. It was real Claire, just as real as me sitting here next to you."

"But you're here now. Doesn't that mean it was only a dream?" Claire snuggled closer. "Lay with me awhile. We're together and nothing can ever separate us again." She whispered beside her sister's ear. Reality was slowly waking her up with the aroma of Arthur's morning coffee wafting into her room. "We have a big day ahead of us. Maybe today will be the completion of our assignment." She didn't have a clue as to how it was going to end, never having completed one before. She rolled to the opposite side of the bed to get up. "Wake up sleepy head." She looked down at the curled up form of Rachel in her pajamas. She walked around the end of the bed, leaned in close to her, and whispered in her ear. "Possum," she breathed heavily on her. Rachel smiled and grabbed her, pulling her back into bed on top of her, tickling her under her arms. Claire thrashed about and flipped over to return the tickle, making her squeal. They both giggled racing to get to the shower first.

"Morning Arthur," Claire walked in and sat down at the counter. In front of her was a stack of pancakes between two plates, waiting for someone to be first to dive in. Rachel sat beside her, grabbing her arm to get the first one. She didn't fight it, having beaten her to the shower.

"Well, you two are in good spirits this fine morning." Arthur laughed. "Today's the big day. Only twelve hours until show time."

They nodded while wrestling with the syrup bottle.

"It's great to be so young and carefree, isn't it? Why, I remember when I was your age or a little older. . ." He paused.

"What? What are you trying to tell us, Arthur," Claire said with her fork halfway to her mouth.

"Just that you should take note to remember this morning. Being on assignment is special because you get to live in a physical body. And in the morning, you can wake up from a bad dream and know it was only a dream, and that you have a day to greet, and things to do in the world."

Arthur raised an eyebrow, expecting a response. So Claire swallowed and in all seriousness, said what she was thinking. "Both of us had a bad dream this morning. Rachel was falling back into the cavern, and I was without wings and was taken away by two angels, who let me fall back into my body when I refused to go without my sister. What does it have to do with your comment?" Arthur smiled his wispy smile.

"Wasn't it great to be able to wake up and come downstairs and eat pancakes? A month ago, that wasn't the case. While you're here on assignment, you get to live in three states: your Angel Self, your physical body, and your dreams. Before, you were trapped inside the worlds you'd created for yourselves. You are together again after all those years, so it's only natural while in this body, to be afraid of losing that closeness. Use those feelings to help you understand how humans feel about life. It's very fragile and under constant assault by outside forces. So, what is the answer to this puzzle? How can you help those in need?"

They shared puzzled looks of the paradox he'd posed, taking a moment to ponder his meaning. "Think like an Angel, while living in the physical body?" They both responded. Arthur's warm smile covered them with light, pausing the morning like in a painting, which captured its essence for all time.

"There you have it," he said. "Spoken like the old souls you are. Now, let's eat these cakes before they get cold."

Arthur sat down and forked one onto his plate, slathering on butter and drenching it with syrup, like he'd never had a pancake for breakfast before – sheer excitement. He always had a funny way of saying things they needed to know before they're actually needed. So she took it as an omen for the day.

Whatever nervousness she had the day before was gone, and in its place was the clarity of a life well lived, and the welcomed sight of her first assignment coming to a close – all thanks to Arthur. Walking into English class, her feet barely touched the floor, and somehow the room seemed brighter and the students more attentive and ready for an enlightening lesson. Even Frank had the same look about him, the look of a hard-earned closure. He'd met his grandfather, made peace with his father, and didn't have to be a father himself just yet. And like her, he was just hours away from an opening night of the very thing he and Linda loved to do. Did it get any better? Jeff handed her a disk in an envelope as she passed by him.

"Rehearsal duets," he said smiling.

"Thank you," she returned the smile and sat at her desk, looking forward to every minute of this day, something that had not happened very much in her life. Ms. Letrell began by introducing the members of the cast, having Frank, Jeff and herself stand up. She said the auditorium seating was already full and the gymnasium was being set up for the overflow with several seventy-inch screens and a sound system.

Claire got so excited, the classroom all but disappeared. She was on stage singing with her sister, totally immersed in the music and the impending completion of her assignment. She'd not heard one word of the lesson.

"Claire. Claire Tate. Class is over now." Ms. Letrell said.

She reentered the classroom, her head still hearing the music. "Yeah. Sorry." Claire fumbled with her backpack, trying to put her English book into it.

"Claire. You were far away during class. Where were you?"

"Oh. Sorry. I was on stage singing." She mumbled as she passed by her teacher.

"Good luck tonight. I'll be there."

"Thank you." She stopped in the doorway, trying to remember where her next class was, shaking the cobwebs from her head.

Mostly, it didn't take. She arrived at lunch, with her tray, standing and staring blankly out into the atrium, looking for her sister. She walked to the middle of the room, slowly turning until she saw Rachel seated with Frank and Linda at the far end of the atrium. She joined them, sliding in next to her sister, rubbing shoulders with Linda, in the next to non-existent space. "Sorry," she said nestling in, and having to set her tray in the middle of the round table, and take her lunch items off one by one.

"Why are you so late?" Rachel asked, trying to scoot over a little for her.

"I got lost," Claire whispered.

"Really? You've been this way all morning?"

"Yeah. Pretty much." Claire looked around the table at Linda and Frank's friends, three of whom she recognized from the orchestra and choir members in dress rehearsal. She smiled as their eyes met. She opened her yogurt cup and ate only a few spoonful's of it and the fruit cup, not feeling hungry at all. Arthur's pancakes had filled her up at breakfast.

"Thank you for all that you did for me," Linda whispered.

It seemed such a long time ago she'd been at Linda's house, almost forgetting it had even happened. She turned to face her, nearly rubbing noses. "You're welcome," Claire said, feeling kinda funny in her tummy – like butterflies. There was something between them. Claire couldn't quite put her finger on, but whatever it was, it made them both comfortable with each other, even in these close quarters. She couldn't eat anymore, so she cleared her tray and went to class early.

Lu was waiting for her and leaning on the lab table, only half seated on her stool in anticipation of Claire's arrival. She pulled her stool back and sat down, expecting some new tidbit of gossip from the 'Gossip Queen' of the school.

"Why didn't you tell me you were in the production? I just found out today."

Lu draped herself half on the table and half hovering in Claire's space. "Sorry. I thought you knew. Rachel and I got the parts only because the other two girls were going to be out of town on performance night. It was a last minute thing."

"Yeah, well I heard you can sing circles around them. I'll be there to find out."

"That's nice." Claire turned away watching the clock count down to the bell. "Glad you're coming." It must be hard for Lu, she thought. She's always looking outside of herself, needing to know every little thing about everyone else, never about herself. There must be a reason, but it wasn't her place to know, privacy rules and all. The bell sounded and Mr. Boswell launched into the day's lesson. She was promptly back on stage, dabbling in the details.

Mr. Clark said he'd be brief and dismiss the class early because of the performance. Class was more of a pep talk than a lesson. She thought he looked nervous in anticipation of his co-written and produced musical. He'd never made light of his participation in the creation of it, instead, delivering helpful working points about musical productions to the class. She wondered how it would work out for him and Ms. Newman. Would they get together anytime soon? Before she knew it, he was standing between her and Rachel, after he'd dismissed the class.

"Claire. Are you nervous? You seemed far away during class." His hands leaned on her and Rachel's desks.

"She's been like this all day," Rachel said.

"Perfectly normal to have pre-show jitters." He said. "You'll do fine. Not to worry."

"Thanks. I know we will."

"Well, I'll see you tonight, 6 p.m. Curtain's at 7 p.m."

DO IT FOR LOVE

Arthur was waiting for them by the front door when they walked in, with a hot pizza box perched at the end of his fingertips, and above his shoulder. By all accounts, she thought he was a mind reader because she and her sister had talked of pizza on the way home as they passed a local gourmet pizzeria a block and a half away, with its aroma littering the streets. With a smile on his face, and the wink of his eye, she knew the truth of the matter, he was all-knowing, all-powerful, and all the other stuff an Angel's mentor should be.

"Arthur, you are shameless, reading our minds and delivering such a needed treat, and with such grace." She followed him to the dining room wondering if he'd put the idea of pizza into their heads because he'd already bought it, or had he really read their minds long before they passed the pizzeria. He gave her his stoic smile of, "It's a mystery."

"One rule, if you please. Just one piece before your performance tonight. I wouldn't want to be the cause of an overfull belly, leaving no room for the diaphragm to belt out those songs."

He was right of course. She and Rachel would have gorged themselves, not thinking of the consequences. She really hadn't eaten since breakfast, so she was famished, and took the biggest piece she could find, leaving the second largest for Rachel. Arthur took two, closed the box, and put it in the fridge, so they didn't have to look at it and automatically reach for another piece.

"I am so proud of you two. This was a difficult assignment, even for a veteran in the field, and you both did admirably well. Even Sandy said so. Tonight is your night to shine and do the thing you love the most. Let the music carry you away in its arms and sing within your heart. Ms. Newman and Mr. Clark both have told me that your voices make their hearts sing with joy. Remember, what happens on stage tonight is as real as it gets; let it be magical for all you – all ninety-one of you." Arthur kissed the top of their heads as he cleared the plates.

She and Rachel went to her bedroom and lay down together before they had to shower, fix their hair and leave. Arthur was humming some of the songs from the musical as they fell asleep. He woke them a short while later to get ready.

Arthur dropped them at the Auditorium and parked, just before 6 p.m. They went directly to the dressing rooms with the other cast members to get ready for first Act. They listened to the orchestra members tuning up and warming up the choir. Ms. Newman came in to wish them luck and tell them they had fifteen minutes until the curtain went up. They stopped by her station to get their headsets and check in with Jeff at the sound mixing board for a test of their wireless mics. He wouldn't activate their mics and its feed into the auditorium's sound system until just before the curtain went up. She and Rachel assumed their places on the platform, being helped into their winged costumes and harnesses by a crewmember. Two minutes before the orchestra began the opening music, they were lifted into position, and their mics were activated. "Are you nervous," she said in her thoughts. "A little," Rachel replied. "Me too." And the opening music began.

Act I

Claire's heart pounded in her chest when Arthur's song, Do It For Love, began to play. She'd forgotten it was the opening music. "Apparently you were asleep during the last dress rehearsal," Rachel chuckled in her thoughts. "Is this how it's going to be? A running commentary throughout?" Her sister sighed into her mic, and even though the people on stage couldn't hear the auditorium's sound system, she knew her sigh had been heard by all. Claire almost shushed her. The choir introduced the Voices of their Angels in charge with a melodic serenade, rising and falling to emphasize keywords:

(stage dark except the heavens' soft glow silhouetting the angels on the raised platform)

Heavenly voices
We are aware this is your first time
and have made allowances for that.
Please adhere to the Angelic Rules
and this will be a joyful experience for all.
Remember, if you need help with anything at all
we are here to listen and advise whenever you call.
So go forth and enjoy your first assignment on Earth

Claire was sure that Rachel was about to burst out laughing at their marching orders. Arthur must have written them as a comic send off into the grips of the physical realm. But, they had to sing now, so the both composed themselves and focused on their opening song.

What Will I Be
(Choir voices rise with orchestra at song introduction)
Could it be
that you and me
will forget how to fly.
Here we go

ready to hit the ground at a run.
But what will happen to us
What if we fail and never return
Will we be stuck here forever
Locked in time and have to live
out our lives always in need of a lift.
Look where they've sent us
out into the cold half frozen to the ground.
Ohoooh, I don't feel so good
I'm ready to go back and hideout
in my little corner of the Angel's Realm.
What will we be.....

The platform touched down and the projected angelic realm on the scrim curtain faded, leaving them in the dark, and able to slip out of their harness and costume. They already had on their tattered clothing for the alleyway scene, as they walked to center stage and sat down leaning against the fence, fluffing up some of the snowflakes on themselves, and sang their duet, Alone Together, before the streetlight brightened. "That went well," she whispered to Rachel. She was shushed by her sister, reminding her their mics were live.

Frank and Linda entered from the wings with Angel the dog, ready to begin the alley scene. Claire hunkered down, leaning against Rachel, with their tattered hoods falling over their faces. She listened to Frank and Linda's dialogue as they approached. She took a deep breath, carefully letting it out silently and out the side of her mouth, away from the mic. Claire saw the dog first. It was sniffing at the fence like it was ready to raise a leg. Rachel's body was shaking, trying to smother the ensuing laughter poised on her face. It was everything she could do to contain her own laughter at the sight. Angel cooperated and veered away from doing his deed, relieving everyone on and off stage.

Billy
"Maybe they're dead."
Kathy
"God Billy! She's as cold as ice. What are we going to do?"

****

While they were being helped into Billy's and Kathy's home, Claire thought it best to stop the inner dialogue with her sister, because she'd almost slipped up twice now, and it was just a matter of time before she blurted some dribble into her mic. "You got that right sis," Rachel agreed in her thoughts. They both took a deep breath and waited for their next cue.

****

(In the Coleman kitchen just before dinner)
Catherine
"Oh my God in heaven, William. They're half
frozen to death. Help me get these rags off of them.
Get the comforters and quilt from the den."
(Mary and Nancy's outer clothing is removed
and they are wrapped in the quilt and comforter.)
Kathy
"I'll make some tea."
Catherine
"Load it with sugar. They're starving."
William
"Maybe I should call the police and let them
take care of all this."
Catherine
"You'll do no such thing. We can take better care
of them here. Now make yourself useful and rub their
shoulders to help warm them."

277

(She motions with her hand, frowning at her husband)

Kathy

"Do you think they'll be alright? I mean
they're cold as ice and look at their eyes.
They don't look right, kinda empty, like they're not here."
(William doesn't do as his wife says, motioning to his son
to follow him into the other room to talk)

William

"You know son, if they die, we'll be responsible for them,
and could go to court if they have a family that gets
angry at us. I think we should
call the police and get them out of here."

Billy

"I think so too Dad. They're just two homeless bums.
Why should we take responsibility for them?"
(William gets the phone from his pocket and is ready to dial
when his wife sees him and waves him back into the kitchen)

Catherine

"William Coleman, you cold heartless man. Don't you dare call
the police. Now, you get our son in here and help us."
(Catherine grabs the phone from his hand and
shoves it in her pocket, eying her husband,
and her son who followed his dad to the kitchen)

Kathy

"We don't need your help." (She pushes her brother aside)
"You wanted to leave them in the alley to freeze anyway."
(Mary and Nancy are jostled by the men fighting
with the women in the household, not a
new occurrence to the Coleman family)

William

"Well, if that's the way you feel, then Billy
and I will go out to eat."

Billy
"Yeah, sis. Who do you think you are?"
(He pushes her into their chairs)

Catherine
"Stop this right now. I won't have you two behaving like this
in my house." (She grabs her son's arm and tries to stop him)

William
"Your house? Who do you think pays the bills around here?
Not you, that's for sure. You just spend my hard-earned money
on stuff we don't even need. You started doing that
right after we got married. Sometimes I think
you're trying to put us in the poorhouse, like them."
(He points to Mary and Nancy
who are eating his food like animals)

Billy
(Snorts like the two pigs eating at his table, elbowing his sister)
"Remind you of someone Kathy?"
(He snorts again imitating he stuffing her face)

Kathy
"You asshole." (She runs off crying)

Catherine
"Leave me alone."
(She grits her teeth, leering at her husband and son)
"There, there. They won't bother us again.
Would you like some more?"
(She gives them more stew and hot rolls, and
sits down at the table)
"What happened to you? Are your parents . . ." (She stops)
"I'll take care of you." (She pours more hot water in their cups)

Kathy
(Enters kitchen blowing nose loudly and sits down)
"My brother is such an asshole."

Catherine
"I won't have that kind of talk in my house.
Would you get them some cookies."

Kathy
"Do you think they're from our town?"

Mary
(Slurps some tea and clears her throat)
"Our father beat our mom and threw her out and then us.
He was drunk.
That was three days ago and no one would take us in."

Nancy
(Wiping her mouth on her sleeve)
"Our father's a drunk and Mom's
a drug addict. Thank you for taking us in.
I don't think we would have lasted the night."
(Coughs hard almost gagging)

Catherine
"Well don't you worry. You're safe now. Let me take you to
your room. You can have a nice hot shower and Kathy will give
you some of her clothes. Don't you worry
about my husband or son. They won't bother you.
Here, take some cookies with you."
(Catherine and Kathy help them to Billy's bedroom
and return to the kitchen)

William
(Coming back into the kitchen with his son
after the women have left)
"I can't believe the nerve of those two homeless girls,
they ate my lunch for next week."

Billy
"And all the cookies are gone too."
(He shakes the empty jar and walks out with his father)

****

Claire and Rachel sat backstage listening to the Coleman family argue loudly in the kitchen. Their mics would be off for a few minutes until they become Angels again and ascend back into the heavens to talk with their superiors and ask for help with the Coleman family. What she loved about this scene was that it was all a setup for an epic battle between brother and sister, one that would last until after dinner. She thought the best part was that Frank and Linda had the chance to air their dirty laundry on stage and in front of a thousand other people. They were good at it, infectious even, stirring similar feelings in their audience to the boiling point, making some so uncomfortable they were cheered that evening – for them being such disagreeable children. It all set the tone for Act II and the opening split stage with Kathy singing about their little chat with the Higher Ups in her bedroom, and Billy from his place on a sofa in the living room, with his father snoring away on the love seat next to him. It would really shake little Billy up in the morning, not quite being able to put his finger on what had happened, but really angry about having to give up his bedroom to the two strangers, and then not sleeping much at all. His only memory of the event, his stupid dream that they were angels, would aggravate him all day. To Kathy, her dream was one in which her position on taking in the two homeless girls was vindicated, greatly buoying her up in the morning

****

(Everyone is called back into the kitchen to help cook dinner)
Catherine
"Now don't let that burn Kathy.
You have to stir it constantly."

Kathy

"You're hovering mother. I know
how to cook spaghetti sauce."
(Kathy chugs from the wine bottle when no one was looking)

Billy

(Aside to his father)
"I still think you should have called the police. I mean,
I even have to sleep on the sofa. They took my bed! "

William

"Yeah, I know. I think I'll be next to you. Your mother is
really pissed at me." (He makes a face and swears)
"Damn homeless bums."

Catherine

"I heard that. There'll be no more of that talk. Mary and Nancy
are our guests, and you will treat them as such."
(Slaps Kathy's hand as she starts to take another drink of wine)

Billy

(Cutting bread on the countertop for garlic toast)
"Yeah, maybe they'll take after my sister the alcoholic."(Laughs)

Kathy

(Throws her shoulder into him, almost making him cut
himself)
"Yeah, your girlfriend said she needed tweezers to find" . . .
(squeals)
(Runs to other side of kitchen to avoid Billy and the knife)

Mary & Nancy   (Sneak out the window, being unable to listen
to any more, and ascend to the heavens for help)

Catherine

"That'll be enough you two. Someone's going to get hurt.
Why can't we act like a normal family and like each other?"
(Everyone stops what they're doing and stares at Catherine)
(Orchestra plays opening bars to Catherine's solo)

Family Ties
Life is too short
Don't let it pass you by
Family is really all we have.
Someone to love and share
Heartache and joy
Family is the real Mc Coy.
No one can love you like family
Friends can come and go
But your family always stays
True to you and who you are
Someone to lean on in times of need.
How could you go wrong with that?
Family ties us all together
Now how can you ever beat that?
Family is really all there is
So what's so bad about that.
(Everything is peaceful for one second,
then the ruckus resumes)
Billy
(Chases sister around kitchen with knife)
William
(Arguing with wife about calling police)
Catherine
(Sits down at the table in the middle of it all)
Everyone
(Yelling incomprehensible phrases, flailing arms everywhere)
Coleman's
(In a split stage, still yelling and arguing; with Mary and Nancy
arguing in
the heavens with the Higher Ups; back and forth in quick
succession
with Rachel calling their boss a "Dumb Ass" (done with

absolute silence
on the stage) A quick crescendo of the orchestra and choir;
then dying out
slowly with a full orchestra, sfz punctuation of the final chord,
including kettle drums)

Curtain End Act I

(Children's choir enters and sings with choir & orchestra)

Claire let out a long sigh when the orchestra began playing for the children as the platform descends to the stage floor. She and Rachel ducked out from under their wings' harness and left their headsets on the Director's table, collecting a hug from Ms. Newman, along with the other cast members.

"They love it," Ms. Newman told the cast. "You're doing an excellent job, all of you. Now let's get ready for Act II."

The audience was very boisterous and easily heard from the backstage area after the intermission music had finished. Claire was so relieved she'd not made any mistakes, like she had in the south of France by rescuing the young girl from the river. It was constantly in the back of her mind, that she was prone to making errors, disastrous ones at that. "Really Claire, is this necessary?" Arthur's voice sounded in her head. "Sorry," she whispered.

"Sorry about what," Mr. Clark stepped out from the other side of a wing curtain.

Startled, Claire's eyes widened, and the tingles ran up her back. "You scared me, Mr. Clark. I was just talking to myself about not worrying, and sometimes I answer myself." She shrugged her shoulders.

"Well, I thought you and Rachel did an outstanding job." He tapped his headset. "Heard every heartfelt word. Gotta run. Enjoy the rest of the show."

"I will," he'd already turned and walked away. "Where are you, Arthur?" She asked in her thoughts.

"Right behind you," he answered.

She whirled around, startled a second time, to find him standing a foot away from her. "Did you have to sneak up on me. Mr. Clark just got through making me jump." She wrapped her arms around him giving him a bear hug. "Thanks. I needed that." Her voice muffled on his chest.

"You're welcome. I just wanted to tell you that Sandy thinks you two are doing great. Says to tell you to be on the lookout for a little surprise in Act II. Well, I'm needed back at my post. Enjoy yourself, Claire."

She didn't know what to do with herself, so she picked up her headset from the Director's table, and went to stand beside the platform to wait for her sister. She stepped onto the platform and readied herself, going over her lines and the sequence of events for Act II. Rachel joined her after a few minutes, and they were lifted into position for their return from the heavens.

Act II
Mary
(Making a commotion on the descending platform)
"Did you have to get into an argument and
call our boss a 'dumb ass'?
What are we going to do now?
We're descending back into the madness at the Coleman family
home, and we've been defrocked, decapitated,
or whatever you want to call it. We've lost our wings
and powers; we'll never be able to help them now."
Nancy
"Sorry. I couldn't help myself. At least now I can
go eat more of Catherine's cookies and not worry
about gaining weight. I just lost fifty pounds."
Duet Mary&Nancy
(Orchestra plays opening bars)

My Faith
My faith has fallen on hard times
What can I do
Alone in the darkness and frightened to the core
Would you lend a hand and lift me up
Turn on a light so I can see
***

(Choir answers back)
Rise my love and you shall see
Is not the will that restores
But Faith that opens doors
***

My heart lays heavy
Burdened by my will
Can't you see my life
Broken on the floor
***

Rise my love and you shall see
Is not the will but Faith that opens doors

Mary
(Sneaking back into bed at Coleman home)
"Shh. I don't want to wake them, it's only 4 a.m."
(Mary and Nancy fall asleep and Kathy comes into their
room to plead her case for them to help her family.
(Orchestra plays opening bars)
I Know Who You Are
Kathy's solo
You must know I believe in you
I heard you talking to the angels
As you ascended into the sky
Can you help us to live
A more useful life

I'm so tired of all the bickering and fighting
Can't you make it all go away
I believe that you can cure all of our ills
If we only believe in you
****

(Morning – family gathers in kitchen for breakfast,
Mary and Nancy enter last)

Catherine
"Today's a new day. So let's try to work
out our differences better than
we did last night. Now, who wants pancakes?"

Kathy
"I'll help Mom."

William
"I'll get the morning paper."

(Billy sets the table and sits down as Mary and Nancy come in)

Catherine
"Good morning. Did you sleep well? (They nod)
"Breakfast will be ready in a few minutes."

Mary
"Thank you, Mr. Coleman, you've been most
kind to us. But we can't stay
any longer. Mr. Coleman, we can't help what we are.
We didn't choose this
for ourselves. It was thrust unto us by
unloving parents. So, thank you for
taking us into your home and giving us shelter
and caring for us. We just can't stay."

Catherine
"They'll be no more talk of leaving. You're
welcome to stay here as long as you need to.
I've never told anyone this, but I was homeless
once a long time ago. I ran away from home and

was stuck in a strange place, with no one to help me.
I was so alone, all I did was cry, until someone cared enough
to stop and help me. So, I know how you feel.
(Orchestra plays opening bars)

Every Heart Needs A Home
Catherine's solo

When I was young and full of myself
I got angry and ran away
I'd never been so alone
And had no one to care for me
And hold me tight in their arms
Someone who loved me
Without needing anything in return
My heart had no home
And no one to love
Until my guardian angel
Came for me
And gathered me up
In her wings
She lead me to William
Who loved me at first sight
It was then that my heart had been found
Never to be lost again
(Catherine kicks her husband to sing with her)
Every heart needs a home
So tell me what I can do for you
(There's a knock at the door by the social worker that William
called yesterday, he lets her in, while Mary and Nancy overhear
and leave to hide by the platform)

Wanda

"Good Morning. My name is Wanda Loveless,
and I work for County Services.
I was called about two female homeless minors.

I have the paperwork all ready to accept them, if you'll
just sign this statement saying you found them in the
alley behind your home last night and called us. We can help
them better than anyone, with our county's new
prison facilities that have a separate wing for
the homeless and women fleeing from domestic violence.
Oh dear, I mean pristine facilities. I'm so sorry."
(In the background, the orchestra has been playing the Jaws'
movie heartbeat, softly at first, gradually gaining volume
and speed. It sends Wanda packing and leads into the
music for three songs sung with different lyrics by:
Catherine & William in the kitchen; Kathy & Billy in the living
room; and Mary & Nancy from outside)

Catherine & William sing Regrets
Where did it all go wrong
How could have we made it right
Somewhere there's got to be answers
***

Kathy & Billy sing their version
Why do they have to be so controlling
What did we ever do that was so wrong
Can't they see we want to be good
But how can we do that if we're not ourselves
***

Mary & Nancy sing What Kind of Angel Am I
How can we ever help if we can't even help ourselves
Thrown from the heavens out on our ear
Without even so much as a goodbye
Dumped on this world without our wings and no way to help
***

Catherine & William
Sometimes I still think that if we could have
The chance to do all over again we could get it right

Life doesn't come with an instruction booklet
So what chance did we ever have

***

Kathy & Billy

Every time that something goes wrong
We get the blame and it's always the same
The same old story of we're too young and they know best
So we have to wait until we move out
To make all the right moves just like them

***

Mary & Nancy

What kind of angel am I if I can't even help
Those in need who are troubled in doubt
What good am I when all alone
And you won't even help

***

(Sung by three groups: parents/children/angels – repeat order)
Give us / the room / to stretch our wings
Give us / the power / you entrusted to us
Let us / live free / to breathe in the love
Hold out / your hand / to lead us in life

***

(Sung by all)
How can we know if we don't know love
How can we live without your love
Open my heart and set my course
Take the time to give my all
Now does that sound right or wrong
Or am I off course

***

(They all look hopefully at each other and continue preparing
breakfast; eating in silence, Kathy eyes

Mary and Nancy – wants to say something,
but gets cut off by her father William)

William
"I can't believe the nerve of that county worker,
what was her name?"
(All in unison) "Wanda Loveless."
(Loudly directed at William)
William
"Calling it a prison for the homeless." (Catherine eyes him)
"Maybe you should stay with us for a while."
(He continues smiling)
Catherine
"Yes, good idea." (She slaps a pancake on his plate)
William
"I'm sorry." (He looks up at his wife and then gets up and
walks to the fridge to get a jar of jam and then faces his family)
(Orchestra plays opening bars)
What Good Am I
William sings
What good am I
Is this all I'm good for   (Holding up jar)
Surely there's more
I must be good for more
Than just this jar of jam
I love my family
More than anything else
Why can't I show it more
Here they are
Right in front of me
Waiting to hear an
I love you
Why is that so hard

What good am I
If I can't say the words
I love you all

Catherine
"We love you too." (They surround him by the
fridge as do Nancy and Mary)
Kathy
"Oh Dad, you know we do."
Billy
"Of course we do."
(Everyone is silent for a moment)
Catherine
"Let's go shopping."
Kathy
"Yeah. Dad, could I borrow some money?"
Billy
"I just got paid." (Holds up cash from his pocket)
William
"My treat today." (Cups his hands around his son's)
Mary & Nancy
"We don't need anything." (Everyone talking at once as they
rush to get ready)
Curtain
End of Act II

(Children's choir enters singing)

Claire walks into the wings and sits on a stool to listen to the children sing. All the choirs of the local grade schools and Jr Highs have been practicing for several months for their presentations between acts. Rachel stands next to her, her arm around her shoulder.

"That went well, I thought," Rachel whispers.

They lock eyes, feeling the full impact of the children's voices and the orchestra playing softly in the background. "Yes, I'd say so." Claire slips her arm around her sister's waist, pulling her close. "I'm so happy inside right now, I could burst. I can't wait to see what tomorrow will bring."

"Shh. They're almost finished." Rachel kisses her sister's head.

"Places everyone." Ms. Newman speaks in their headsets.

Act III
(Home late from shopping - after sunset)
Catherine
"That was fun. Thank you, William." (She kisses him.)
Billy & Kathy
"Yeah. Thanks, Dad." (They take their bags to William's study)
Mary
"Thank you, Mr.. Coleman. We are most grateful. (Waiting by the living room
sofa with coat in hand)
"We're going for a short walk, if you don't mind
Catherine
"Oh. It's cold outside. Are you sure?"
Mary
"We won't be long." (They exit and reappear at the platform, which is illuminated softly. The rest of the
stage is lit in a soft silhouette)
Mary & Nancy
"Can you hear us?" (They call up to the heavens
with no response)
Nancy
"I guess not. They're not interested in helping us anymore. Sorry about the dumb-ass, comment." (She hangs her head)
(Orchestra plays opening bars)

293

Sisters Forever
Mary sings
We're kin you and I
Joined at the hip
Ever since birth
Our love together will never fade
Sisters Forever
That's who we are
***

(Orchestra plays opening bars)
Alone Together – Nancy sings
Secluded in love
We wait together
Our hearts beat as one
Alone Together

Mary sings
Even if we fail
At this one small task
We will still be
Sister Forever
Of that I am sure

Nancy sings
Abandoned in life
With no one to call
This is how it will always be
Alone Together for all time

Duet
But together we are strong
Inseparable without a doubt
Sister Forever – forever strong

We may be alone and abandoned
But we will always be
Sisters Forever – Forever Strong

(Light from above)
Heavenly choir answers (Loudly)
The Voice Speaks:
"We are pleased you have called out for help. Return to
the Coleman residence and keep Faith."

Mary & Nancy
"OK. We're back."   (They shrug their shoulders and step
off the platform. The light above dims)
Catherine
"Good. Dinner's ready." (They join the Coleman's at
the table and Catherine serves them)
Mary & Nancy
"Thank you all so much for taking us in and caring for us.
You've been so very kind and we have no means with which to
thank you, other than keeping you in our prayers
William
"You've already done more than you know. I am
grateful and I do apologize for my behavior yesterday."
Mary
"No need to, but thank you."
Kathy
"Did you have a nice walk?" (She raises an eyebrow)
Mary
"Yes, thank you. We needed to talk alone.
Ms. Coleman, this roast chicken is divine."
Catherine
"Please. Have some more."

Mary

"Thank you no. We're very tired and want to
go to bed early. May we be excused?"

Catherine

"Of course. Sleep well." (Mary and Nancy take their plates to
the sink and retire to their bedroom.)

Nancy

"What does it mean – Keep Faith. Does it mean that
(They sit on the bed) we'll get our wings back
and be able to go home?

Mary

"I think we're done helping at the Coleman home.
"It's not up to us any longer. (They hear the Coleman family
retiring early to bed)
We've done all we can without having our wings
They'll need a miracle to undo the years of strife."
(Kathy sneaks up to their door to listen)
(Orchestra plays opening bars)

Breath of Life

Mary and Nancy sing

Life is such a funny business
Never knowing what will come next
How could we possibly know
The first thing about helping
Stripped of our wings and power
Helplessly lost at sea
Barely able to catch our breath
Keep the Faith they said
But took all of our power
And simply said to just
Keep Faith
How can we live without them
Lost and alone in a world not our own

If they want to help us
Then they must give back our wings
Let us fly free and we'll
Do whatever you ask

Nancy
"I can't breathe." (Gasping, then faints.
Mary lies beside her sister)
(Kathy is crying outside their door)

Mary sing/talks & is crying
Why won't you help us
I know that you can
Help us, please

---- the stage goes dark ---
heavenly choir voices are softly singing

Multiple Staggered Strobe Flashes
The orchestra accentuates with drums,
horns, etc., and choir voices
Stage goes Dark
(A split stage with Mary and Nancy move to the platform
as a soft early morning light wakes the Coleman family.
Mary and Nancy are now with wings and are lit
from above, as they fully extend their wings.
Kathy wakes and finds the bedroom empty. She rushes to
find her parents at the kitchen table)
Kathy
"Did you see those Flashes of light last night?"
Catherine
"What Flashes."

William
"Yeah. What Flashes."

Billy
"Morning" (He wanders in yawning)

Kathy
"I heard them last night talking about getting their
wings back. And then I fainted during the Flashes.
(Family stares at her)
You didn't see that?"

Catherine
"Well, maybe – I had a dream and heard a
choir singing far away."

William
"I had the same dream. The voices were heavenly."
(Rubbing his face to wake)

Billy
"I slept like a baby."

Kathy
"They're gone. I think they were angels. And I think
they were our Christmas Gift – You know Mom – The one
you asked for at Thanksgiving – To bring our family back
together."

Catherine
"Maaay-bee you're right. Maybe they weren't
just two homeless sisters." (Looks at everyone, perplexed)

Family   (Gasps and laughs hysterically at the thought,
while the choir voices sing and
Mary and Nancy are watching with wings spread wide)

Curtain

(Orchestra plays opening music softly while
the choir chants lyrics from musical, rising and falling)

*****

(Stage curtain raises and backstage curtain raises
revealing the choir and orchestra.
Mary and Nancy are out front with wings spread wide)
(Orchestra plays opening bars of closing song)

Do It For Love – All sing
The light in your eyes says it all
You've found what you've been longing for
Your life will never be the same again
Because you gave yourself away in love
If you want to find your life
Then you've got to give it your all
Never hold back what makes you feel alive
Live for love and give it all away
And you'll never live alone again
Reach out and embrace all that you are
And life will respond and fill your sails
So give your love away
Reach out and help and
Do It For Love

Curtain
(Orchestra continues to play during curtain calls)

CHRISTMAS PARTY

At the last curtain call, Claire's head was swimming with an exuberance that their assignment was finished. She and her sister had done a good job. The audience was still cheering and calling for another curtain call, but Ms. Newman said three was more than enough. She turned to face the choir members and the orchestra behind them, saying thank you for their important part in the musical, bumping into Frank center stage. His face was aglow.

"Good work there, Ms. Claire Tate. I think they liked it."

"Yes, it was good wasn't it?" She winked at her sister behind him. Rachel smacked him in the behind as she stepped beside her sister. It made Frank Richards laugh.

"I probably deserve a lot more."

"Indeed," Rachel said, patting him hard on the chest. "Maybe later."

"Remember," Mr. Clark said above the din. "Some of you are performing at the Christmas party that's already begun in the gymnasium." "Also, there's a special guest I want you all to meet. I'll be up at the bandstand with him shortly."

Mr. Clark pointed at Frank and Linda, and then her and Rachel. Claire remembered from several days ago that Dr. Rideout was the special guest from the Theater Department at American University; someone who Frank and Linda were hoping to impress.

Arthur came from behind them, gathering them up in his arms, squeezing them all together.

Claire let out a squeal of delight, not having to see his face to know it was him. Arthur twirled them around in his arms, putting some color on her face. The heat overtook her and made her dizzy with delight, knowing that Arthur, her mentor, was responsible for much of the success of their assignment.

"Arthur, I can barely breathe." Rachel gasped.

Claire was so consumed by the love she felt for him to notice she was out of breath. It was the same feeling she remembered from the south of France so long ago. She'd fallen in love with her mentor from the first moment they'd met, feeling just as overwhelmed now as she was then. She was embarrassed and completely taken with the likes of him. He set them both down, letting out a breath from his effort.

"Congratulations to the both of you. You knocked their socks off out there."

"Yeah well, you Flashed them all pretty good Arthur." Rachel giggled.

"Really? Everyone?" Claire questioned. "I didn't even notice."

"It was only Frank and Linda. No need to exaggerate Rachel. In any case, it completed the assignment."

"What about Ms. Newman and Mr. Clark? Were they included too?" Claire asked.

"Well, maybe just a little." Arthur winked.

Arthur's little grin said it all for Claire. He was happy his assignment was complete as well.

"So, now what? Another assignment to prove our worth to the Ranks of Higher Ups?" Rachel asked.

"Not yet. Now it's time to party and enjoy ourselves."

Arthur gathered them and led them off stage, maneuvering their way backstage, where they met up with Ms. Newman and

Mr. Clark talking with several members of the choir, cast, and orchestra. Claire went right up to her teachers and hugged them both.

"Thank you so much for the opportunity and for helping us give our best. I can't tell you how much it meant to me."

"We are both very proud of you both, and of all the cast, crew and all of you." Mr. Clark waved his arm to the group.

"You're the best," Ms. Newman said. "And we'll see you at the party."

They continued on their way across campus to the gymnasium, following the sounds of Renovatio, the band playing at the Christmas party. Renovatio, Latin for renewal, was an ethnic mix of seven widely accomplished musicians, each playing no less than three instruments. The mass of students in the hallway, slowly gaining access to the gym, was charged with energy, this being the last day before Christmas break. They melded into the crowd and were carried along through the doors, emerging into a river of youth, which branched in three different directions. They chose the middle, hoping it would lead to the bandstand at the far end of the gym.

"Hey Claire," Lu yelled over the band. "You guys were great. You made me laugh and cry, and that flashy thing was too much."

"Thanks, Lu. Glad you enjoyed it. This is Arthur, our legal guardian, and just about the best Dad, anyone could ever have. And my cousin, Rachel." Lu's mouth moved, but she couldn't hear anything over the band – it was so loud it hurt. They all retreated as far as possible off to the side.

"Dr. Rideout should be here somewhere." Arthur waved his arm at the masses and laughed. "Look for Ms. Newman and Mr. Clark, he'll be with them."

Rachel took off back towards where they'd entered without a word. Claire pulled on Arthur's jacket sleeve to get closer to his ear. "So, what's this surprise trip you have planned? Someplace warm and sunny I hope."

"Probably not warm, but maybe sunny. We're going to Salt Lake City, Utah to see a fellow Angel, Bernard. You'll like him. He's an old hand at working with people and has trained countless new recruits. We'll be leaving the day after tomorrow. We'll be flying there on an airplane."

Arthur gave her a crooked little smile, like this was some Angelic joke – flying by means of a machine. "Sounds interesting, but why don't we just arrive and skip the flying business?"

"You'll see." Arthur pointed into the crowd.

Claire couldn't see what he was pointing at, but after a few moments, Rachel appeared with their teachers and Dr. Rideout following behind. Frank and Linda weren't far behind. Walking beside Dr. Rideout was a tall, dark, and handsome young man. He was every bit the size of Frank's father.

"This is the head of the Theater Department at American University, Dr. Rideout. And this is one of his students, Gordon Evers." Mr. Clark introduced his guests.

While everyone was shaking hands and greeting each other, Claire was sizing up this Gordon character. She was thoroughly taken with his presence, and so was her sister. When it came time for her to say something, she balked as if greeting a person was suddenly like leaping across a Grand Canyon.

"Mahalo," dribbled from between her lips, turning her beet red. She had no idea what she'd said and began to laugh, covering her face with both hands, trying to hide from her gaffe. Claire stood naked in their presence, more embarrassed than was possible for a person to bear. It only got worse when no one said a word until Gordon smiled and thrust his hand out towards her.

"Mahalo," he grinned.

Claire was laughing so hard her eyes teared-up and she was

having trouble catching a breath. In any case, it infected everyone, because they were all laughing now. She shook Gordon's hand limply, having little control of her body yet. "Sorry," she said after a moment, gathering some semblance of composure. "I'm pleased to meet you both." She was still shaking, trying to subdue her heaving diaphragm.

"Claire, Rachel, your performance was wonderful. You each have a gift that I hope you pursue. It's why I am offering you both dual enrollment next semester. I want you to consider taking classes at American University and participating in our Spring Musical, Adam & Eve. Gordon here is cast as Adam, and I'd like it if you both try out for the part of Eve, with one of you being the understudy. Please think about it over Christmas break." Dr. Rideout said.

Claire was stunned. An offer to participate in a college production. "Yes, thank you, Dr. Rideout, we will." Rachel elbowed her for talking for the both of them.

"I accept," Rachel shoved her hand into his.

"Wonderful. If you will excuse me, I have a production of my own, which requires my attendance. Good-by."

"Gordon's your next assignment you know," Arthur whispered in Claire's ear.

Her eyes bugged out at the very thought of being on stage with him, after what she'd just done; saying mahalo, Hawaiian for thank you, in place of hello. Gordon had made her feel giddy, like a wild-eyed schoolgirl, which she was technically, never mind the whole Angel thing. But, what on earth could be wrong with his life that it needed the attention of two rookie Angels?

"For him to know and us to find out." Rachel laughed.

Photo by Kim E Morgan

About the author

John was born in Evanston, Illinois, and raised in the rural community of Glenview, where he was free to roam in the fields of his imagination. Embellished stories of his everyday life, became a mainstay to entertain his friends and neighbors during his youth. His imaginative tales wouldn't find their way to paper though until he retired from carpentry in 2008. Then, the floodgates opened, and the stories began to flow. He calls himself a dreamer and says:

"If a man's life is about the sum of all his parts, then I am happy that this story came through me. It is, by enlarge, a snapshot of my worth; older, yes; wiser, maybe; young at heart, you bet. What life requires of us is passion, and that is why Grading Scale was written, with passion, from my heart to yours."

Website – jcmorganauthor.com